Black
Lab Press

Cottage *on* Oceanview Lane

AN *Emerald Cove* NOVEL

LILLY MIRREN

WELCOME TO EMERALD COVE

Read the series in order...

CHAPTER 1

MEG

*T*he cool breeze lifted Meg Taylor's red curls from the back of her neck, tossing them wildly. She smiled and tented a hand above her eyes to squint at the curling waves. She should've brought her darker sunglasses. The ones she wore didn't cut through the glare enough for her to properly see what was going on, but she'd sat on the dark ones last week in her car and hadn't had time to buy a replacement set before the wedding. She was always doing things like that. It's why she didn't buy expensive sunglasses; they rarely lasted long.

The blare of the bullhorn startled her, and she laughed to herself. As the wife of Brad Taylor, international surfing champion, she'd have to get used to that sound. The voice of the announcer cut through the buzz of the crowd, detailing the water conditions, wave size, and backgrounds of the competitors as arms curved beside surfboards, pulling the surfers into the depths.

She blocked out all the noise and scanned the group of distant, colourful corks bobbing on the ocean's surface to find her husband.

Her husband.

She liked the way the words sounded. Even in her head, they sent a thrill of delight along her spine that tingled and made her heart leap. They'd only been married a week and decided to honeymoon in Hawaii so Brad could compete in the Oahu championship before they headed home to Emerald Cove on the sunny northeastern New South Wales coastline.

It felt strange to be here, watching Brad on her own. Usually his parents would come too, maybe his brother. She'd gone with him to two other events, but always with his small entourage. Never on her own. Having just the two of them made this competition feel special in a way the others never had. At twenty-four and twenty-two years of age, they were now Mr and Mrs Taylor, and she was his entire support crew.

She rested a hand on her backpack. Water, snacks, a towel... She hoped she had everything he'd need. He was so relaxed about the whole thing he hadn't been much help. All he'd wanted to do was stay in the beach cottage they'd spent the past week inside. She'd objected - why come all the way to beautiful Hawaii to honeymoon if you were barely going to step foot outside? But she hadn't really minded. Her cheeks flushed with warmth at the memory of his kisses, of exploring each other the way they'd been able to do - unfettered, unchecked. She loved him so much. In ways she'd never imagined she'd be able to love someone else.

"Hi, Meg!" One of the other Australian surfers' wives, she couldn't remember the woman's name, sauntered past and waved, her blonde hair bobbing in a thin ponytail down her tanned back.

Meg waved in return, offering the woman a smile. "Nice day for it."

The woman nodded. "Brad's looking good, I think he's got a chance today."

Meg grinned. "I think so too. See ya."

The woman disappeared into the crowd, and Meg's attention returned to the group of tiny surfers floating beyond the break, waiting for the perfect wave.

The waves this week had been bigger than any waves she'd ever seen in her life. Emerald Cove was renowned for having great waves, but even Emerald Cove waves couldn't come close to the waves in this bay.

She lowered herself into a chair and foraged around in her bag for her hat. Her skin wasn't as fair as her sister's, but it was fair enough that she did her best to protect it from sun damage when she thought of it. Though, since arriving in Hawaii a week ago, she'd already noticed the sun didn't burn as harshly as it did back home in Australia.

With the hat firmly ensconced on her head, she studied the ocean once again. Several of the surfers had caught waves to shore. Most had crashed out, as the thick lips of the waves curved towards the churning ocean below, taking the surfers with them.

The sky was clear today, but the wind was high and the waves were unpredictable and rough. White water sprayed in the air as another wave crashed. The announcer cautioned everyone to be careful out there, and Meg's heart skipped a beat.

Brad was a professional. He surfed every day, had for most of his life. He'd grown up in Emerald Cove and moved to Brisbane after high school. She remembered him from when they were kids. She'd had a huge crush on the tanned athlete, who was so filled with confidence it made her heart ache just to watch him laughing with friends, playing touch football on the beach or surfing the biggest waves. When he moved away, she'd thought she'd never see him again. Then, a surfing competition in Emerald Cove had resulted in an encounter with Meg that'd changed both their lives.

That'd been over a year ago, and since then, their whirlwind romance had taken Meg by surprise. She still couldn't quite believe that world surfing champion Brad Taylor had fallen for her and was now her husband. She was just a hairdresser, a nobody, from the tiny beachside hamlet of Emerald Cove. Yet he loved her. The realisation surprised her during chance moments, whenever she let her mind wander back to memories of a childhood filled with pain, doubt and unfulfilled wishes.

"Can you believe these waves?" Alice Levin pulled a beach chair up beside her and sat with a huff, looping her arms around knees folded against her thin chest.

"I know, it's crazy."

"It's Hawaii." Alice chuckled. "Glad I'm not competing today though."

"Did you think about surfing?" Meg often felt out of place in the group of Australian surfers, since most of the wives were surfers themselves or at least knew something about the sport. She knew almost nothing. She'd surfed herself, of course, having grown up at the beach, but had never competed or even watched a competition before the one where she'd met Brad.

He'd told her that her complete lack of interest in him or his sport was what'd sparked his interest in her, that and her wild red curls.

"Nah...now that we have the three rug rats, it makes it pretty tricky if both of us compete. We tend to try and take turns, that way one of us is watching the kids." Alice's husband, Nick, was one of the older men in their crew of surfing champions. He was a household name, but in Meg's experience, he was down to earth, a thoughtful husband and a loving father to their three small children, who were, at that moment, seated on a picnic rug eating snacks out of a basket.

"I'm sure it's hard to manage it all..."

"You've got no idea." Alice sighed and ran a hand over her blonde hair. Freckles were scattered across her tanned face, and her blue eyes flashed above a pair of round sunglasses that hung low on the bridge of her nose. "They're only quiet while they have food in their mouths, so I figure I've got about three more minutes to talk, then I'll be on my feet chasing them again." She laughed.

When Meg turned her attention back to the surfers, she was dismayed to see Brad had already ridden a wave to shore while she'd been speaking with Alice. She sighed, then watched as a jet ski pulled him back out beyond the break.

"Oh, I missed it."

"Sorry, I'm distracting you."

"It's okay." She flashed a smile in Alice's direction, even as the woman jumped to her feet and rushed off after her escaping toddler.

The sun beat down on Meg's shoulders, and she reached for the sun cream to slather another thick layer over her exposed skin. The wind helped to keep the heat from becoming oppressive but was wreaking havoc with the tents and other structures that'd been set up by the event organisers. Men were hammering stakes into the sand, working to hold the temporary shelters in place. A few stray hats bowled across the dunes behind the crowd.

Meg inhaled a slow breath as memories of the morning washed over her. Before they'd caught a taxi to the surf competition, they'd risen early and spent an hour snorkelling in the small bay by their cottage. She'd seen some brightly coloured fish as well as the typical silver ones. More than that, she remembered the feel of Brad's skin against hers as he enveloped her in an embrace or tickled her ribs with his fingertips, sending goosebumps up and down her body.

If marriage was going to be anything like it'd been during their first week, she could hardly believe how blissful her life had become. Brad was the kind of man she'd only ever dreamed of meeting. She'd been raised in Emerald Cove, moved with her parents to Port Macquarie when she was sixteen, then left home the very first moment she could manage it after dropping out of school. She'd hated it there, in large part because she'd left her friends behind in the Cove, and the fighting between her mother and father had become unbearable. She hitched a ride back to Emerald Cove with a family friend and landed a hairdressing apprenticeship at one of only two salons in town soon after. She'd lived a quiet life since.

Brad had changed all of that.

Nothing about her life was quiet any longer. She travelled the world to watch him surf. Her life was filled with the laughter and buzz of his friends and family. Even her boss had wondered out loud whether she'd continue working at the salon after they were married. Brad told her she didn't need to keep working; his competition earnings were increasing with every event. The two of them would be able to live a good life together on what he made; she could quit and come out on the road with him full-time.

But things in her life had changed so quickly she'd decided to hold onto her job for now and only travel with Brad when her schedule allowed. She wasn't sure she was ready to change everything all at once. But maybe next year...

The announcer's voice caught her attention. It was Brad; he was riding a wave. She focused on the small figure in the distance, determined not to miss it this time. He stood on his board at the crest of the wave. Her heart skipped a beat. The wave was enormous. The water seemed to stall for a moment in its descent, then curled behind Brad as he slid down its smooth face.

He amazed her. She could never do something like that. Even just watching, it sent her heart into her throat. It was terrifying, the amount of water that pursued him down the wave. He curved his board this way, then that, even as she clenched her hands into fists at her sides. *No, don't do that,* she begged him in silence. The wave was too big; he didn't have time for tricks or moves, just had to get to the bottom and out of the way of the curling water. The lip of the wave curved, wide, thick and falling rapidly.

As it fell, it enveloped Brad. She couldn't see him at all. A gasp rushed through the crowd. When the sound reached her, her breath caught in her throat and her skin was instantly covered in a clammy film of sweat.

The announcer paused, then continued his rambling as the crowd waited with a collectively held breath for Brad to emerge from the remnants of the spent wave.

Meg lurched to her feet and stood there, frozen in place, her hands still fisted, her heart thundering.

"Come on, let's go." Alice rushed over and grabbed Meg by the hand, the toddler planted firmly on one hip. "We've got to go and make sure he's okay."

Meg couldn't speak. Her tongue was stuck to the roof of her mouth. She only nodded and ran in step beside Alice as the woman tugged her along by the hand down the beach.

She couldn't see him. The sand sucked at her feet. Each footstep felt like running through molten lead. There was a tent set on the far end of the beach where the officials were located, along with the first-aid crew. She fixed her eyes on the tent, willing her body to carry her in that direction. She'd lost feeling in her limbs; her face was numb too. This couldn't be happening. It was Brad. Her strong, athletic husband. He could handle anything. He'd be fine. He'd emerge from the waves laughing, shaking the water from his long, sun-bleached hair.

When they reached the tent, one of the men was barking orders into a radio. The others had left the tent, all but the row of judges who were on their feet, peering at the place where Brad had been. Tables strewn with folders and pens had been abandoned. Loose sheets of white paper caught on the wind and sailed past Meg as she fought to find her breath.

"Where is he?" she asked, her pulse loud in her ears.

"I don't see him..." replied Alice beside her, adjusting the child on her hip.

No one responded. The sound of the waves crashing, the whistle of a gust of wind, the noise of the bullhorn, all drowned out her voice. Everyone's attention was fixed on the stretch of water where jet skis circled.

The set of enormous waves had fallen into a lull of temporary relief as the swell slowly rose and fell. The jet skis were joined by kayakers, paddle boards, and everyone in the water circled, peered, yelled. Meg shook her head, slowly at first, then faster until her brain rattled against her skull.

No. No. No.

Where was he?

He couldn't drown. Not on their honeymoon. She couldn't lose him now. They had plans, big plans for their lives together.

She craned her neck, squeezing Alice's hand even tighter, feeling the woman flinch. Then, one of the kayakers let out a shout. It seemed the entire beach was watching in silence, so the shout rose on the wind and carried to shore. The man leaned over and hauled a body onto his kayak, then signalled to one of the jet skis. The vehicle accelerated over, and two men shifted the body onto the jet ski.

It was Brad, but he wasn't moving.

The swell rose tall behind the jet ski, and Meg watched as the driver glanced at the towering wave, then leaned forward over the handlebars. The small machine hummed along the water's surface, rising as the wave built, growing, heaving, building. Meg's eyes widened, and her throat tightened. She was helpless. There was nothing she could do but watch in despair.

"Oh my word," hissed Alice beside her, staring at the wave. "That wave's going to knock the jet ski for six... Get out of there!" She shouted the last, though the man riding the jet ski couldn't hear her. The toddler fussed, and she set the child down by her feet.

As the crest of the wave tipped forward, the jet ski finally seemed to pull away and reached the shoreline as the wave thundered behind it.

Meg released Alice's hand and ran. She stumbled down a grassy embankment, then plunged into soft, hot sand and tumbled forward. A lump filled her throat.

"I have to stay positive, Brad needs me. Focus, Meg, focus," she murmured beneath her breath as she ran.

It seemed an age before she finally reached him. By the time she got there, they'd already transferred him to a stretcher and set off down the beach in the direction of the parking lot with Brad prone between six stout, tanned men. Half wore wet suits; the others were in shorts and t-shirts.

"Stay back please!" one of the men shouted.

"He's my husband," she said. Her voice seemed alien; she almost didn't recognise it.

"Stay with us, Mrs Taylor," said one of the men carrying the stretcher. He grunted as they lifted it up the sandy bank, careful not to tilt it so far that Brad might fall. "Talk to him."

She nodded, her eyes filling with tears. Talk to him. What did that mean? Was he alive? He didn't look alive. His eyes were shut, and he wasn't moving. His hair, normally golden and soft, lay lank, dark and wet across his eyes.

"Brad, I'm here, honey," she said, but the words came out choked.

There was an ambulance waiting for them in the parking lot. When had it arrived? Or perhaps it'd been there the whole time. She didn't know. There was so much she didn't know about any of this. These weren't the kinds of things she should be thinking about right now. She should be enjoying her honeymoon in her husband's arms.

They transferred Brad into the ambulance, and one of the paramedics ushered her in behind him. She sat on a small, hard seat in the back of the ambulance as the paramedic shouted questions at Brad while checking for breath and a pulse.

Through it all, Meg stared, frozen in place. She reached out a hand to rest on Brad's leg.

"It's going to be okay," she whispered, though she knew he couldn't hear her. "It's all going to be okay. You'll wake up soon, you'll be fine, we'll laugh about it all. You'll see. And then we can go snorkelling again tomorrow before breakfast, and you can call me your adorable little piggy when I order the bacon and eggs again. Come on, Brad, wake up."

CHAPTER 2

SARAH

*T*he main highway to Emerald Cove was nothing more than a single-lane paved road, barely wide enough to fit two cars side by side. The edges of the pavement fell away to gravel, then blowing plains of seagrass that billowed and swayed its way over rises and dunes until it met a few straggly coastal shrubs that shielded the beach from view.

Sarah Flannigan had travelled the road more times than she could remember. She'd spent her childhood in the town, but it'd been fifteen years since she'd lived there.

The top of her convertible Mercedes was up today. The weather was beautiful, and the sun shone bright in a brilliant blue sky with no clouds to be seen from horizon to horizon. Still, December wasn't the best time of year to be exposed to the sun in Emerald Cove.

It'd turn her skin beet red inside of ten minutes - a sad fact she'd lived with throughout her childhood years.

Fair skin and beach living didn't go well together, which was exactly why she always wore a large hat, these days often coupled with long-sleeved cotton shirts even when the weather was so warm that sweat trickled down her spine.

She had worn one today and had the AC cranked in her car so high it was blowing her hair back a little from her shoulders.

It'd been a long drive. They'd had to stop a few times for fuel and food. She checked the rear-view mirror - the moving truck was still behind her. At least she hadn't lost them in the traffic, turns and bends that'd gotten them through Grafton and Ballina. The new stretches of highway made all the difference; the journey hadn't been as bad as she'd remembered it. These days, she mostly flew to the Gold Coast Airport and hired a car from there when she visited home, but this time, it was different. This time, she was staying.

She sighed and switched on the radio, swivelling the dial until she found the local station. The announcer's voice brought childhood memories swarming back, one on top of the other. Riding in the back of the car with a group of teenagers singing at the top of their lungs. Evenings in the bed of a truck parked at the beach, a bonfire lighting up the blackness of the country night, laughing over the boys who'd gone skinny-dipping, then streaked through the glow, hands covering their privates.

There were so many memories. Her stomach clenched. Was she doing the right thing? It seemed crazy for her to sell everything, pack up her entire life and move home to the Cove now. Everyone told her so. She'd almost listened. But then, something inside compelled her to keep going, to keep moving, to run home and stay there. At least for now.

She needed a sea change. A new lifestyle, away from the bustle of the urban sprawl.

Heck, she needed more than that. She needed a new life. Something completely different than the one she'd been living. She couldn't pinpoint the exact moment she'd come to that realisation. Everything she'd done since she was eighteen years old had been leading her in the direction she'd taken. She'd wanted the high-profile career, the handsome and successful fiancé, the impressive friends and exquisite cocktail parties.

After spending her childhood in a beachside hamlet where the idea of a cocktail party involved small, red frankfurters in a napkin with lashings of tomato sauce, she relished the sophistication she'd found in Sydney. It was the life she'd longed for as a teenager while seated on the beach watching the ocean crest and sigh as her friends splashed and dove beneath the waves.

She slowed the car as she approached the outer limits of Emerald Cove. A sign marked the start of the village, though there was nothing else to signal the presence of a community. No buildings in sight. No other traffic either. When she reached the turnoff, she pulled her convertible to the side of the road, careful to give the truck behind her plenty of space.

A piece of paper, with the company logo of the publishing house she worked for etched along the top, was folded on the passenger seat. She unfolded it and read her hurriedly scratched instructions. She could get out her phone and use GPS, but the real estate agent had assured her it would do no good. Her new cottage wasn't located on the digital map, and she'd find herself lost in no time. She didn't remember the cottage from her childhood, since it was located outside of the main part of town on a hilltop overlooking the ocean. At least, that was what the photographs on the realty website had shown.

Whispering the directions beneath her breath, she set the paper back in place on the seat and pulled onto the road with a quick glance over her shoulder.

Oceanview Lane was little more than a rugged, half-paved track. It pulled off to the left of the main highway, with a wattle tree blocking the street sign so that she only saw it at the last minute and had to flick on her blinkers quickly so the moving truck didn't careen into the rear of her car as she braked and swerved.

"Sorry!" she whispered with a quick wave of the hand. No doubt they were cursing her after a long day on the road and several unscheduled stops so she could check her email. She was waiting to hear back from a client on a manuscript she'd been editing, but so far, they'd remained silent.

She shook her head. Time to switch off from work and focus on what she was doing. But how should she do that exactly? She'd hardly taken a holiday in almost ten years; she wasn't sure she knew how to turn off her working brain and focus on her private life. Perhaps it was something she should've done long ago, although it'd only been the past year or two that the effort of always being on duty, always having more work to do, never turning off her brain, had begun to wear her down.

The convertible bumped and jolted its way down the lane. A few potholes looked big enough to swallow the small vehicle whole, but she dodged them just in time. There were four other driveways before her own. She counted them. The agent had told her the fifth driveway was the one, and she turned down it while leaning forward over the steering wheel as far as she could to see the way ahead.

There was a narrow gate, rotted timber propped open. Brushes and shrubbery dwarfed a broken fence line that circled the property. In the centre of a small garden stood a cottage. It was pale grey with a dark roof. The walls were covered in a climbing vine and mould, and the garden was overgrown, like a mop-haired child.

Sarah parked in a patch of tall grass and helped signal the truck to park in front of the cottage.

"This it?" asked the driver.

She nodded, fetched the key from the glove box and opened the front door. It creaked and stuck a little. She shoved it with her shoulder, and it flew open, releasing a musty smell.

With a cough, she stepped aside, pressing her hands to her hips, and watched as the movers deftly ferried every one of her possessions into the small structure. Within a half hour, everything was inside and the truck was pulling out of the driveway.

Sarah stood in her new living room and looked around at the piles of boxes and plastic-wrapped furniture with a shake of her head. She didn't have the energy to do any unpacking after a twelve-hour drive.

The house seemed more rustic, older than the photos had indicated. Her agent had assured her it was in liveable condition, but standing in the middle of the largest habitable room, she wasn't so sure. She tiptoed around the house, giving it a quick tour, hoping not to find anything living inside that didn't belong there. She was gratified to discover that the only other residents than herself seemed to be a few spiders. And once she'd opened the windows, the musty smell subsided reasonably quickly.

Sarah threw herself down on a covered couch and tugged her mobile phone from her jeans pocket. It was hot. Already she'd sweated through her t-shirt, and the jeans clung to her damp legs.

There were several calls from Jeremy. Her nostrils flared and stomach tightened. Never mind. She'd ignored his calls for weeks; she could continue to ignore them until he finally got the picture and gave up. It was a surprise to her he'd carried on for this long. Surely, he knew she wouldn't call him back by now. Having her phone on silent was the only way she could survive his unrelenting attempts to contact her, though it did mean she missed most of her work-related calls. That was a frustration she could do without.

Her mobile service only had one and a half bars, then a moment later, it disappeared entirely, replaced by an *SOS Only* message on the screen. She wondered if the service was always so bad at the cottage. She'd have to get wireless installed soon. She'd never be able to manage her work with such sporadic service.

Outside, the rotting porch seemed ready to collapse beneath her feet at any moment. She grimaced as one of the boards shifted, then shuffled onto another. The boards might've been past their prime, but the view was impressive. She stared out over a deep blue ocean. The sun travelled down the western sky behind her, sending shafts of pink and orange light over the shifting sea, imbuing it with a magical glow.

Her eyes widened, and a satisfied smile spread over her lips. This was what she'd been looking for. She could stand living in a small, musty cottage with rotting floorboards for this view. It was incomparable.

In her pocket, her mobile buzzed. She startled, then tugged it free to stare at the screen. Three full bars. Apparently, the porch was the best place to get service. There was a message from her mother.

Let me know when you get in. I'm so excited!

She smiled to herself. When she'd first told Mum she was moving back to Emerald Cove, there'd been complete silence on the other end of the phone line. Then, disbelief had echoed through her carefully chosen words.

"Don't do anything rash, love. I didn't mean for you to drop everything to come to my rescue. I'm sure I can figure things out..."

"No, Mum," she'd said in a steady tone. "You need my help with the cafe after Dad ran off and left you in the lurch."

"But just a quick trip should do the job."

"Don't you want me to come home?" she'd asked then, her throat tightening. She wasn't sure she wanted to do it herself. Part of her was aghast at the idea, told herself she was crazy to drop a thriving career as the hottest young editor on staff at one of the top publishing houses in Sydney. She'd even heard talk of being on the fast track to head editor. Head editor of Greenmount Publishing - it was what she'd been working for, dreaming of.

"Of course I want you to... but I don't want you to give up the life you've built. Not for me. I'm so proud of you, and I know you love it there. You'd hold it against me..."

"No, I won't." And as she'd said the words, the objections in her own mind had stilled. This was something she had to do. Wanted to do. "I want to be there for you, Mum. The way you've always been there for me when I needed you. And besides, I could do with a change of scenery. It's getting a bit..."

She didn't know how to finish the sentence. What was it getting? Constrictive? Difficult? Frustrating?

If only Jeremy would stop calling, maybe then...

She sighed and texted her mum back.

I made it. At the cottage now.

This place was a chance to start again. She'd help Mum get the cafe back on track, to get over Dad leaving her for a younger woman. And she'd give herself a second chance at the same time. After all, she'd managed to convince her boss to let her work from home. She could juggle her editing load from hundreds of kilometres away, and she could enjoy this amazing view while she worked.

You should come for dinner. I'm at the shops now, I'll pick us up something.

Sarah studied the screen, even as her stomach cramped with hunger. She hadn't eaten anything other than a hastily scarfed burger since breakfast. Mum's cooking was one of the things she'd missed most about living so far away from the Cove.

I'll unpack a few things then come over.

It felt strange to be living somewhere close enough that she could just pop over to her old childhood home. Strange in a good way? She wasn't sure yet. It might take some time to get used to her new living arrangement.

Great. See you soon!

Sarah shoved the phone back into her pocket and

stepped inside the cottage. She immediately missed the fresh, brisk breeze from the porch. The stale, musty smell inside made her nose twitch. She pressed both hands to her hips and studied the mess.

Boxes everywhere.

It was hard to know where to begin. But she should at least try to find some pyjamas and her toothbrush. With a sigh, she set about reading the labels on the boxes and pushing them into like piles. She located her bathroom box and with a grunt carried it to the bathroom. Mouldy tiles and stained walls greeted her. She eyed the bathtub slash shower with suspicion. Did she dare stand barefoot in it? Perhaps she'd take a change of clothes over to Mum's with her, shower there and scrub down this shower tomorrow. With that resolved in her mind, she bent to unpack the box.

Ugh, where were the box cutters?

She did her best with the tip of one of the keys on her keychain, and the box was soon open. Another glance around the room and she decided to leave everything in the box until she'd had a chance to thoroughly clean the place. Perhaps she should've invested in a hazmat suit?

She shook her head, grabbed her toiletry bag from the box and padded outside to find the shoulder bag she'd purposefully packed with the things she'd need the first night in the cottage. It was all well and good to have these things prepared ahead of time, but you had to find the darned bag for it to be helpful. Now, where would the movers have put that bag?

CHAPTER 3

CINDY

"You ready to order that turkey yet?" Marg asked, tugging at the fingertips of her rubber gloves before reaching down to grab a handful of shaved smoked ham beneath the sparkling glass of the deli counter.

"Yes please. You know what I want. I'll need to pick it up the day before Christmas Eve."

"Got it," Marg replied with a wink. "I'll set aside the best one for you, Cindy. Nice and plump. You gonna have enough guests to manage it this year? Or are you thinking leftovers for a week?" Marg chuckled at her own attempt at a joke as she wrapped the ham in butcher's paper.

"I've got Sarah here this year," Cindy replied with a smug dip of her head. "And the other kids will be coming too."

"Oh yeah, that's right. Sarah's moving back to the Cove, you said?"

Cindy smiled. "She's here. Made it already. I just got a text from her that she's at the cottage."

Marg handed Cindy the package, her blue-tinted hair pulled tight in a bun. Cindy knew the moment Marg got home that bun was coming out and the frizzy hair Marg was known for around town would tumble around her shoulders. "Well, that's nice. Everyone's talking about it, you know? Sarah Flannigan moving back to the Cove. Who would've thought? I mean, she has that high-powered career in the city, and we've barely seen her for years. I wonder why..." Marg's brown eyes narrowed.

Cindy swallowed and shook her head slowly. "I guess she missed home. Thanks for that, Marg. Don't forget about my turkey, will you?" The last thing she wanted was for everyone in the Cove to be talking about her personal life again. She'd managed to get through two months of constant chatter, questions, condolences and pitying looks everywhere she went after Andrew ran off with Keisha. The thought of giving the town more fodder now by revealing that Sarah had come home to the Cove to save her beloved cafe was more than she was ready to deal with.

Marg issued a mock salute. "I'll write the order down now. Don't you fret, your Christmas turkey will be here."

"Day before Christmas Eve..." Cindy called over her shoulder as she pushed the wobbling trolley away from the deli counter.

"Day before Christmas Eve!" Marg confirmed with a wave.

Cindy sighed as she hurried down the closest aisle.

She loved Marg but wasn't ready to deal with the entire town knowing the reason for Sarah's move to the Cove yet. No doubt they'd figure it out soon enough. In the meantime, she wanted some time to enjoy it.

Excitement bubbled in her gut.

It'd been more than a decade since any of her children had lived in Emerald Cove. She'd raised them all here but had known since they were young they wouldn't stay. All three of them were smart, ambitious and hardworking. The Cove didn't have anything to keep them here.

And now Sarah was back.

Even though she couldn't be happier about the prospect of seeing her eldest daughter on a regular basis, she couldn't help worrying. Why was Sarah back in the Cove? Other than the obvious reason of her asking for help, there had to be more to it than that. Sarah could've taken a few days, visited and gone over the cafe's books before returning to her life in Sydney.

Her announcement had come two weeks earlier that she was moving back - for good - though Cindy still didn't quite believe that to be true. Cindy hadn't been able to speak for a full minute.

Moving back to the Cove? For good?

Sarah had assured her she'd heard correctly.

"But Sarah, love...you've always said you'd never move back. You couldn't wait to get out of here. It's too small, nothing ever happens here. Those were your exact words."

"Things change, Mum."

That was her entire explanation. Things change.

Cindy shook her head as she reached for a can of baked beans. Yes, she knew things changed, but she didn't know Sarah could. Her eldest had always had a strong will and a determined way about her. She'd decided on Sydney and a career in publishing, and she'd gone after it until she had it. Nothing could stop her. Cindy was proud of her daughter's achievements. She couldn't help worrying, of course. That was a mother's prerogative, she often told herself. Andrew would say, stop worrying, Cindy. Everyone's fine. Life is good.

What did he know?

Apparently, he'd been plotting to leave her behind her back, suggesting life for him wasn't as good as he liked to let on. Though she still couldn't figure out what it was about his life that was so unbearable. She took care of him, took care of everything. He had it easy. She ran the cafe her parents had left her in their will when they passed, and it provided them with the income they needed after he retired from his job as a financial planner. All he had to do was keep the books.

Now that he was gone, she couldn't figure out what all those numbers meant. Perhaps she should've kept up with the cafe's finances, but she hadn't expected her husband to leave her. Not in her sixties. They'd been through so much together, raised three children, built the business. To be alone at this time of her life wasn't part of the plan.

She grabbed a bunch of fresh flowers, added it to the trolley and headed for the checkout.

No time to dwell on the past, on what she'd missed and how she'd managed to ignore the warning signs in her marriage. She'd done enough of that over the previous two months. She had a meal to cook now. Sarah was used to getting takeaway for dinner, and she wouldn't find much of a variety of restaurants in

Emerald Cove. Cooking meals was one of the ways Cindy showed her family love, and she relished the idea of being able to do it more often for Sarah. With a smile, she set the full bags of groceries one by one back in the trolley and headed for the car.

CHAPTER 4

MEG

*M*eg paced to the other side of the ER waiting room, then back again. She rubbed the tips of her fingers against her eyes, pressing deep into her eye sockets, then sighed.

What was going on back there? When would she find out whether Brad would live or die? So far, they hadn't given her anything definitive. He'd made it to the hospital, but only just. The paramedics had resuscitated him twice in the ambulance on the journey from the surf competition to the ER. Still, he was breathing when she told him goodbye with a hurried kiss before he was wheeled through the swinging glass doors at the end of the room. Doors she now kept glancing at, waiting to hear something, anything about how he was doing.

She'd never had to manage anything like this

before. Usually there was an adult to turn to when a tragedy unfolded. Someone who could make the phone calls, tell her how to feel, remind her that she wasn't alone. Only this time, she was alone. Very alone.

Her heart thundered in her chest, which felt tighter and more constricted by the moment, as if every breath was harder to take than the one before it. She leaned against the wall, stared at a pamphlet about breast self-examinations tacked to a corkboard, and did her best to calm her breathing.

Brad would be okay. He had to be okay. This couldn't be the story of their marriage, their lives together. It couldn't end now, on their honeymoon. They were supposed to spend decades together, grow old, have children, grandchildren...walk on the beach together hand in hand, into the glowing sunset.

This didn't make any sense.

Her phone buzzed on the hard, plastic seat where she'd left it. The room hummed with activity. Children squealed and cried, waiting their turn to see a doctor. Mothers did their best to occupy the active ones. A young boy held an obviously broken arm while his mother filled out paperwork beside him, her face gaunt.

Again, Meg's phone buzzed, this time spinning in a circle on the seat. She strode to the chair and picked up the mobile, swiping the screen to answer.

"Vicky?" Her voice broke on the word, thick with tears.

"Honey, where are you? What's going on? I saw all these missed calls from you, then I put on the news and Brad was...was in an accident."

Tears coursed down Meg's cheeks at the sound of

her friend's voice. "He fell, on the way down the wave. It was a giant and crushed him. He's in surgery now, I don't know what's happening. They told me he needed surgery on his neck and back, and that he was in critical condition. It doesn't look good... I'm here all by myself. I don't know what to do!" The words spewed from her mouth, punctuated by sobs. She slumped into the chair, pressing a hand to her eyes.

"Oh, honey, I'm so sorry." Vicky's voice cracked with emotion. "Do you want me to come to Hawaii? To be with you?"

"No, there's nothing you can do. I've already spoken to Brad's parents, and they're on their way. They'll be here tomorrow, and they'll help... I just wish we hadn't come here. I wish we'd honeymooned somewhere else and forgotten about this comp. I should've said something, I didn't want to do it, but I thought it would make him happy..."

"Meg, honey," Vicky's voice interrupted her with a firm tone, "this isn't your fault. You did nothing wrong. Brad knows the risks, he surfs these kinds of waves all the time. It had nothing to do with you, it was an accident."

"But what if he was distracted, didn't prepare himself for the competition the way he usually does. We went snorkelling this morning, and his coach wasn't happy about it. Told him he should've been at the beach preparing, getting his mind on track. Oh, what if it's my fault?" Meg burst into tears. It was the first time since the accident she'd let herself be overcome with emotion, and now the tears fell unchecked down her tired cheeks.

The swinging glass doors pushed open, and the

doctor who'd spoken to her earlier emerged, pushing his white mask down from his face. His forehead was lined, and Meg couldn't read his expression. Her heart seized.

"Vicky, I've got to go. I'll call you later."

She hung up the phone and faced the doctor with a sharp intake of breath.

"Mrs Taylor?" he said.

She nodded. "Yes."

"I'm Dr Benson. Brad's out of surgery, and he's stable for now."

She let out a rush of breath. "Oh, thank you, Dr Benson. Thank you!"

He offered her a half smile. "Don't thank me yet. We're not out of the woods. I'm afraid he's sustained some serious neck and back injuries. We did the best we could to fix the damage, but we may have to do further surgeries when he's stronger and more likely to survive them."

Her brow furrowed. "What do you mean? He might not survive?"

Dr Benson pressed his hands to his hips. "No, he may not survive. We had to close him up because his blood pressure dropped, he was too weak to continue. We'll try again if, or when, he is strong enough to handle the surgery."

Meg's vision blurred. She shook her head. This couldn't be happening. Brad was young, he was strong and fit. Surely, he'd make it through.

"So, what are the chances of him recovering?" Her voice sounded calm, but inside she was quivering from head to toe, her legs threatening to give out beneath her.

"I really can't say. The damage to his spine could be

permanent, we have to prepare for that possibility, but as I said, we really don't know."

"Permanent? Do you mean paralysis?"

He nodded. "And that's likely the best outcome. At this stage, we're simply hoping he'll make it through the night."

CHAPTER 5

CINDY

*T*he Seaside Manor Bed and Breakfast was only a few hundred metres away from Cindy's home. She and the owner, Diana Jones, had known each other since childhood and had been fast friends all that time.

Cindy stared up at the back of the building where creeping vines blanketed one side of the bed and breakfast. The back door was solid timber, painted in a rust-coloured red. A winding footpath curved away from the house, flanked by the cottage garden Diana spent so much time in and was so proud of. It was lush and colourful at this time of year. They'd had plenty of rain in recent weeks, and the gardens around the Cove reflected it with their dark greens and vibrant pinks, yellows and reds.

Cindy pushed open the back door and stepped inside. The sweet scent from the bunch of flowers she'd bought for Diana followed her inside, immediately filling the hall with their soft aroma.

She knew where to find her friend and manoeuvred her way down three steps and through a narrow opening. She knocked on a dark timber door.

"Come in!" called a high voice.

She opened the door, smiling. "Hello, Di, I brought you those flowers you wanted."

"Wonderful!" Her friend stood from behind the desk where she was working to embrace Cindy. "Good to see you. How're you going getting ready for Sarah's arrival?"

Cindy slid into a seat across from Diana and handed the flowers to her friend who promptly pulled a vase from the sideboard and filled it with the arrangement of pink and purple carnations and soft white baby's breath.

"She's here! She's at the cottage doing a bit of unpacking, and I've been shopping, and she's coming over soon for dinner, so I can't stay long."

"Sounds wonderful. I can't believe she's actually here." Diana sat in her chair and steepled her hands on the desk.

"Me either. I can't help…" She stopped, frowned.

"What?"

Cindy exhaled a slow breath. "I hope she didn't give up her entire life just to help me."

Diana shook her head, shrugged.

"I don't think I could live with that - knowing she might've given up her career for me. It's always meant so much to her. And what about her fiancé?" Cindy's eyebrows arched. She'd always liked Jeremy.

"Ex-fiancé," Diana reminded her.

"Yes, of course, ex-fiancé. Still, they were good

together. Now, in the course of the two months since her father's disappearing act, she's broken off her engagement and left the city behind, along with her career. Something's not right."

"Maybe it impacted her more than she's letting on," Diana said.

"Perhaps... She and Andy were pretty close."

"I still can't believe he left you for that...woman!" Diana sniffed. "It's an absolute travesty."

Cindy couldn't even summon enough emotion to feel anything about her ex-husband. Well, technically he was still her husband, though he didn't act like he was and she preferred to think of him in the past tense.

She chuckled. "Leaving me for his much younger assistant - it's very clichéd."

"The ultimate cliché," Diana agreed with a dip of her head. "And with the hair..."

"And those nails," Cindy added. Generally, she didn't like to criticise, but in this particular case, she felt she should have a little bit of latitude. Though it gave her a queasy feeling inside. She shifted gears. "Regardless of She-Who-Won't-Be-Named, the way he left -without a word - it wasn't like him."

"I think it was exactly like him," Diana said with a flair of her nostrils.

"I know you never liked him—"

Diana interrupted her. "He wasn't good enough for you - when we were kids or now. He doesn't seem... genuine, even when he's being as sweet as pie. And to leave you with all that credit card debt..."

Cindy's lips flattened into a straight line. She'd spent more than twenty years defending her husband, and it'd become something of a habit that was hard to break. However, he had made the transition a little easier for her by leaving behind a flood of credit card debt she'd known nothing about and which seemed to grow each passing day as new bills arrived in the post. Why had he continued to grow his financial planning business if he wasn't making a profit? The irony would've made her laugh if she wasn't so anxious about what she should do now. And with the mortgage on the cafe — she might lose everything.

"Well, perhaps you've been right all along. I should've listened to you, I suppose. Although we did have a lot of good years, and then of course there's the kids. I can't regret my children - they're the best thing I've ever done." Cindy meant every word as her throat tightened. She couldn't imagine her life without the three children she'd birthed and cared for, even if they'd spent the past decade living in various parts of the world far away from Emerald Cove. She told herself their independence was a sign she'd done a good job raising them.

"Your children are wonderful," Diana admitted. She'd never been able to have children herself and so had taken on the role of doting adopted aunt to Cindy's. "And I'm so glad Sarah is back, I can't wait to see her. Everyone's talking about it, you know."

Cindy grimaced. "I know. They can't help themselves. They see drama and intrigue where there is none. I do hope they leave her alone, for at least a few weeks until she settles in. You'll put out the word, won't you?"

"Of course," Diana said with a determined nod. "I'll make sure everyone knows to give her some space for a few days."

"Weeks," Cindy corrected as she stood and smoothed her skirt with both hands.

Diana inhaled a deep breath. "I'll do my best, but you know how exciting it is for us all...the big-time editor back from the city. No one understands why she broke off the engagement to such a rising literary star, and we're all curious."

Cindy frowned. "Poor Sarah. There's no way we can keep the local gossips off her back, is there?"

"I'm afraid not." Diana stepped out from behind her desk and embraced Cindy with a peck on the cheek. "Not to worry, Sarah can hold her own, and she's used to them."

"I suppose that's true. And she has been living in Sydney, navigating the cutthroat corporate world for the past decade."

"Yes, she has. She'll be fine," Diana replied, looping her arm through Cindy's and walking her to the back door.

"Only, I wish I knew why she'd decided to move back here out of the blue like that. I hope it wasn't only for my sake, but then if it wasn't - what was it?"

As she walked away down the winding garden path, past the red- and white-capped gnomes and the stained fairy statues, she couldn't stop thinking about Sarah, her runaway husband and what on earth she'd do with herself if she lost the cafe.

CHAPTER 6

SARAH

*I*t'd taken every ounce of strength she had to get the mattress from the place where it'd been wedged between boxes and the closet against the wall onto the floor at her feet.

Sarah puffed hard, then slid onto the mattress, her booted feet careful to stay off the freshly added sheets. The mattress was surrounded in boxes and bags, but at least she now had somewhere to sleep that night. That was, if she didn't decide to stay over at Mum's instead. The idea of sleeping in her old bed for the night was a lot more appealing than a mattress on the floor. She'd put the bed together tomorrow and get some things put away. It'd feel more like a home then.

Outside, a kookaburra laughed, the sound echoing through the scrub around the cottage. The wind whistled through the eaves, sending a shiver down her spine. That was another thing she'd have to learn to get used to - the wind seemed to blow constantly on the outlook over the jagged cliff face where the cottage perched.

She set her clock radio on top of one of the boxes and found an outlet to plug it in. Nothing. There was no electricity. Of course, she'd intended to make the phone call before she left Sydney but hadn't gotten around to it. There were so many other more pressing issues. And now she was without power. Another thing to add to tomorrow's growing list of to-dos.

There wouldn't be much point setting up her laptop yet then, even though she'd assured her boss she'd be working tomorrow, the next day at the latest. She hadn't connected the internet yet either.

With a sigh, she ran a hand over her hair, smoothing it back into the long, brown ponytail that hung almost to her waist. Then, with a heave, she stood and padded to the kitchen. By the time she'd found a few of the more necessary kitchen items, like the kettle of course, a box of tea bags, cereal and some long-life milk, along with a bowl, spoon and cup, all stashed in a small box marked, "Unpack first - Kitchen", she felt much better. There was no refrigerator, so nowhere to put the milk yet. Still, seeing her cup and bowl on the bench gave her a small sense of satisfaction.

With a nod, she grabbed the overnight bag she'd packed in Sydney, along with her purse, and headed for the car, locking the cottage behind her. She wasn't sure what the local etiquette was anymore. When she was a kid, no one locked their doors in the Cove. But she'd been living in Sydney for almost fifteen years, and door locking had become an instinct more than anything else. She wasn't sure she could go back to leaving everything open the way she had in the past, especially since her closest neighbour here seemed to be at least one hundred metres away through scrub and bush.

The drive through town was nostalgic for her. So many memories popped into her mind as she turned down the main street, then onto side roads that led to the place she'd called home for so many years. The time Vicky had fallen off her bike and broken her funny bone, the time Adele, her younger sister, had announced she was in love with little Brad Taylor beneath a particularly gnarled-looking gum tree and proceeded to spend the next six months mooning about him and following him around.

The memories brought a smile to Sarah's face.

She pulled into the driveway at the house on Broadwater Terrace, her eyes watering. She'd avoided visiting Mum since Dad left. Hated the idea of seeing her in that big house all alone. It wasn't right, didn't seem normal somehow without Dad there. He'd been retired for the last two years, so even though she didn't visit often, when she did, he was always there, puttering around the place, fixing this or fussing with that, the latest mystery novel never far out of reach.

It made no sense at all to her that he'd gone from retirement and mystery novels to running off with his former assistant. The fact that he hadn't called her to talk to her about it angered her, but it seemed petty to hold onto that given the fact that he hadn't talked to Mum either. Sarah had spoken to her father since he moved out, but he never wanted to talk about the breakup, never wanted to answer her questions about why he'd given up on his family that way. His stubbornness and seeming lack of compassion confounded and angered her, but she'd always been a peacemaker when it came to her dad. He was standing on a precipice ready to jump and leave them all behind for good. She didn't want that, so she'd swallowed her retorts to try to coax him back, away from the edge, talking about nothing in particular, laughing over frivolous stories and hoping all the while he'd open up on his own if she gave him enough space. But so far, he never had.

She shook her head as she parked, then climbed out of the car. Mum seemed to have coped fine with the split, though you could never tell with her. She kept her emotions in check most of the time, only letting them show when they'd built up so much they exploded all over everyone. It was a trait Sarah found particularly galling in her otherwise genial and happy mother.

Mum answered the door before Sarah had even finished climbing the front steps, with a wide smile, then a breath-stealing hug.

"There you are! I was about to send out a search party," she said, stepping aside to let Sarah through the doorway. "Come on in, you must be starving."

The entryway was spacious, and Sarah stowed her overnight bag there for now. Suddenly a feeling of intense fatigue washed over her. She followed her mother down the hallway.

"And how do you like the cottage?" Mum asked, glancing back over her shoulder.

"Um...it's very rustic."

Mum chuckled. "Yes, it is. I had a look at it from the outside, couldn't get in without the keys of course, and I wondered if you'd really gotten the right impression over the internet. Still, it's got a wonderful view."

"That it does. It's worth it just for that view. Still, I think I'm going to have to get someone in to help me renovate the place pretty quickly. I can't live with it the way it is... I think I even saw mould. It's funny, a few months ago, I never would've considered the cottage. I wanted a house, kind of like this, I guess - something big, regal, spacious. The type of home that could host dinner parties and wow guests. But something's changed, I've changed. I don't want that anymore."

"It's too much, my darling, too big, too empty now... I'm not sure I want it either, truth be told. It seems hollow somehow to build the perfect home with someone who, it turns out, doesn't love you the way you thought he did."

Sarah shook her head, throat tight. She laid a hand on her mother's arm as they paused for a moment in the hall. She cleared her throat. "So, now I have an old cottage in desperate need of renovating. Maybe I can renovate my life while I'm at it." She laughed, a shrill sound that echoed with unshed tears.

Mum squeezed her hand. "Well, I have a number for a guy. He's one of the locals, in fact I think you probably went to school with him if I remember correctly. Anyway, he's very good at that sort of thing. I'll give you his details, don't let me forget."

"Great, thanks, Mum."

Sarah's eyes strayed to the photographs that lined the walls of the hall as they walked. Different shapes and sizes, some with black frames, others white. All with memories attached.

There was a photograph of her year twelve formal - she'd worn an off the shoulder black dress, her long, brown hair curled around her shoulders. Her skinny date stood uncomfortably beside her in a dinner suit, hair parted in the middle, hands clasped in front.

Next, a photograph of her with her brother and sister at Falls Creek ski resort. None of them were recognisable, since all wore beanies, goggles and scarves pulled up around their chins, along with thick, puffy jackets. Snow swirled around them, but even though their faces couldn't be seen, she remembered the wide smile - she'd always loved to ski. It was something she'd continued doing as an adult. Each winter, she travelled to Falls Creek, or to Queenstown in New Zealand, to ski. It was one of her favourite pastimes, and it'd all started here, with her family.

A lump formed in her throat.

Her family wasn't the same any longer. How could Dad walk away from what they shared together, the love they'd built over so many years? It didn't make sense.

How could he leave Mum like that?

"Have you heard from Dad?" Sarah asked as they stepped into the kitchen.

The scent of fresh bread filled her nostrils, and her stomach growled in anticipation.

Mum shook her head, opened the refrigerator. "No, I haven't."

"Don't you think that's strange?" she asked.

Mum pulled out a jug of lemonade and set it on the kitchen bench, then opened a cupboard to search for glasses.

"Strange? Yes, I suppose I do think it's strange. I think it's downright bizarre for a man in his sixties to run off with a woman half his age when he's finally retired and can do all the things he's promised his wife they'd do over the many years of our marriage." Mum's voice dripped with sarcasm as she set the glasses on the bench and poured lemonade into them.

Sarah grimaced. It wasn't fair on Mum to bring up Dad. Only, she hadn't heard from him in a while. She didn't intend on calling him again herself, since she was angry with him and he should know that. She'd hoped instead he might call, show that he actually cared, let them know he was okay, beg for forgiveness and ask to come back. Something like that, anyway.

Mum handed her a glass, then leaned against the bench to sip her own. "Why do you ask?"

"I'm sorry, Mum, I shouldn't have brought it up."

Mum sighed. "No, it's fine. I get it, you want to understand. But I'm not sure there's anything to understand other than your father has always been a selfish man. He does whatever feels good to him and doesn't think about the consequences for anyone else." Mum's mouth clamped shut, and her nostrils flared. "I shouldn't have said that, I know he's your father...but that's how I feel."

Sarah's eyes widened. She'd never heard her mother criticise her father before in her life. Was that how she'd always felt about him?

"I suppose you're right... I've never considered it quite like that before. He always did what he wanted and didn't ask any of us for our input, but I didn't think it'd come to something like this. In spite of everything, I believed he loved us."

Mum laid a hand on Sarah's arm. "Oh, honey, he does love you. This isn't about you, Adele or Ethan, it's about him. When parents get divorced, it's only because of their relationship with one another, nothing to do with the kids."

Sarah quirked an eyebrow. "I know, Mum. I'm not

ten years old. It's okay, I get it. I didn't realise you were already on track for divorce though. Maybe he'll come back…"

"Let's sit in the lounge room, love. There's something I need to talk to you about, and I've set up some lovely antipasto for us in there."

* * *

THE PLATTER ON THE SMALL, square coffee table took up almost the entirety of the table's surface. It was covered from one side to the other with rolls of ham, turkey, pastrami and salami, green and black olives, spoonsful of hummus and baba ganoush, water crackers and tiny breadsticks.

"This looks amazing, Mum. Thanks for throwing it together. I know you've probably had a long day at the cafe already, you must be tired."

Mum sat on the loveseat across from the armchair where Sarah's body slipped into the most familiar and comfortable position, with one elbow leaned on the armrest.

"Yes, well, I'm used to being on my feet at the cafe for most of the day. I've done it for as long as I can remember. I started helping out my parents when I was about five years old, taking orders from the customers. Mum always said the customers loved it, me standing there with my little notepad and pen, making markings on the paper that no one else could understand but me." Mum sighed, reached for a breadstick and took a bite. She continued around her mouthful. "It's a part of most of my life's memories, that place."

Sarah set down her lemonade on a side table and

reached for a cracker. She dipped it in the hummus and chewed with contentment.

"You sound like you think you might lose the cafe, Mum. You told me on the phone it wasn't going well, that you were losing a lot of money... What's going on?"

Mum leaned back in her chair, crossing one leg over the other. The skirt of her floral dress fanned out around her, and she combed her almost silver hair back from her face with one hand.

"That's what I wanted to talk to you about, love." She inhaled a slow breath. "It seems your father accumulated some debts before he left me."

"What?" Sarah's brow furrowed.

Her parents never had financial problems, not in as long as she could remember.

"But Dad was a financial planner. That makes no sense. What were the debts for?"

"Yes, I had the same reaction. And I don't know why he took out the loans."

"Loans? There's more than one?"

Mum nodded. "There's a significant amount of credit card debt on a card which, unfortunately, is in my name."

"Oh no." Sarah's heart fell.

"Yes, and then there's the loan he took out against the cafe... I only just found out about that one. I haven't told anyone else... I can't seem to quite believe it. I put your father's name on the cafe when we were young and in love. He asked me to do it, so I did. Now, of course, I regret that choice. He seems to have racked up debt against the cafe, and since he's run off and I don't want to lose the place, I'm going to have to pay it back. At least that's what Byron down at the bank tells me."

Anger stirred in Sarah's gut. How could Dad do that to Mum? She knew he had his flaws, they all did. But to do something like that, she hadn't thought him capable. He'd taken Mum for granted; even she'd been able to see that. But to be so unconcerned about Mum's well-being - she hadn't expected that from him. She'd believed he loved her in his own way. He was the fun one, always up for a good time, and for his kids, that meant a lot of laughs and plenty of good memories, but now that she thought about it, he'd left Mum in the background cooking, cleaning, doing the dishes, running the cafe, managing the large, sweeping gardens that surrounded the house, taking care of everything while they had fun together.

"I'm so sorry, Mum."

Mum shook her head, patted Sarah's arm. "I know. I didn't want to say anything over the phone, I suppose I couldn't quite believe it myself. And I only found out about the loan yesterday when I got a bill in the mail. I've been checking the P.O. box, which is where your father had all his business mail sent over the years, and I suppose he never closed it after he retired. There was a bill from the bank, and it just about took the wind from my lungs. I had to go in to see if it was really what I thought it was."

"I'm here to help, so let me know what I can do." Sarah wasn't sure exactly how she could help, but she intended to do everything she could to save the cafe. She couldn't allow her father's selfishness to take the one thing her mother had left.

"I'm so grateful, my darling. Thank you for coming. I don't know if I've said that to you yet, but thank you.

I didn't mean for you to move to the Cove, of course. I'd hoped you'd come and help me out for a few days..."

Sarah shook her head. "It sounds to me you need more than that. If you'd like me to, I can take a look at your finances and see if I can figure out a way forward."

"That would be wonderful. I'm hopeless with those things, I look at the numbers and my head gets all light and my thoughts spin around trying to figure it all out. I thought I might pass out at the bank. Byron had to sit me down and get me a glass of water." Mum shook her head, squeezed her eyes shut for a moment, then pushed a smile onto her face. "But I'm sure you'll figure it out and it'll all work out fine."

"You said the cafe was losing money. That might make things a little more difficult. What's going on?" Sarah's eyes narrowed. The cafe had always pulled its weight. It was the main reason the family had lived so well over the years.

"I don't know exactly. You know I always run the place within a budget. I'm careful about spending. I don't ever do anything too risky. But lately, we've been making a loss, and I can't figure out quite why."

Sarah dipped her head, reached for an olive. "No worries, Mum. We'll work it out. That's why I'm here."

Mum sipped her lemonade. "I've been meaning to ask you - is there another reason you moved back to the Cove?"

Sarah cocked her head to one side. "Other than to help you?"

Mum nodded. "I mean, you could've done that from Sydney. I didn't intend for you to uproot your entire life. You have a career to think of and a fiancé."

"Ex-fiancé," Sarah corrected, her stomach tightening into a knot. It was hard knowing how much everyone in her life loved Jeremy. He was perfect; she wasn't. He was a catch, and she was the lucky woman who'd somehow managed to reel him in. So, telling her family and friends she'd ended things had resulted in a lot of blank stares and arched eyebrows, not to mention clucking of tongues.

The clucking tongues had mostly come from Mum and her best friend, Diana Jones, the woman who owned the bed and breakfast next door. Still, Sarah had noticed the way the people in her life reacted to the news - they didn't understand, couldn't understand her reasons. And honestly, she didn't have the energy to explain it to them. Didn't want or need their sympathy. She hated that Jeremy had made her feel like a victim. That wasn't her. Sarah Flannigan wasn't about to be the jilted woman, the one waiting at home in the kitchen while her husband philandered about town, who was caught by surprise when he left her for a younger model thirty years from now.

She understood how Mum had let it happen; she'd almost followed her mother blindly down the same path. But when Dad left, when he destroyed their family and broke Mum's heart, he'd helped Sarah wake up to what her future could easily become - and bile had risen in her throat at the thought she could end up just like Mum.

"Sorry, ex-fiancé. Although why did the two of you break up? You never really told me what happened there."

"It's complicated," Sarah replied, pressing her lips together. What should she say? He cheated on her, more than once, and she'd finally figured it out? He didn't listen, didn't prioritise her, always had to have things his way. That she'd been too smitten to see it until her parents separated, when she realised she was following so closely in Mum's footsteps that she might smack into her the moment Mum stopped moving forward?

She couldn't say that. It'd hurt Mum's feelings. Mum wouldn't respond, would press her lips together, her eyes glistening, then leave the room to "tidy" the kitchen. But Sarah knew her well enough to see through the facade. It would break her mother's heart if she told her she'd ended things with Jeremy because Dad had walked out on her and Sarah was afraid she'd end up the same way.

"I'm sure it is...but I'm worried about you. That's all."

Sarah sighed. "There's nothing to worry about, Mum. I'm fine, I came here to help you. That's all there is to it. And yes, I suppose I needed a change in my life. My career is important to me, but it's not everything. The breakup helped me to see that there were some empty spaces in my life, things I'd been overlooking because of Jeremy. But we weren't right for each other."

"But you seemed so happy together," Mum objected.

"He was a lot more like Dad than you realise, Mum. I can see the patterns now, and at first, I loved that about him. He was fun, always the life of the party, but when it came to serious matters, he left them to me to deal with. I thought that was normal, just how couples operated. It's how you and Dad were. But when Dad left you, it made me think. I didn't want to spend my life with someone who wasn't able to put my needs first sometimes, who might run off with his assistant in his sixties and not give my happiness a second thought."

Mum's lips had formed a thin line as Sarah spoke. Her eyes bright, she spoke, her voice thick with emotion. "Well, if that's the case, you did the right thing. Marriage is forever, at least in my mind it is, and spending your life with someone who's fun but inconsiderate quickly becomes a strain."

"I had no idea...all these years...I didn't know Dad was like that. I saw him as the happy, life of the party, affectionate one. You were always serious, busy, getting things done, but Dad gave us his attention."

"I know, love. I know. He was great to spend time with, it's why I fell in love with him. I would've liked to have more fun with my kids as well, but I didn't have a partner to share the load. And now I realise he wasn't pulling his weight with our finances the way I thought he was either. It's very frustrating to look back on your life and realise so much of what you thought was true was actually a lie." Mum's voice thickened, and she let her eyes drift shut.

Sarah squeezed her arm. "Well, your kids weren't part of that, Mum. We love you, and we're here for you. At least, I am. I don't know what those other two slackers are doing."

Mum's eyes popped open, and she laughed. "I haven't told them yet. I don't know what to say... They love your father so much."

Sarah smiled. "It's fine, we can work this out together."

"Thank you, my sweet girl." Mum shook her head. "I never thought I'd find myself bankrupt and single in my sixties."

"Maybe you can look at this as your chance to start over. I mean, you've never tried Tinder before. Now you can. The entire world of online dating is out there, just waiting for you. See, silver linings." Sarah chuckled as she shook her head.

Mum laughed, her eyes glistening with tears. "Wonderful. Just what I've always wanted."

CHAPTER 7

SARAH

"No, I need the internet connected now. I can't wait two weeks, I have work to do." Sarah squeezed her eyes shut and pressed one hand to the top of her head, the other holding her mobile phone firmly against her ear.

On the other end of the line, an operator with a strong but unrecognisable accent assured her the internet should be connected within the next two to four weeks.

She sighed with exasperation. She stood on the deck, the cottage's back door open behind her. In front of her, the ocean stretched blue and sparkling, like jewels had been scattered over its surface. The setting sun still shone bright, even as a cool breeze lifted her hair from her neck. She shivered and tugged her jacket more tightly around her thin body.

"Just try to get it done as quickly as possible please.

I can't be stuck without internet access, and there's hardly mobile phone coverage here. I didn't realise I was moving out of reach of technology, for heaven's sake!"

She turned off the phone and shoved it into her pocket with a groan. It was her third call to her internet provider in the past twenty-four hours, and she still hadn't made any headway.

"That sounds frustrating," said a man's voice behind her.

She spun about with a gasp, eyes wide to see a stranger standing in the open doorway.

"Sorry, didn't mean to startle you. The front door was wide open, and I could hear you out here talking. Didn't realise you were on the phone. I'm Mick McIntosh. We spoke earlier?"

He shoved out a hand for her to shake, and she took it with a gulp of air.

"You scared the life out of me."

"Sorry about that." He chuckled. "You're Sarah Flannigan, right?"

She nodded, shook his hand. "Sorry, yes, I'm Sarah. Mick McIntosh...that name's familiar. Mum said we went to school together."

He nodded. "I remember you."

"Really?" She cocked her head to one side. "You do look vaguely familiar." Floppy dark blond hair fell over his green eyes, and he had a wide jaw and muscular build. Exactly the kind of man most women swooned over, but not her type. Still, she'd have thought she'd remember someone who looked like Mick did from her high school years.

He laughed. "I'm glad I made such a lasting impression on you."

Something in his smile sparked a memory.

"Oh yeah, I remember you now. You were shorter, and skinny...with braces."

His lips pursed. "Yep. That sounds about right. But you haven't changed a bit."

Her cheeks flushed with warmth. She wasn't sure why his words had such an effect on her, but she felt an urgent need to change the subject.

"I'm sure that's not true. Anyway, I think you can guess why I asked you to meet me here." She raised an arm and swept a wide gesture towards the cottage, the warped floor still cluttered with unopened boxes. Framed pieces of art leaned up against the stained walls, and broken shutters on dirty windows let in a few shafts of light that stabbed at the dreary darkness in the cramped space.

He nodded. "You want to remodel the place."

"Yes, I've recently bought it and want to make it liveable, light, airy - more modern but still with a hint of history. Does that make sense?"

He nodded. "Got it."

She walked him through the cottage, talking in detail about what she wanted changed, redone or built. She intended to extend the deck, since she wanted to spend as much time as possible out there taking in the spectacular scenery. Also, the kitchen, currently a single bench with a tiny and ancient stove in it and a half dozen cabinets, would need to be enlarged, and the space opened up to let in more light.

By the time they'd finished discussing the work she wanted done, her head spun.

She slumped onto a box, and he sat on one beside her, taking notes with a pencil in a notebook.

"Old school, huh?" she commented.

He nodded with a grunt. "Yeah, I prefer it that way."

"So have you lived in the Cove ever since high school?" she asked.

He shook his head without looking up. "Nope. I went to Canberra to study architecture, then worked in a firm there for about five years. Hated every minute of it." He laughed. "I missed the beach too much. So, I came back here. But as you can imagine, there isn't a lot of call for architects in Emerald Cove. So, I do some architecture, but mostly I do renovations and draft work."

She stood and stretched her arms over her head with a yawn.

"Tired?" he asked.

She smiled. "Actually, I feel great. I've slept the last two nights at Mum's place, in my old bed. There's something deeply satisfying about sleeping in your childhood bed, even if it is small. Except, the boy band posters on the walls give me the creeps. So many white teeth, and so very young!"

He chuckled, shoved the pencil behind his ear and stood. "I can understand that. All the brightly coloured clothing, perfectly combed hair and pouty smiles, it's freaky."

She laughed. "Yeah, it is. So, what do you think about this place? Are we going to be able to make it happen?"

He shrugged. "Yeah, we can definitely do every-thing you want done. I'll put together a quote and get it to you tomorrow. Does that work?"

She smiled. "Perfect. Although, how I'll get the quote without access to email is anyone's guess."

He cocked his head to one side. "How about I swing by with it. I can leave it at the front door if you're not home. Give me a call when you've had a chance to look it over."

She nodded and shook his outstretched hand again. "Thank you. I really appreciate you coming. I already feel a lot better about the cottage. It was a little overwhelming at first, and I wasn't sure where to start or if my ideas for it were even possible. So thanks."

He smiled, revealing a set of his own white teeth - only, unlike the creepy teeth on her old bedroom wall, his weren't perfect. His two front teeth crossed a little in a cute, boyish kind of way. "No worries. I'm glad I can help." He started for the front door, then turned to flash her another grin. "Oh, and welcome home to the Cove."

"Thanks," she said.

He dipped his head, then left. Sarah watched his truck pull out of the driveway from her front door, her eyes narrowed and nerves, or something like them, spinning in her gut. Who would've thought Mick McIntosh would grow up to look like that?

She shook her head and was about to step back inside the cottage when another car pulled into her driveway. She hadn't seen so much traffic on her little street since she arrived.

She tented a hand over her eyes and squinted against the brilliant pinks and oranges of the sunset to see who it was. When Vicky Hawkins stepped from the car with a wave, a lump formed in Sarah's throat. She ran to her friend and threw her arms around her. She hadn't realised how much she'd missed Vicky until the moment she saw her sweet, round face.

Vicky laughed. "Hey, Sarah, how are you?"

Sarah inhaled a quick breath. "I'm good, how are

you? I wasn't expecting to see you. I've really missed you."

"Me too, I'm so glad you've moved home. I didn't think I'd ever see the day when Sarah Flannigan would move back to the Cove. Everyone's talking about it. We haven't had this much excitement since Dotty Harris streaked nude down the main street after her Alzheimer's diagnosis."

Sarah laughed. "Great, so I'm listed in the gossip columns alongside Dotty Harris, huh?"

"You bet," Vicky replied with a grin. "I come bearing gifts!"

She pulled a bag of takeaway food out of the car, along with a bottle of sparkling wine.

"Oh, I could kiss you," Sarah said, reaching for the wine. "Let's go inside, I'll see if I can find some clean drinking glasses."

* * *

THE OVERHEAD LIGHT blinked on in the kitchen. Sarah smiled in satisfaction. At least she'd managed to get the electricity connected, and she'd be spending her first night sleeping in the cabin tonight as a result. She told herself she couldn't stay at Mum's forever. She had her own place. Although it was hard to give up the fridge full of food and the comfortable furnishings for her box-strewn, mouldy, musty-smelling cottage.

"I really like what you've done with the place," Vicky said, glancing around the kitchen and living area. Both spaces opened into one another, providing a wide, spacious area that Sarah imagined would look great once Mick was done with it. But for now, it had the appearance of a homeless shelter.

"Thanks," Sarah replied, crossing her eyes.

She searched for some clean glasses for the wine and found two plates and a pair of forks as well, then carried them to her coffee table, which she'd managed to pull into the centre of the room. She set down the plates, glasses and wine bottle. Vicky added the take-away bag and began removing plastic containers filled with Chinese food.

"Mmmm, Chinese. My favourite!"

"I know," Vicky replied with a grin. She filled both glasses with champagne, handed one to Sarah and raised her own. "To new beginnings, and to my gorgeous friend moving back to town after so many years away." Vicky's eyes glimmered with unshed tears, and her smile wobbled. "It's good to have you back."

Sarah's throat tightened. "I never thought I'd say this, but it's good to be back."

She leaned forward to hug her friend, then they each toasted with a mouthful of the sparkling wine.

Sarah began spooning the steaming hot food onto their plates. "So, how are things in the veterinarian business?"

Vicky chuckled. "Business is booming."

"You're amazing. I don't know how you do it. Day in, day out, treating sick animals."

Vicky shrugged and took a bite out of a spring roll. "I love it. I couldn't imagine doing anything else. Today I got to help a prized mare give birth. She had a difficult time of it, would've died if no one was there to help her. There's definitely some satisfaction in that."

"Good for you. I can't even imagine how stressful that must be. I get to deal with egotistical authors all day long." Sarah chuckled.

"It's not that bad. Is it?"

Sarah sighed. "No, of course not. When I say egotistical authors, I really mean my ex-fiancé. Unfortunately, even though I ended our engagement, I'm still his editor. And since I'm currently avoiding his calls, it makes for an awkward editor-author relationship."

Vicky's eyes widened. "I'd say so. Wow, how do you navigate that?"

"Move to a small seaside town as far away from him as possible..." Sarah laughed. "Seriously, it's been challenging. I'm hoping a little bit of distance will help. He won't accept that the relationship is over, but it is. We couldn't make it work. He's too much..."

"What?" Vicky asked.

"Never mind, tell me more about you. What's going on in your life?"

Vicky inhaled a sharp breath. "Actually, you know how Meg and I have become good friends...?"

Sarah nodded. "I remember her - she was a sweet little girl. Isn't she dating Brad Taylor?"

"Well, she's not a girl now, and they were married last week."

"Wow, I feel old." Sarah grimaced. "I remember her riding her bike around town, her little red pigtails bouncing on either side of her head. She was very cute."

"She's still cute." Vicky sighed. "She and Brad have been so happy together, so in love, and they're on their honeymoon..."

"That sounds nice," Sarah said.

"It would be, except Brad's had a surfing accident. They're in Hawaii, and I haven't had a recent update, but I think it's bad."

Sarah's eyes widened. "What? Oh no!"

"Yes, I'll let you know when I find out more, but I

feel so bad for poor Meg. She was so excited about their trip. The wedding was lovely, they're head over heels for each other. I hope he doesn't...anyway. No point talking about what might happen or could go wrong. We have to stay positive until we hear more." Vicky's voice broke, but she coughed to clear her throat and kept going. "So, as you can see, it's never dull around here, even if it is a small town."

"You know what they say about small towns..." Sarah began, still shaking her head over Vicky's news.

"No. What?"

"Small town, big drama."

Vicky dashed a tear from the corner of her eye and chuckled. "I've never heard that."

"I made it up. I think it's going to catch on." Sarah smiled and patted Vicky's arm. "I'm sure he'll be okay. He's young and strong. We should check the news later, maybe they'll have a story about what's happened. After all, he's a big-time surfing star these days." She inhaled a slow breath, eyes narrowed. "It's still hard for me to comprehend, little Brad Taylor is a superstar."

Vicky took a bite of chow mein and chewed thoughtfully. "I know. I used to babysit him."

"Really?" Sarah laughed.

"Yeah, and now his wife is my best friend. Who would've thought?"

Sarah's smile faded. It was childish to hold onto a title, but she'd always been Vicky's best friend. Moving away had meant losing that closeness over a period of time. It'd been her own fault; she'd been so caught up in studying, building a career, falling in love, climbing the social ladder...she hadn't looked back. She'd neglected their friendship. It was one of her biggest regrets.

"Well, please let me know if you hear anything."

"I will," Vicky said. "I tried calling her back a few times, but she's not answering her phone. I don't know if that means she wants to be left alone, but I need her to know I'm here for her. It's so hard to know what to do."

Sarah nodded, then continued eating her meal. There were so many people she'd lost touch with over the years. It was strange to be back in town, strange to be eating takeaway with her childhood friend in her very own beachside cottage. She wondered how long it'd take her to get used to it.

And would she ever get used to the fact that her father had abandoned his family for his assistant, stranding her mother with a mountain of surprise debt?

At least there was something concrete she could do to help Mum on that score. She couldn't fix Mum and Dad's relationship. She couldn't bring him back or mend their family. But she could do her best to figure out why the cafe was losing so much money, plug the leak and work out a payment plan for the bank.

CHAPTER 8

CINDY

*C*indy stared wistfully at the copy of People magazine on the small, rectangular table in the centre of the waiting room. There were several stories inside the magazine she'd love to read - one in particular about the Duchess of Cambridge and a lovely cerulean dress - but she didn't dare pick it up. She'd made it a rule, years earlier after a particularly nasty bout of gastro, never to touch magazines at a doctor's office.

She sighed and stared instead at her own hands, twisted together in her lap. She could do with a manicure. But that was always the case since she worked at a cafe. It was impossible to keep her hands and nails in good shape when she washed them so often and used them to carry, wipe and scrub all day long.

It was worth it though. She loved her restaurant - the Emerald Cafe. Her parents had named it that when they'd first opened it fifty-five years earlier. She remembered the day. They'd buzzed with excitement. It'd been smaller then, more cramped, with a kitchen that would barely count as anything more than a sink and a cupboard. But they'd been so proud of it.

Of course, since then it'd undergone several remodels and upgrades, until now it was the largest and busiest cafe in the small tourist town.

"You can go in, Cindy," Helen said. The receptionist was seated behind a long mahogany desk and doubled as a nursing assistant whenever Dr Miller needed one.

Cindy smiled and strode towards the closed door with a nameplate on it that read, "Dr Athol Miller M.D."

She knocked once, then pushed the door open and stepped inside.

"Good morning, Cindy. How are you today?" Athol stepped towards her, kissed her cheek.

She blushed. It was awkward seeing her doctor again after everything that'd happened. Athol and Andrew had been best friends. For all she knew, they were still. Maybe he talked to Andrew; they could still be in touch. Part of her wanted to know, wanted to corner him until he confessed. The other part of her wanted to stay naïve. Athol was her friend as well, had been for thirty years. She'd been the one to comfort him and ferry him meals every week a decade earlier when Cheryl died, after more than twenty years of marriage.

She offered him a hesitant smile. "Hi, Athol. I'm fine, thanks."

"Take a seat," he said, returning to his own seat behind a desk with a glowing computer monitor.

"Thank you." She sat, crossed her feet at the ankles

and folded her hands in her lap. She stared at her wrinkled fingers. When had they gotten so old? One of the strangest parts about growing old was not recognising parts of your body when you looked at them, thinking for a moment that you were seeing someone else.

Athol's mouse clicked a few times, his eyes on the screen. "Let's see…the last time you came in was a year ago for your annual check-up. Is that what we're doing again today? Or is there something else?"

She inhaled a quick breath. "Just the check-up. I had this appointment set months ago…or I wouldn't have… I'm sorry this is a little awkward."

He studied her, his brow furrowed. "Because of Andrew? Is that what you mean?"

She nodded.

"Well, I haven't spoken to him since right after he left. I called him one time to give him a piece of my mind and haven't spoken to him since."

Cindy's eyes narrowed. "You haven't?"

He smiled. "Nope."

"I thought…that maybe you were still in touch. I wasn't sure I should even come today." Her lips pursed.

"Well, I'm glad you did. Now, let's take that blood pressure of yours. It's always perfect, I'm sure it will be again today." He fitted the cuff round her arm and pumped the bladder.

Cindy studied the floor by her foot, then glanced at Athol's face. He was studying the numbers, his blue eyes narrowed behind a pair of black-rimmed glasses.

"You really gave him a piece of your mind?" she asked.

He nodded, smiled. "Yes, I did. After I realised he'd run off with Keisha, I called his mobile. He answered, told me we should catch up sometime, stay in touch, you know how he is - always smiling, always ready to have fun. I used to love that about him." He hesitated, then unwound the belt from her arm. "Perfect blood pressure, as always."

She nodded, rubbing her arm where the belt had been. "Yes, he was good at that. Not so good at being a faithful husband, or dedicated father, it turns out."

Athol tapped at the keyboard with a nod. "I told him I thought he was a fool to leave you for someone as vain and vapid as Keisha. That she was bound to leave him the moment someone richer and younger came along, and he should turn around, speed home and beg you to take him back. He didn't listen, of course. He laughed and told me to relax, that life was like a theme park, and if you didn't change rides every now and then, you could get sick."

Cindy huffed, her eyes narrowed. "He said that?"

Athol chuckled. "Yes, he did. It reveals a lot, if you ask me. You were always too good for that man, Cindy. Far too smart, beautiful, sweet... He didn't deserve you. Of course, none of us saw that about him when we were young. He's charming and fun, we all fell for it. But I've struggled to remain friends with him for years now."

"I noticed you weren't coming around as often..." Cindy replied thoughtfully. "I figured it was because you were grieving Cheryl."

"There was some of that," he admitted. "But mostly, it was because after she died, I couldn't stand to ignore the truth anymore - which was that Andrew Flannigan was a selfish, conceited man, and I didn't have much in common with him. I grew up, he didn't. It was hard to maintain a friendship with someone like that. To be honest with you, the only reason I kept coming to dinner was because of you."

Cindy's brow furrowed. "Really?"

Athol smiled and laid a hand on her arm. "Yes, really. When Cheryl died, you were there for me. You've always been so kind - I know Cheryl appreciated your friendship, and so do I."

Her throat closed around a growing lump. She smiled as tears threatened. "Thank you, Athol. I appreciate your friendship as well."

"Of course," he replied. "I'm so sorry for the way Andrew treated you. But I really believe you'll be better off in the long run. You're an amazing woman, and he didn't deserve you."

Cindy sniffled. "Thank you. I really miss seeing you. It's been far too long."

"I'm still around," he replied.

"Well then..." she said, unable to continue. She smiled and linked her hands together. It meant a lot to her to hear that Athol valued their friendship and wanted it to continue, that he supported her and was on her side. One of the advantages of living in a small town was that you were never quite alone. She knew everyone who lived in the Cove, but she only had a few true friends, and Athol was one of them. She'd thought he wouldn't want to see her again after Andrew left and mourned the loss of his friendship in silence, alongside every other feeling that raged. To know that he was still her friend, after everything that'd happened, choked her into silence.

So, instead of saying anything more, she patted his arm with a wobbly smile.

CHAPTER 9

SARAH

*S*arah stood in the doorway and waved goodbye to Vicky as her friend's car pulled out of the drive. The car was soon shielded by bushes and trees, the darkness of night having replaced the usual dappled sunlight that shone through their branches.

With a shiver, Sarah tugged her cardigan more tightly around her shoulders against a frigid breeze that rose from the ocean, up the cliffside and around the cottage. A constant wind was something she'd have to grow accustomed to if she was going to live with an ocean view.

She turned to head inside the cottage when a rustle in the garden caught her ear. She hesitated on the threshold, glancing back over her shoulder. Her eyes narrowed, sensing movement. She skipped down the stairs, her eyes fixed on the place where she'd seen the flicker of something - tan, brown, dark. Maybe a tail.

"Hello?" she said.

A low growl rose against the hush of waves as they curled to shore at the base of the cliff.

"Come on out, I won't hurt you."

Perhaps it was a possum, though they didn't usually growl and were more likely to be found on a tree branch, fence post or traversing a power line. It sounded more like a dog.

With her hands on her hips, she studied the bushes as her eyes adjusted to the dim lighting. Definitely a dog. And it was hungry, starving in fact.

She hurried inside the cottage and fossicked through the fridge, looking for something that might entice a dog out of hiding. There wasn't much in there other than the packet of bacon and dozen eggs she'd bought for breakfast. Though she realised now it was a bit ambitious to imagine she'd be up for cooking a hot breakfast any time before noon. She wasn't much of a breakfast eater at the best of times, instead preferring a cup of coffee and perhaps a small yoghurt with fruit if she was particularly hungry.

She grabbed the packet of bacon, sliced it open with a knife and dropped the meat into a large, white bowl. Then she carried the bowl outside and set it on the ground next to the bushes where she'd last seen the dog.

It wasn't there.

Her lips pursed in disappointment.

Oh well. There wasn't anything she could do about it. Though she hated to see any creature suffering.

She left the bowl where it was and returned to the house, her thoughts already turning to what was left to do. She still hadn't finished unpacking, there were a few pieces of furniture she hadn't managed to slide into place yet, and she wanted to check to see if she could access the internet, though she didn't like her chances given the provider had mentioned a vague and infuriating time frame of two to four weeks.

She sighed and padded into the kitchen, sat at the bench and booted up her laptop.

It wasn't long before she realised she wouldn't be logging into her company's network anytime soon. She sighed, closed the laptop then tiptoed to the front window. Pushing aside the musty-scented, retro print curtains, she peered outside. The dog stood over the bowl, front knees bent as it devoured the bacon in several large gulps. She could see it more clearly now; it was a medium-sized dog with a dark brown coat. Its ribs showed through the patches of hair that clung to its thin sides, and its tail was firmly wedged between its back legs.

Sarah smiled, watched for a few moments then tiptoed back to the front door. She stepped outside. The dog raised its head and studied her.

"Hey there," she said. "What's your name? Huh?"

The dog didn't move.

Sarah walked a little closer, slowly, her eyes fixed on the dog. "I'm not going to hurt you."

The dog spun in place then sprinted for the tree line.

She sighed, pressed her hands to her hips. She'd hoped she might find a collar, perhaps with a tag on it and a phone number to call. Though from where she was standing, the dog didn't appear to be wearing one. Most likely it was a stray, looked like it had been for a while. And it certainly wasn't comfortable around people.

The wind tugged at her blue cardigan, pushing in gusts that shook the bushy branches of the squat trees surrounding the cottage with an almost constant rustle.

She headed inside and locked the front door behind her. Her life had certainly changed since she'd left her high-rise unit in the city. The noise of traffic and people had been replaced by the whistle of a cool sea breeze and the sighing of trees, and her social life, once filled with the vibrant, artistic and upwardly mobile people of inner Sydney, had been replaced by a stray dog who had no desire for her company.

She shook her head and flicked off the main light. With a shiver, she wrapped her arms around her body and hurried to the bedroom. The warm blankets she'd found in one of the many boxes that lined her wooden floors were calling her name.

CHAPTER 10

MEG

*M*eg studied the small cartons of eggnog clutched in her hands. This wasn't exactly how she'd planned to spend her first Christmas as Brad's wife - drinking eggnog from cartons bought at the hospital cafeteria. Then again, none of this had been part of the plan.

Her heart ached for a moment; she allowed herself that much before she walked back into the room to face what was inside. Past the nurse's station, there was the door. Only slightly ajar, waiting for her return. A light flickered against the doorframe - the television was on, it was always on, though the sound would be on mute and no one would be watching it.

Even the glimpse of the doorframe accelerated her heart rate. It was no use; she wasn't good at this kind of thing. She'd never liked conflict, and that was what her life had become now. Conflict. Arguments. Shouting. Things crashing against walls or onto floors. Tears. Hidden moments in the small adjoining bathroom as she rocked silently, her mouth pressed to a wadded-up jacket or shirt or whatever she could find to stifle the sounds of her grief. This was her life.

For now, she reminded herself. It wouldn't always be this way. This wasn't how her marriage would be. It couldn't be.

Tears threatened, and she pushed them down with a determined breath, straightened her shoulders and walked into the room with a cheerful smile.

"Christmas is saved, I found eggnog!"

Brad continued to stare at the wall furthest from the window. His mother, Sharon, smiled at her, arms crossed. His father, Des, lowered the newspaper to peer over it in her direction. He was the only man she knew who still liked to sit and peruse a real newspaper, rather than scrolling through pages on his phone.

"That's wonderful," Sharon said.

"Thanks, sweetheart," Des added with a wink.

She nodded and set the cartons on the small table that hung over Brad's bed on a set of squeaky wheels. She pushed it a little closer to Brad, the wheels emitting a creak.

"Brad…look, eggnog. You love eggnog."

She opened one of the cartons with both fingers pressed to the cardboard until it popped. Then she shifted the table closer to Brad's nearest arm, it lay pressed to his side in the bed. Her gaze traveled over the covers to where his legs stretched, straight and still beneath the cream covers.

Meg glanced at his mother, who nodded her encouragement. "We'll make this Christmas special in our own way. I might see if I can find somewhere that'll serve a better Christmas turkey than the cafeteria." Sharon reached into her purse where it was hung on the back of the door and pulled out her mobile. "There has to be somewhere nearby we could buy something decent to bring back to the room."

Anger emanated in waves from Brad like heat from summer scorched tarmac. Meg watched him, her brow furrowed. She couldn't get through to him and didn't know what to do. He'd always been so open with her, so affectionate, full of smiles and laughter. Never like this. Never sullen or silent.

"That sounds good," she responded to Sharon while continuing to watch Brad for some indication he was listening to their conversation. He remained unmoving, his eyes fixed on some invisible spot on the wall.

She sighed, crossing her arms over her chest. The past two weeks since he was admitted to the hospital had been the hardest of her life. At first, she'd been desperate, praying for Brad to make it through the emergency surgery.

Then, there were two more surgeries in the days that followed, days in which they'd almost lost him more times than she cared to remember. His doctors had worn harried expressions, barely slept. Nurses had rushed here and there, and she'd sat alone in the waiting room, chewing her nails to the quick, tapping her heels against the floor and answering the phone. So many phone calls, eventually she'd turned it off. She couldn't concentrate on conversations, not while Brad was lying on an operating table somewhere in the hospital, possibly dying.

His parents had arrived on the third day. Had rushed into the waiting room. His mother's hair flew out behind her, wispy and blonde; his father's eyes were red-rimmed.

"Where is he? What's the update?" Sharon had questioned the moment she saw her and enveloped Meg in a crushing embrace.

They'd been amazing since then, helping her stay positive, getting her food, coffee. They'd checked her out of the beachside cottage where she and Brad had honeymooned and got her a room at their hotel near the hospital, bringing her clean clothes back with them. Eventually they'd even convinced her to go back to the hotel to get some sleep, once Brad was stable and the surgeries complete.

She'd collapsed into the bed with dry eyes and slept without moving, waking twelve hours later with pins and needles in one ear and sheet marks creasing the side of her face.

Two weeks later and it was Christmas Eve. Thinking about it had her throat aching. She'd planned for them to wake up in their unit by the beach at home in Emerald Cove on Christmas morning, to open their gifts over a cup of coffee and then drive to Brisbane to spend the day with his family. Something so suburban, so simple, had filled her with delightful anticipation.

It was everything she'd never had as a child, everything she longed for. Growing up with parents who fought, separated, got back together only to start all over again, and a mother who barely spoke to the extended family, she'd longed for a normal Christmas, filled with family, laughter and lazy conversation. Instead, they were stuck in a hospital, and her husband hated her. Or, if he didn't, he was giving a good impression of it.

The door to the room swung wider, and Brad's

doctor stepped inside, a clipboard in his hands. He studied the page a moment, then regarded the room with a smile.

"Good morning, Brad, good morning, Meg, Sharon, Des... How are we all on this Christmas Eve?"

For the first time in an hour, Brad's eyes shifted from the nonexistent spot on the wall and moved to study the doctor's face.

"We're doing well today, thanks, Dr Benson," Meg replied. "Brad ate some breakfast, and I found eggnog in the cafeteria."

"That's good news."

Brad's eyes seemed to darken; his lips shrank into one thin line. He wanted to say something, make an angry retort but was holding back in front of the doctor, Meg could tell. He'd spent the past week, at least whenever he was conscious, either in complete silence or spitting angry words at her and his parents. She linked her hands together, her fingers twisting.

Dr Benson moved close to the bed and began fixing a blood pressure sleeve around Brad's arm. He studied Brad as he worked.

"How are you feeling today, Brad?"

Brad huffed. "Same."

"No changes?"

Brad shook his head.

The doctor ran through a series of tests. When he pulled back the covers to press a small instrument to the soles of Brad's bare feet, Meg held her breath. She watched, eyes wide, waiting to see some reaction, a movement, anything to show the swelling in his back had gone down.

When the tests were complete, the doctor slid

Brad's covers back over his legs and sat on the end of the bed with a smile.

"You're looking good, Brad. Your stats have improved, the infection we were fighting is gone, and you're getting stronger every day. We'll be able to let you go home before too much longer."

Sharon's hand flew to cover her mouth.

"Really, doc?" Des asked, standing all of a sudden.

"There's some physiotherapy still to do, but yes. I'm happy with your progress. But there's something we need to talk about today, Brad. I'd like to do it in private, if that's okay with you."

Brad shook his head. "No, they can stay. I've got nothing to hide from them."

The doctor nodded. "Fine, if that's what you'd like."

"It is."

"As you've no doubt realised, the swelling along your spine is going down. You're on the way to recovery. However, you still haven't gotten any feeling back in your legs and feet. From the hips down, you continue to experience paralysis. I'm afraid, from what I'm seeing, the impact of your injuries may be permanent."

Silence followed his statement.

Sharon looked at her husband. He moved to her and slipped an arm around her waist.

Meg's thoughts froze. She couldn't process what Dr Benson was saying. Permanent? That couldn't be right. He'd been telling them for over a week the swelling was impacting on his nerves, his muscles' responses. She'd been concerned but not worried - it would resolve in time. That was what they'd all said. It would resolve. There was a risk, of course, she'd heard the words, but she hadn't listened, had clung instead to the idea of them getting through this, going home to restart their lives together with the horror of the accident behind them. This couldn't be happening. There must be a mistake.

Her gaze flicked to Brad's face. He stared at his feet, two lumps beneath the covers, unmoving.

Dr Benson was talking again, but Meg couldn't seem to focus on the words enough to understand what he was saying.

Brad's gaze met hers for an instant, then clouded with anger. His lips curled into a sneer. He reached out a hand and slapped the cartons of eggnog. The one she'd opened flew across the room, splattering the beverage across the floor and up the wall. The other cartons landed with several thunks.

Sharon gasped, hid her head in Des's shoulder. Des's eyes glimmered, his lower lip trembled. He swallowed as his gaze landed on his son's reddened face.

Dr Benson stopped talking, stood and wiped his hands down the length of his white coat.

Meg felt tears rising, her throat tightening. She couldn't cry in front of Brad; it only made him worse, angrier somehow. He hated to see her cry. She squeezed her eyes shut a moment, holding her emotions at bay, then ran from the room.

Outside she leaned against the wall, heaving to catch her breath. It wasn't fair, wasn't right. He was young, fit, strong. He was a professional surfer; it was what he loved, what he spent most of his time doing.

Tears welled and coursed down her cheeks. She had to be strong for him, but outside of the room, she'd allow herself this moment to be weak, to be afraid. She buried her face in her hands.

A few moments later, someone walked from the

room. They hesitated beside her, and she felt a hand on her shoulder. She looked up to see Dr Benson standing there, a look of compassion warming his face.

"It's not the end of the world, Meg. I know it seems that way now. You're young, these things can feel, in the moment, like they're everything. But they're not. Brad is otherwise a healthy, young man. He'll have to learn how to navigate the world again, but the two of you can still have a full and happy life together."

She rubbed her hands over her face, the tears drying beneath her palms. "We had so many dreams... travel, adventure, children..."

"In all likelihood, there'll still be children...if you want them. And the other things too."

She studied the doctor's face, warm brown eyes, long, pointed nose, thin lips with the slightest tilt of a smile lighting up one corner.

"Really?"

He nodded and patted her shoulder gently. "Yes, it's all a possibility, it might be more difficult, but it's not impossible. I know it's a lot to take in right now, and you feel as though your world has come crashing down around you, but you both have a decision to make - will you face this with courage and get on with your lives, or will you let it knock you down and keep you there?"

She sniffled, wiped her nose with the back of one hand. "I don't know... He won't even talk to me."

"Give him some time. Don't give up on him, it's the death of a big dream for him... Competitive surfing is out of the picture for him now. But I hope he'll be able to see that there's the hope of other things ahead for him, things that he might even enjoy just as much."

She shook her head. "I doubt that." Her throat was thick with tears.

"I have to get going, but I'll see you tomorrow and we can talk more if you'd like."

She watched as Dr Benson walked away down the wide hall. The beep of machinery echoed through the buzz and hum of nurses striding with purpose, patients working their way slowly from their rooms to the cafeteria, their hospital gowns flapping with each step, and visitors shushing rowdy children who sat with hands folded in little laps, lips pouting in protest.

With a sigh, she strode back into the room, blinking away the last of her tears.

CHAPTER 11

SARAH

*T*he tick of the grandfather clock set a rhythm that had Sarah's foot tapping beneath her mother's solid blue gum timber desk. She chewed on the end of a pen, her eyes narrowed as one finger traced a column of numbers scratched in her mother's hand.

"Have you never heard of a computer?" Sarah murmured around the pen.

"What's that?" Mum called from the nearby kitchen.

The scent of roasting meat drifted through the office doorway.

"Nothing, just wondering why you're still using this old ledger book to keep track of your accounts for the cafe," Sarah replied with a grimace.

Mum stood in the doorway with a ladle in one hand. Her grey hair had been styled into perfect waves that looked as though a wind had come through and blown her locks back from her face. She wore a pink ruffled apron around her neat waist, paired with a dark pink top and white capri pants. Sarah only hoped her legs would look so good when she reached her sixties.

"I've always done the books that way, and I wouldn't know where to start using the computer for it... I guess we could try...but honestly, it's fine the way it is."

Sarah cocked her head to one side. "Is it? I can't for the life of me figure out what's going on. What is this, here?" She pointed a finger at one line item.

Mum leaned forward, studied it with a squint. "I can't see without my glasses, but it's probably a personal expense."

"So why is it listed against the cafe?" Sarah asked.

Mum shrugged.

Sarah continued working a while longer, getting more concerned and confused with each moment that passed. From what she could see, it looked as though the cafe was in debt. A lot of debt. And she couldn't figure out why expenses were so high, given the incoming revenue was decent.

"Mum, what's all this debt," she called.

Her mother's head popped through the doorway again. "Oh yeah, that."

"What's going on?"

Mum's lips pursed. "That's the debt I told you about — you know, from your father."

"I wanted to talk to you about that," began Sarah, "how on earth did he manage to do it without your knowledge?"

"I don't know, and he won't return my phone calls." Her mother's smile tightened. "As I mentioned before, when we were first married, he convinced me it would be good for tax purposes if I added his name to the business. So, I did. I can't imagine what I was thinking - I mean, it's my business. Why would I add his name to it? Anyway, I'm talking to a lawyer about getting him removed. But in the meantime, he's managed to practically sink the cafe in debt, and I didn't know a thing about it — I should've known, but I didn't."

"Oh, Mum, I'm so sorry." Sarah's heart ached for her mother. The cafe was more than a business to her; it was the legacy passed down by her parents, it was the place she'd spent most of her childhood and in turn where she'd raised her own children.

Mum disappeared back to the kitchen. Her voice echoed through the doorway. "It's Christmas Eve, can't you do this another time? Don't get me wrong, I'm so grateful you're helping. I really am at the end of my rope with all of that...but your brother and sister will be here soon. I'd love it if you'd come out to the kitchen and sit with me while I cook. You can even open a bottle of red if you like."

Sarah sighed. "I guess I can stop. It's not as if I actually understand any of it. And it's giving me a stomach ache..." She ran fingers through her dark hair, sending it cascading down her back.

With the ledger shut, she followed her mother back into the kitchen and sat at the bench. Mum handed her a bottle of shiraz and two wine glasses, and Sarah opened it and poured them both a drink. They clinked the glasses together.

Sarah smiled at the grin on Mum's face - Mum loved this stuff. Loved it when her family gathered under her roof, and soon she'd have all three of her children in one place. Sarah knew it was everything her mother had hoped, for her first Christmas without Dad. At least, she imagined it was, and the smile seemed to confirm it.

"Cheers," they both said at the same time.

Sarah chuckled, then sipped the wine as Mum went back to basting the roast.

"It smells amazing, Mum."

"I hope it tastes as good," Mum replied.

"It always does, and I'm starving. I haven't eaten anything all day in preparation." Sarah tugged at the waist of her skirt. "I wanted to make sure I had plenty of room for the feast."

"Thanks for bringing the pavlova."

Sarah grinned. "You're welcome. All I did was put whipped cream and sliced fruit on top of a meringue I bought at the market."

"Still…one less thing for me to do. And it looks delicious."

"So, how are you feeling?" Sarah asked.

Mum set down the basting brush and wiped her hands on the apron. "What do you mean?"

Sarah waved a hand around as she took another sip. "I mean, without Dad. This will be our first Christmas without him. Are you okay? Do you want to talk about it?"

Mum's nostrils flared. "I'm fine. In fact, I was thinking just this morning how great it was not to have to get up and make someone breakfast before finishing off my Christmas shopping. And I've managed to get the staff at the cafe up to a level where they can run the place without me some of the time, so I'm pretty content all around. I had a lovely day of shopping and cooking, and even had time for tea with Diana."

"Sounds great, Mum. But the others will be here soon... Don't you think it'll feel a little strange without him?"

Mum hesitated. "I guess that's probably true. Although, don't worry about me, I'm fine. I hope you kids adjust, I know it's a big change for you. I'm sure you miss him."

Sarah sighed. "I do miss him, but I'm still so mad at him for what he did. I don't understand it. I thought I knew him..."

"We all did." Mum's hollow voice surprised her.

Sarah got up and met her mother in the middle of the kitchen. She laid a hand on her arm. "I'm sorry, Mum. I know it's hard for you to talk about, but I don't think we can go through Christmas without acknowledging that it's our first time without him."

"It's fine." Mum patted her hand. "I know you want to talk about him, you miss him...but honestly, I don't. I don't want to talk about the fact that he's not around, and I don't miss him." Her eyes flashed. "He made the choice, it's his loss. And I get to have the three of you all to myself."

Sarah embraced her mother, enjoying the feeling of safety and warmth she always felt in her arms.

Mum wiped her eyes with her sleeve. "Do you think you could throw together a few nibbles for me?"

"Sure," Sarah answered.

Mum pulled a platter from a cupboard and handed it to her. "There are nuts, biscuits and chocolates in the pantry. Cheese in the fridge."

With a bob of her head, Sarah got to work arranging the items on the platter.

"Are you settling into the cottage?" Mum asked as she reached into the oven with a pair of tongs to turn the baking potatoes, pumpkin, capsicum, beetroot and sliced onions.

"It's okay. It still doesn't really feel like home, with boxes jammed into every room and so much mess. I think it'll be great when the renovation is finished though. And there's a dog..."

"What do you mean, there's a dog?"

Sarah laughed. "This mangy dog showed up outside the cottage a couple of weeks ago. I gave it bacon, and now it keeps coming back. It won't let me near it, of course. So, I haven't been able to find out if it's a boy or a girl, but it stands in the distance, eyes begging for more food."

Mum pressed a hand to her heart. "Oh dear. I hope it's not vicious."

Sarah huffed. "No, Mum, it's not vicious. It's a stray, but I wonder where it came from. There are only a few houses around my area, otherwise mostly bushland. I guess it could've come from town, though that's a long way to run for a dog."

Mum's eyes narrowed. "I think the man who used to live there owned a dog of some kind, a mutt. I remember seeing it when I took him soup one time."

"Really?"

"Yes, but that was a few years ago now. He died from a stroke in the end. Perhaps it's his dog. I don't know if anyone would've thought to collect the poor animal, since Phil died in the hospital after a long stay. Maybe his dog was forgotten in all the craziness. I don't think he had any relatives, so it's entirely possible your dog lived in that cottage before you."

Sarah crossed her arms over her chest. "That makes a lot of sense. It certainly seems to feel at home there, hangs around on the edges of the clearing a lot. Do you remember its name?"

"Hmmm...let me see." Mum tapped fingernails in a steady rhythm on the stone bench. "Odin, or Owen, or...Oscar. Yes, I think it was Oscar, but I could be wrong. Anyway, worth trying it out, see if the dog responds, I suppose."

"Yeah, thanks, Mum, I will." She really had no desire for a dog; they were nothing but work. Still, she wasn't sure she could do anything about it. Oscar, or whatever his name was, didn't seem to want to move on. He'd hung around the cottage for two weeks, in the shadows, just out of reach but never far away. Maybe his name would help her get a little closer to him. If he was going to be a part of her life, he'd need a bath at the very least.

The sound of the front door opening caught their attention, and Sarah hurried to meet her siblings.

"Merry Christmas!" she called, hugging them one at a time.

Adele kissed her cheek, her hazel eyes glowing. "It's good to see you, sis."

"You've shrunk!" Ethan declared, throwing his arms around her and spinning her wildly.

Sarah laughed. "No, you've grown."

"Oh, that makes more sense," Ethan replied with a wink, his brown hair perfectly mussed.

They wandered into the living room, chatting and laughing together. Sarah watched with a smile as Ethan and Adele put down their luggage and embraced their mother. She hadn't realised until that moment how much she missed them.

CHAPTER 12

REBECCA

*R*ebecca Mair studied the sea with a frown, inhaled a long, slow breath, then continued walking as the water hurried back into the ocean, leaving a dark path in the sand. Waves curled to shore then chuckled with bubbles and froth as they enveloped her bare feet.

She crossed her arms over her chest, feeling the cool wind from across the ocean in the dimming twilight. It was cool here; at least that was a bonus. After the stifling heat of Sydney's western suburbs, she enjoyed the feel of a sea breeze on her cheeks.

In the distance, a family played cricket on the sand. A young boy bowled the ball, his arm flinging awkwardly forward. The ball bounced once on the hard sand, then a man, most likely the boy's father, hit it with the flat side of the bat. It dribbled over the sand as the man ran towards a set of wickets that'd been stuck at odd angles, pushed down beside the remnants of a sandcastle.

A woman ran after the ball, her laughter carrying on the wind to where Rebecca stood. A young girl crouched by the wickets ready to catch, hands poised in front of her coiled body.

She wanted to smile, but it'd been so long since she'd felt any desire to, the urge dissipated before her lips had the chance to curve. The sudden realisation of how long it'd been since she'd smiled, or felt happy enough to try it, made Rebecca shake her head. She pushed her hands deep into the pockets of her denim capris and kept moving, shoulders hunched.

She turned to head up the beach towards the line of shops and small buildings. Her new unit was up there, above a fish and chip shop. It smelled like fried food and vaguely of smoke in her small, dark living room, though the single bedroom that jutted off one side of the narrow kitchen was a little better.

She'd shut all the windows when she left in hopes it might improve while she was out, though she thought it unlikely given the fact that the structure had steeped in the aroma for years, possibly decades given the paint-chipped, rusted and stained look of the place.

When she reached the street, she glanced at her unit, the curtains drawn shut, giving the two street-side windows a sleepy look, eyelids drawn partially closed over tired eyes.

On the ground level, the neon of the fish and chip sign blinked bright in the dim twilight. Diners sat around on mismatched chairs, phone screens captivating their attention while they waited for their meals to be served steaming hot and wrapped in butcher's paper.

With a long breath that drew into her lungs as though it'd been an age since the last, Rebecca spun on her heel and continued down the street rather than face the silent emptiness of her new home. As she walked, the street grew busier. Soon she found herself in the centre of downtown Emerald Cove. Walking through the hamlet from one side to the other only took about fifteen minutes, so she wasn't sure she could call it a town.

A woman pushed a pram past her, glanced up and offered a smile, her eyes glinting with curiosity. Two men, deep in conversation, turned to look at her as she passed the cafe they were seated in. A group of children playing hopscotch on the pavement stopped to look, and one pointed in her direction. They all fell silent as she passed.

Emerald Cove was a tourist town; surely they were accustomed to strangers. Or perhaps the locals had already learned she was here. She wouldn't be surprised; she'd heard that everyone knew everyone else's business in the seaside village. A new police officer was bound to capture the attention of the people who lived there, especially after what'd happened to the cop whose shoes she'd be filling.

She could feel eyes boring into her back as she walked and stiffened her spine in response. She hated the feeling of being watched, of attracting attention. It was exactly the reason she'd chosen Emerald Cove, to fade into the background, to disappear. She didn't want attention and certainly didn't need it.

It was at times like these Rebecca wished she could call her mother, talk to her about the lonely stone that'd taken up residence in her gut and wouldn't seem to shift no matter what she did. Talk to her about starting over in a new place, with new faces, new names, a new chance to screw things up all over again.

With a grimace, she studied the outside of a small shop - the sign read, "Emerald Cove Foodstore". She swallowed, certain that she'd prompt a deluge of gossip by walking inside. With a shrug, she strode through the automatic door, a bell jangled over her head. Faces tilted in her direction, curious but kind enough. She didn't hold anyone's attention for long, and as she selected fruit to add to a basket that swung over her arm, the breath that'd caught in her throat released with a quiet sigh. She could do this. Could start again, rebuild her life. It wasn't what she'd wanted or planned, but it was her chance to make the kind of life she needed, even if she had to do it alone.

Christmas Eve alone was harder than she'd thought it'd be. She'd planned on letting this holiday pass without a second thought, but the decorations that marked every storefront, filled the shelves and hung from the ceilings, along with the cheerful piped music made it difficult to overlook.

At the checkout, the girl who served her looked about twelve years old, though Rebecca knew that couldn't be the case. Now that she was twenty-eight years old, anyone under the age of twenty looked like a baby. By most estimations, she was still young herself, but after everything that'd happened to her over the past few years, she felt ancient. As though she'd lived five lifetimes.

"Merry Christmas," the girl said with a grin as she pushed groceries over the scanner.

"You too." Her lips tightened. Why did it matter whether it was Christmas or any other day of the week? She had no intention of celebrating Christmas this year, since Christmas was for family and she had no one to share it with. It shouldn't bother her. She was surprised by the emotion that welled up in her throat.

"You visiting?" the girl asked, mousy blonde hair falling across brown eyes.

She studied the name tag pinned to the girl's thin chest.

Martha, How can I help you? it said.

"I've just moved here," Rebecca replied, tugging her credit card from her purse.

"Oh? Well, welcome to Emerald Cove."

The lump in Rebecca's throat grew. She wasn't accustomed to kindness. It was the one thing she had no defence against.

"Thanks."

"You the new copper?"

Rebecca nodded. "That's right."

The girl's lips pursed. "Don't worry, it's pretty quiet around here. You'll love it. And never mind what anyone says. Okay?"

Rebecca's eyes narrowed. What did that mean? What would they say to her that needed prior warning?

"Thanks, I think it's going to be great." She took her bags, one in each hand, and - with a nod of her head - left through the swishing doors.

"See you around," called the girl behind her.

CHAPTER 13

MEG

*T*he gift in her hands felt like a stone. Meg turned it over, swallowed and fingered the red ribbon she'd tied around the gold paper. It wasn't much, just a watch, but it told time, had an alarm, could even be connected to Brad's mobile phone if that was what he wanted.

It'd been hard to think of a Christmas gift for him. Everything he loved had something to do with surfing or sport. The gift she'd bought him before they left on their honeymoon was stashed in the closet at their apartment in Emerald Cove. A brand-new wet suit with his name scrawled along one sleeve in blue. She couldn't bring that out now; it'd only make things worse.

"I got you something," she said, holding it out to him.

He glanced her way, which was more than he'd done in hours.

"Thanks." He took the box in one hand, let his hand fall to the bed and returned to staring at the window. The glass panes were covered by thin white curtains; beyond them lay a parking lot, concrete and vehicles stretched out to meet a busy street where the blare of a horn punctuated the steady hum of engines.

She slipped her hands together, her fingers twining with one another for comfort. "Don't you want to open it?"

She offered a hesitant smile. He sighed, shook his head.

"Come on, it's Christmas."

His gaze was steely; anger boiled beneath the surface. She could almost feel its sting in the look he shot her.

"You don't have to... I just thought we should celebrate at least a little bit. Nothing big, you know. Your parents are out getting Christmas lunch, they found a place that serves roast. They should be back soon. So, why don't you open your present before they get back?"

She was sitting on the end of his bed and slid a little closer over the covers until she could lay her hand on his where it held the gift.

He shifted his hand so hers fell off, landing on the soft covers alone. Her eyes smarted with tears as her hand slid back to find solace in her own lap.

"Fine," he said. He tugged the paper from the gift, studied the watch with a frown. "Thanks."

She smiled. "You're welcome. I hope you like it. The sales guy said that it even works underwater."

His eyes narrowed. "Is that so?"

She grinned. "Yep."

"And when exactly do you think I'll have need to use that feature? Huh? All the underwater diving and swimming I'll be doing?"

Her heart dropped as her smile vanished. "I…uh… sorry, Brad. I didn't think…"

"Forget it," he snapped. He pushed the watch onto his wrist and fitted the clasp in place. Then his eyes drifted shut. "Can you just leave me alone?"

She stood to leave, then turned back to face him, her cheeks flushing with warmth. "I'll go, but you don't have to talk to me like that. I didn't mean anything by it, and you know that. I love you and wanted to give you a gift, wanted to celebrate Christmas with my husband. Is that a crime?"

His eyes opened, and his gaze landed on her with a flash. "Your husband?"

"Yes!" She was shouting now, releasing the pain of everything that'd happened, the accident, the surgeries, the hours spent pacing across hospital tiles not knowing what the future might hold, the silence, the anger that simmered beneath the surface of Brad's sullen rejection of his new normal. "Yes, you're my husband. You're supposed to love me, to treat me with some kindness. But all you've done is shout at me, push me away… You won't even let me kiss you. What's wrong, Brad? Talk to me, tell me what's going on in that head of yours. I need to know."

His nostrils flared. He pushed his hands on the bed to leverage himself up higher against the pile of pillows that cushioned his back and head. "You want to know what's going on in my head? Trust me, sweetheart, you don't want to know that." He chuckled, a sinister, horrible sound that chilled her to her core.

"Yes, I do," she whispered, unsure that it was the truth when she saw the look in his eyes.

He shook his head. "Fine, I'll tell you. I'm angry - it's not fair. This isn't right. Why did this have to happen? I don't want to live like this. I can't live this way. Without surfing, the beach, the outdoors, I have nothing!" His voice rose with each word until he spat the last at her.

She strode to his side, took his hand in hers and squeezed it so he couldn't pull away. Tears blurred her vision, and her throat tightened so much that it ached. "Nothing? That's not true, you have me."

He jerked his hand from her grasp. "I don't want you."

When his eyes shut, she gaped and tears cascaded down her cheeks. "You don't mean that. You're upset, that's all it is. I'm your wife, we promised to love each other forever."

He sighed, focused his gaze on her face, his voice chill. "That wasn't me, it was a different person. I'm not the guy you married any longer. I'm half a man, not even that. I'm nothing. You didn't sign up for this, and neither did I. I don't want to be married, I don't want you. I want to be left alone." He squeezed his eyes shut. "*Please* go away."

Meg stumbled from the room, tears blinding her. She reached out both hands to grasp the doorframe as she went, then spun into the hallway with a gasp, pain squeezing her chest, her throat, her gut. He didn't mean it, couldn't mean it. Where was the loving, kind, patient man she'd married only weeks earlier? He'd genuinely loved her; she was sure of it. Only, now he wanted to push her away right when he needed her the most. She'd thought their love was stronger than that, that the bond they shared was special. Maybe she was wrong. Maybe she'd been wrong all along.

She leaned against the wall, sliding to the floor until her legs were bunched against her chest, her arms wrapped around them. Sobs wracked her body, and her heart ached in a way she'd never experienced before, in a way she didn't think was possible.

"Meg, honey?" Sharon's voice roused her.

She lifted her head.

"Meg, are you okay?" Sharon rested a hand on Meg's shoulder as she squatted in front of her. "What's wrong, honey?"

Meg's tears only fell harder at her mother-in-law's kind words. "He doesn't want to be married. Doesn't love me anymore. He said so."

Sharon shook her head slowly, lowered herself onto the floor beside Meg and set down a paper bag that smelled of roast meat and gravy beside her feet. She slid an arm around Meg's shoulders and gently pushed Meg's head onto her shoulder, then stroked her hair back from her face. "Oh, honey, you know he doesn't mean that. He's been through so much, is facing a whole new way of life that has him in so much pain, so much sorrow. He's grieving the life he had, the life he wanted, and you were a part of that."

"Has he said anything to you?" Meg asked, sniffling.

"He doesn't want you to have to live your life taking care of him."

Meg raised her head, her eyebrows knitting together. "But I'm his wife. If someone has to take care of him, it should be me."

"But you're both so young, he doesn't think it would be fair. Besides, he's in too much pain to make any sense at the moment. He needs some time to come to terms with what's happened."

"What can I do? Every time I go near him, he yells at me and tells me to go away." Meg inhaled a long, deep breath as her sobbing subsided. She rubbed the back of her sleeve over her nose, wishing she'd thought to bring a box of tissues with her when she ran from the room.

As if reading her thoughts, Sharon dug around in her handbag and gave Meg a small pack. Meg pulled out a tissue and blew her nose, a loud honking sound that brought a smile to Sharon's face.

Des stood silently nearby, a brown paper bag in each hand, his moustache drooping at the ends as if in solidarity with how they were all feeling. The Santa hat on his head stood in stark contrast to the white hospital walls and his red-rimmed eyes.

"I think the best thing for you to do right now would be to go home to Emerald Cove. You can start working on getting things ready for him. You've got a second-floor unit, so that's not going to work. You'll have to get settled somewhere that's wheelchair friendly...there's plenty to keep you occupied. And it's probably the best thing for you, for now."

"Go home? But I can't leave him..." She couldn't abandon him, even with the way he was treating her. It didn't seem right.

"As I said," Sharon continued, "Brad needs some time to process everything, and we'll be here with him. The doctor says he can travel in a couple of weeks, and we'll bring him back to Brisbane with us where he can access the best physiotherapy. Then, when he's ready, he can join you in the Cove."

Meg's lips pursed. It made sense, but something

inside her rebelled against the idea of leaving her injured husband behind in a foreign country.

"I don't know..."

"You have to get back to work, you'll be the sole breadwinner...at least for a while," Des added in a gentle voice.

"That's true... My boss has been amazing, but I know they'll be suffering without someone to fill in for me if I stay much longer."

"Brad will be fine, we'll take care of him," Sharon said, patting Meg's arm.

Meg leaned over to embrace Sharon. "Thank you. I don't know what I would've done without the two of you here to help."

Sharon blinked back tears. "We're family now, honey. We love you, and Brad does too... He'll come around. I'm certain of it."

Meg wasn't so sure. She'd seen the hatred in his eyes, heard the acid dripping from his words. How could they ever get back to the place they'd been a few weeks earlier - blissfully in love, unaware of anything but each other? Thinking about it brought fresh tears to her eyes, so she shoved the memories of their brief honeymoon back down into the depths of her mind. She couldn't function, couldn't do the things she needed to move forward, if she let the images of their passionate few days as husband and wife hover in her mind's eye.

Sharon stood with a grunt, and she and Des carried the paper bags filled with their Christmas lunch into the hospital room. She heard Sharon wish Brad a Merry Christmas and his murmured response. Why couldn't he be so kind to her? He was taking out his frustrations, pain and grief entirely on her. He must blame her in some way for the accident, for his injuries. But that didn't make sense.

She'd spend Christmas with him, then she'd pack up the hotel room and head home to Emerald Cove. The thought buoyed her spirits for the first time. She missed home, her friends, her work at the salon. Missed the quiet happiness of her life. The life she'd thought she'd be returning to with her husband by her side. She'd decorated the unit with a Christmas tree and fairy lights, hung mistletoe over the front door, made the brand-new king-sized bed and covered it with the newly purchased blue-striped doona, all the while smiling at the thought of sharing her life, her home, her bed with her new husband when they got back from Hawaii.

And now she'd be going back alone.

She stood, wiped the tears from her cheeks with the sleeve of her cardigan and braced herself. Then, with her head held high and a smile pushed onto her face, she strode into the hospital room.

CHAPTER 14

SARAH

*T*he smell of eggnog lingered in Sarah's room, and the empty glass sat as a reminder on the bedside table, next to a plate with crumbs from the sugar cookie in the shape of a Christmas tree she'd eaten the night before while watching a few minutes of *The Santa Clause* before falling asleep.

She ran a tongue over her furry teeth and slung her feet over the side of the bed. She should've taken the time to brush them. Now a foul taste in her mouth pushed her to the bathroom where she reached for her toothbrush. She yawned and tugged the hair back from her forehead to study the wrinkles that'd extended themselves around the corners of her eyes in the past few years.

With a grimace, she added toothpaste to her toothbrush and cleaned her mouth vigorously. It was strangely comforting to sleep in her childhood bedroom on Christmas Eve and wake up on Christmas Day in the same place she had for so many of her formative years. It'd been late by the time they'd finished eating dinner, then dessert, and talking over everything that'd been going on in each other's lives that they'd missed with so much time apart.

There was an ache in her chest for the old days, the times when she, Adele and Ethan spent almost every waking moment together, when they'd ride their bikes down the road in front of the house, past the bed and breakfast, through Emerald Cove to the beach with towels slung over their shoulders. They'd run down the too-hot sand, then fling themselves into the ocean to dive through waves, body surf, laugh and tumble all the way to shore, only to begin all over again.

They'd had so much fun together, knew everything there was to know about each other and now hardly saw each other at all. That was how it was to grow up, she supposed. Still, she missed them and made a decision to call them more often. Even if talking on the phone wasn't nearly the same as seeing someone in person, it was better than nothing.

As the hot water from the shower ran over her head and down her back, Sarah wondered again whether she'd made the right choice by moving to the Cove. In the weeks since she arrived, she'd barely gotten any work done. With the renovation, family commitments, helping her mother with various odd jobs and the cafe books, she found her time each day ran out before she had time to do much, and even when she did sit down to work, internet access was sporadic.

Finally, last week, she'd had broadband connected, but by then, most of the staff in the office had taken leave for the holidays and she couldn't reach any of them. She stepped out of the shower with a frustrated sigh and slung a towel around her dripping body.

By the time she'd dressed, she could hear voices in the kitchen, along with the muted tones of Christmas music. She found her family seated around the outdoor dining table on the expansive back deck. Birdsong warmed the morning air, the warble of a magpie, the chatter of a noisy miner.

She sat with a grunt, smoothing her hair back from her face with one hand. "Good morning, all. Merry Christmas!"

"Merry Christmas," Adele replied with a smile as she spooned yoghurt over a bowl of cereal.

Sarah reached for the muesli and filled a bowl with it, then poured cold milk on top.

"Did you sleep well?" Mum asked.

Sarah nodded, yawned. "Yes, thanks. I always sleep like a log in that bed. I love it."

"So, Mum, are we going to open presents after breakfast? We used to do it first, then have breakfast when everything was opened..." Ethan grinned.

Mum chuckled. "Ah, I miss those days, when you were all so excited to wake up at the crack of dawn. You'd rush out to the tree and gather around it, whispering so loud you'd wake your dad and me..." She faltered, her smile fading. "I guess those days are behind us."

Sarah's lips pursed. She hated what her father had done, but there wasn't anything she could do about it.

"How are things in Darwin, Adele? Is it as hot as they say it is?" she asked her sister, hoping to change the subject.

Adele swallowed a mouthful of cereal. "It's hotter.

Ugh. I'm so glad to be back in Emerald Cove with the sea breeze and the cooler weather. But I do love it up there. It's a pretty young population, and I'm getting the chance to fly a lot more than I would down this way."

Adele had finished her pilot training right out of high school and moved to Darwin soon after to get as many hours in the air as she could. As the baby of the family, she'd always pushed herself to stand out, be different, do the unexpected, and training to be a pilot was her way of doing that. At least, that was how it seemed to Sarah, who'd always done what she could to protect her little sister. Now there was nothing she could do; it was completely out of her hands.

"Any interesting men in Darwin?" Sarah asked.

Adele grinned. "Lots. But no one in particular, if that's what you're asking."

"And how about you?" Ethan asked, taking a bite of toast. "I heard you ended things with your writer fiancé. I'm kind of out of the loop... Care to bring me up to speed?"

Sarah's cheeks warmed. She didn't like talking about her love life, though she'd known the questions would come. "He wasn't right for me, that's the gist of it. I suppose we could've kept going the way things were, but I wasn't happy."

"Is that why you moved back to the Cove?" Adele asked.

Sarah exchanged a glance with her mother. How much had Mum told her siblings about what was going on with the cafe and the debt their father had left her? She didn't know and so figured it best to keep things as vague as possible until she'd had a chance to talk to her mother about it.

"I wanted to be here to help Mum. It was also convenient to get out of Sydney, since Jeremy hasn't accepted that it's over yet. I needed some space, that's true, but also wanted to come home for Mum."

Ethan studied his toast, and Adele's lips pinched together.

"And she's already been a big help," Mum added. "We're going to have so much fun together."

Sarah offered a tight smile. The tension in the air was palpable. What bothered her siblings so much - the fact that their father had run off with a younger woman, or that she was talking about it at Christmas?

"Thanks, Mum, I hope having me here will make a hard situation a little easier for you."

Mum nodded. "Thank you, sweetheart. It does."

"Do you mean because of Dad, or is there something else going on?" Ethan asked around a mouthful of toast.

"Because of Dad, the situation Mum's left in—" Sarah started.

"He's coming back," Adele interrupted. "You know he'll come back. He's not thinking clearly. That woman has obviously confused him, or tricked him, but he'll be back. He loves you, Mum, and he loves us. He's going to remember that soon, and he'll come through that door, all smiles..." She inhaled a long, slow breath. "I know he will. It's going to be okay."

Mum's face clouded, and her lips pursed. "Yes, darling. Of course."

Sarah frowned. "But what if Mum doesn't want him to come back? He's completely ruined everything. He can't come back now, can't expect things to go back to the way it was. That's not how this works."

Adele stopped chewing, stared at her sister with

wide eyes. "What do you mean? Why would you say that?"

Mum left the table, hurrying into the kitchen. With her back turned, Sarah couldn't tell if she was crying. She sighed, rubbed a hand over her face.

"I'm sorry, I shouldn't have brought it up - not on Christmas morning. Let's have a nice day together, we can talk about it another time."

Ethan's eyes narrowed. "No, it's too late for that. What did you mean? Why wouldn't Mum want Dad to come back? That's what we all want, isn't it? This is our family, he's made a mistake, but we can't write him off over it."

Sarah leaned back in her chair. "You're right, we're not going to write him off, but Mum doesn't have to take him back. That's not how relationships work. He's always going to be our dad, he's not always going to be her husband."

"They're getting a divorce?" Adele asked, her voice cracking.

Sarah sighed. This wasn't her place; it wasn't her conversation to have. "You should talk to Mum about it."

Mum returned then, sat at the table. Her eyes glistened, but otherwise she looked the same well-groomed, put-together woman she was minutes earlier. Her grey hair was curled just so, her makeup was minimalist and stylish, and her pantsuit accentuated her curvy figure just enough without being over the top.

"I hadn't wanted to talk about your father today," she said, "but I know you want to understand what's going on. You love him, it's perfectly natural to be curious."

Adele wiped her mouth with a napkin. "You don't have to, Mum…"

Mum raised a hand. "It's okay. I have to face it sometime. Your father ran off with his assistant…"

"We know that part, Mum," Ethan interrupted.

She smiled. "When he did that, he broke trust with me and any chance of coming home again. He didn't talk to me about what he was going to do, only left me a note on the bench. He packed his things, took anything of value he could find in the house, cleaned out our bank account and left."

Adele raised a hand to her mouth.

"Now, I don't want to speak ill of your father, he will always be in your lives, but that doesn't mean he'll be in mine. I don't want him to come back. I've hardly spoken to him since he left, and even when I have managed to get him on the phone, he's unapologetic. He blames me, for some reason. Says I wasn't there for him, didn't care for him the way he needed…blah blah blah."

Ethan's frown deepened. "I'm sorry, Mum."

"Yeah, that's horrible, Mum. It must've been so hard for you. I didn't realise he left a note, that he didn't explain to you face-to-face how he was feeling. I can't believe he'd do that. I'm going to say something the next time I talk to him." Adele's nostrils flared.

Sarah's stomach tightened. It wasn't the first time she'd heard the story, but it was still difficult to stomach. Hearing how little concern her father had for her mother after so many years of marriage, it made her wonder how marriage could work for anyone.

"No, there's no need for any of you to get in the middle. I'll deal with him in my own way. Now, let's finish breakfast so we can start on the gifts. I've made some delicious peppermint coffee to sip while we unwrap."

* * *

COLOURFUL, torn wrapping paper lay in a neat pile beside her mother. Sarah leaned back against the couch and crossed her feet at the ankles. The carpet was soft, and she caressed it with her fingers a moment before taking another sip of coffee. The rug beneath her had been a part of the family for as long as she could remember. Mum had it cleaned every year, and even though the colours had faded, the Turkish patterns still looked just as she remembered them.

"Thank you for the earrings," Adele said, holding two hoops up to her ears with a grin. "I love them."

"You're welcome," Sarah replied.

It was good to be home. Even better to have Adele and Ethan there. Their family had changed, but it was still family and still warmed her heart. Surely Dad missed that. It wouldn't be the same with just him and Keisha. The fact that Keisha was only a few years older than Sarah herself made her shudder to think of it. It was all too strange, too bizarre to consider.

The front doorbell rang, and her mother's aged Pomeranian launched itself at the door, yapping on high alert.

"Settle, Petal!" shouted Sarah and Ethan at once.

They both laughed. The fact that their mother had named her dog Petal had been an endless source of amusement over the years.

"Who would come knocking on Christmas Day?" Adele mused, her brow furrowed. She stood, smoothed her hands down her pants. "It must be Dad. It has to be."

Sarah resisted the urge to roll her eyes. Even after everything he'd done, Adele couldn't fault her father. He'd always been a hero in her eyes, and it was clear she thought there was some kind of mistake, something that could explain his absence apart from the obvious. She wanted to believe the best of him, but Sarah was afraid she was going to be sorely disappointed.

Even though he was her father as well, and she loved him, she had a different view. She'd seen the way he treated their mother over the years, to him, she wasn't there, didn't matter. He'd been the fun one, she'd been the responsible one, and he never attempted to shift any of the burden onto his own shoulders, even seemed to regard her with contempt at times for it.

When it came to their father, Adele wore rose-tinted glasses, but Sarah saw things clearly. If it was him at the door, she'd be happy to see him but wasn't sure how things would play out with their mother. She shifted in place, her heart rate accelerating.

"Well, look who's come over for a cup of coffee." Mum walked back into the living room, stepping aside to reveal Athol Miller, the family doctor and their father's best friend. Or at least he had been Dad's best friend years ago. Sarah didn't recall hearing as much about him in recent years, though of course she'd moved to Sydney so that was to be expected.

Athol waved a hand. "Ah, Merry Christmas, Flannigans. How nice to see you all. I told Cindy that I'd love to come and visit with all of you on Christmas. I haven't seen you in so long."

Sarah stood to greet him with a gentle embrace. "Uncle Athol, it's so nice to see you. Merry Christmas to you as well."

He chuckled. "You can all call me plain old Athol."

She nodded. "If you like. I suppose we're getting too old to call you uncle, although habits can be hard to break."

He kissed the women's cheeks, shook Ethan's hand, then sat with a grunt in an armchair. Dad's armchair. Sarah noticed the grimace on Adele's face even as she quickly turned away. She knew it was hard on her sister; Adele had been close to Dad, his little girl for so long.

"So, how have you been, Athol?" Sarah asked.

Athol smiled. "I'm getting there. It's been busy at work, but I hired a new doctor. Hoping to get her up to speed before I retire."

"You're retiring?" Ethan asked.

Athol's lips pursed. "I suppose I'll have to at some stage, though I'm not particularly keen on the idea. What I'll do with myself then...who knows." He chuckled. "Your mum tells me I can help out in the cafe, though I'm not sure how relaxing that will be."

Mum emerged from the kitchen with a cup of steaming hot coffee and handed it to Athol. He leaned back in the armchair, crossed one long leg over the other and sipped. "Thank you, Cindy."

Sarah studied him as he spoke. What was going on? They'd had Athol over for Christmas many times in the past, but it was always because he was Dad's friend.

"Have you heard from Dad lately?" Adele asked, shoving her light brown curls behind one shoulder.

At twenty-three years old, she had a young face that gave her the appearance of a teenager, something her passengers no doubt wouldn't appreciate. She was older than her years though, more mature somehow. Being the youngest, she'd felt the need to prove herself.

Athol arched a bushy eyebrow. "Uh…no, not lately. In fact, I haven't spoken to your dad since right after he left."

Creases formed above Adele's hazel eyes. "That's a shame, I'm sure he needs his friends right now."

Irritation buzzed in Sarah's gut. Adele always stood up for their father, even when he was in the wrong. She hadn't asked Mum once how she was coping, yet she was concerned about their father's well-being. It rubbed Sarah the wrong way; even though deep down she cared about him, her anger burned closer to the surface.

Athol shifted in his seat. "Well, that's probably true, I suppose. But…your father and I don't see eye to eye on a few things."

"What kinds of things?" Adele asked.

Ethan coughed. "Adele, that's none of our business."

Beside Ethan on the long leather couch, Mum bit on her lower lip, staring at the coffee cup in her hands.

"No, it's okay." Athol waved a hand and smiled. "I don't mind talking about it, as long as Cindy doesn't mind."

Mum offered a quick nod. "I don't mind."

"Well, for one, I didn't like the way he left things with Cindy. He didn't talk to her, didn't try to work things out, just took off. As you all know, I lost my wife almost a decade ago, and there hasn't been a moment where I didn't wish she was still with me…" His voice broke, but he cleared his throat and continued. "I think he should've appreciated Cindy more than he did. It's not only about him leaving… He took her for granted for years…didn't see what was right in front of him, didn't treat her the way she should be treated." As he spoke, Athol's gaze drifted to where Mum sat. He focused on her, a smile tugging the corners of his mouth.

His grey hair was combed to one side but had shifted into peaks where a hand had run through it. He wore long, khaki pants and a button-down blue shirt, and with spectacles perched on the bridge of his nose, he looked every bit the country doctor. Sarah couldn't help noticing how handsome he was, and one glance at her mother told her she'd recognised that fact already.

Sarah's eyes narrowed. Something was going on between the two of them, and she wasn't entirely sure she liked it. If she was going to pick someone for her mother, she'd have thought someone more masculine, maybe a man who worked with his hands, would suit her. Someone rugged and outgoing, not a quiet, unassuming doctor with pale skin and smooth hands. Though after being married to their father for so many years, perhaps quiet was just what she needed. Athol was kind, gentle and thoughtful, that much she knew from their years of friendship.

Adele had listened to Athol's speech with flashing eyes. She inhaled a quick breath. "I don't think that's very fair. You don't know both sides of the story. Mum can be irritating at times… Dad's put up with a lot from her over the years."

"Adele!" Sarah shouted, her hackles rising. "This isn't the time, and that's completely unfair. We're not going to pile on Mum."

"Well, I don't think we should pile on Dad either. It's not right, he's not here to defend himself."

"You're right, he's not here. He abandoned us. Left Mum on her own. And that's not all—"

"Sarah, there's no need," Mum interrupted, her cheeks flushed.

Sarah swallowed the rest of the words that she wanted to say. About the fact that Dad had left Mum with debts she might never be able to repay. That he'd been draining their finances for years. Sarah had no idea what he'd been doing before his retirement that'd brought him to that place. His financial planning business must've been losing money, but he hadn't let on, and it seemed Mum hadn't known a thing about it either.

She pressed her lips together, her blood boiling. "Fine, we can talk about it another time. But I don't think you should be attacking Mum right now. It's Christmas, we should talk about nice things like sugar plum fairies and puddings, or we could even debate the likelihood that a rotund man in a red suit could squeeze down so many chimneys all around the world in one night, or how he's able to break into houses across Australia since most of us don't have chimneys... And while we're at it, let's address the elephant in the room: why does he bother, now that he can simply shop online and have it delivered?"

Ethan chuckled.

Adele shook her head, her body relaxing.

Mum reached over to squeeze Sarah's arm. "Let's get this mess cleaned up, and we can all relax on the veranda before it gets stiflingly hot."

Sarah collected bits and pieces of wrapping, ribbon and envelopes and wadded them into a ball. She watched as Mum gathered empty coffee mugs to carry to the kitchen, and her heart ached. Mum could've said something, could've railed about what Dad had done; instead she didn't want to destroy Ethan and Adele's view of their father at Christmas. It was just like her, always thinking of her children. Sarah couldn't fault her for it, but she worried about her mother and what the future might hold.

CHAPTER 15

SARAH

*T*he year was almost over. Tomorrow would be New Year's Eve, and Sarah felt she could finally face it. She was ready. She'd unpacked everything in the cottage, found a place for it all, even had a vase of wildflowers in the kitchen to bring a sense of life to the room. She'd never been one to do much decorating; her focus had always been her career, networking, building a life for herself outside of her home. Her unit in Sydney had been austere, modern with smooth lines and neutral tones. But so far, the cottage had a more vibrant, colourful and vintage feel to it, and she loved it.

Nothing really worked, apart from the internet connection which was finally somewhat reliable. She took a sip of coffee and glided in her new rocking chair on the rotting deck - she'd been careful to find the most solid section of the timber floor before dragging the rocking chair out onto the deck. She'd found the chair by chance in town at a garage sale. As she drove past the sale, her gaze had flitted to the chair, and she'd immediately pictured herself rocking in it on her deck, looking out over the ocean, the wind teasing her hair. So she'd pulled over and negotiated with the owner to deliver it to the cottage for her, along with a vintage buffet and dining table with six matching chairs, all in good shape.

Renovations would begin in the new year, and she was excited to see how the place would look given a face-lift. She glanced at the bowl of kibble beside her chair. She'd folded and visited the pet store one town over as well. She'd driven there to buy herself a comfortable armchair when she thought she might as well embrace the fact that she had a dog now. The creature wasn't going away; it visited every day, though it still hadn't let her within arm's reach.

As if sensing her thoughts, there was a rustle in the grass beside the cottage and the stray appeared, his brown fur matted and soiled.

He crept forward, tail pushed down firmly between his hind legs, large brown eyes trained on her face.

"Hi there, glad you could make it. Hope you like dog food. I know you've gotten used to bacon and my leftover steak or chicken, but let's face it, you could probably do with a little more substance and some vitamins or something. I don't really know, I'm new to this whole dog-owner thing." She hesitated, watching as the animal snuck up the stairs and found the bowl next to her chair.

If she reached out her hand, she could touch it. She held her breath, leaned down and peered under the animal.

"Ah, so you *are* a boy, I thought so. Is your name Oscar?"

The dog glanced up at her, crunching through a mouthful of kibble, the wild look gone from his eyes for now.

"Great, let's agree on Oscar. I think it's a fine name. I'm Sarah, by the way, just in case you were wondering what to call me."

Oscar lost interest, dropped his head to the bowl again and resumed eating.

She reached out a hand, let it hover over the animal's bony back. "I don't know about you, but I like my personal space. I'm not big on hugging, or touching, like some people are. But I figure, if we're going to share a home, and it seems to me that's what you're hoping for, then perhaps we should try patting...or maybe one pat. If you're up for it."

Oscar didn't respond. Sarah eyed him a moment, braced herself and gently dropped a hand onto his back. The feel of bones beneath her hand made her heart lurch for what he must've been through, how hard he'd struggled to survive since the previous owner of the cottage died.

The dog lurched to one side but didn't take his mouth from the bowl. Then he shifted and eventually relaxed.

Sarah sighed with relief.

She stroked his fur a few times, feeling the mange, the mud caked into the hair, the sharp ribs. "Well, that wasn't so bad, was it? Just giving you forewarning - I'm going to want to give you a bath at some point. I mean, not today, I get it, you're still warming to me, but before too long. You really need one."

CHAPTER 16

FRANKLIN

*F*ranklin Russell stepped out of the police cruiser, pushed the door shut with his foot and balanced a tray of disposable coffee cups in one hand, a manila folder in his mouth and the strap of a backpack in the other hand.

He grimaced as the effort of shutting the car door made the cardboard tray sway precariously from one side to the other, then leaned against it to steady the cups before heading for the station door.

He studied the double automatic glass doors that barred his way into the station, one eyebrow arched. The doors were his nemesis. Everyone knew it. They all had a good old giggle at his expense whenever he collided with them. For some reason, he was the only member of the team who had an issue with them; they glided open with no problem at all for the others. Only for him, they stuck at times, and if he wasn't paying attention, he'd end up with his nose squashed against the glass.

With four coffee cups held aloft, he couldn't risk being caught off guard again. He stepped forward, and the doors swished open. He hesitated, then passed through the doorway, smiling around the mouthful of papers pressed between his lips.

"Good morning, Sergeant Russell. How are you on this fine day?" The receptionist's cheery voice pierced through the small opening in the centre of a secure glass window.

The day was already growing hot, and the high humidity had a line of sweat forming on his upper lip from the walk between his cruiser and the front door.

"Fine, thanks, Steph. How are you?" He uttered the words around the folder sagging at both ends between his lips.

Stephanie's brow furrowed. "What did you say? Here, let me help you..." She came out from behind the reception desk, through the security door and reached for the folder.

Franklin smacked his lips, dispelling the feeling of cotton mouth, then inhaled a slow breath.

"Thanks, Steph, that's much better. Here, I brought you a coffee. Yours is the one with 'Strep' written on the side."

Stephanie took one of the coffees from his tray with a chuckle, her green eyes glowing. "Thanks, boss, you're the best. I was thinking that a good dose of caffeine was in order. The twins had me up half the night coughing." She shook her head, covering a yawn with the folder.

"Sorry to hear that. Hope they're feeling better soon. Hey, could you buzz me in?" He raised both hands, showing they were full, and she gave a brisk nod, her auburn hair stirring in the messy bun that perched on top of her head.

"New Year's Eve, Sarge. You got any plans?"

He shook his head. "Not really. Working, then I'll head over to Dad's. How about you?"

"We're taking the twins to a pool party in Banora Point. It's going to be a nightmare. But at least there will be fireworks afterwards."

He chuckled. "Good for you, you'll have a blast."

"I'm sure we will, come on inside. You're not the first one in today. Your new Proby is here already, I gave her a tour of the office."

His nostrils flared. "Great."

Steph's pink-painted lips pursed. "Be nice."

"I always am," he growled.

She chuckled, then flicked the ID card looped around her neck against the wall, and pushed the security door open. He stepped through, smiled and opened his mouth. She pushed the file back in between his teeth.

As he walked to his desk, Franklin couldn't help letting her words play over in his mind.

His new partner was here.

In the office, his office, no doubt waiting to meet him. Eager to start the job that shouldn't be vacant. The office looked empty; no sign of the new recruit - probably sitting in the tiny kitchen rethinking life choices.

He'd told the brass he didn't want a new probationary constable, didn't need one. He had everything here under control. There wasn't an epidemic of violent crimes underway in Emerald Cove anyway. He knew how to police the area; heck, he'd grown up on its streets, had built solid relationships with almost every single resident. There wasn't much about his town he didn't know, couldn't take care of himself.

Of course, they hadn't listened to him. Protocol, they'd said. When he'd pointed out the crime statistics, they'd nodded. Good police work, they'd commented.

Still, you need a partner up there.

He sighed, eying the open glass door that led to his office.

The Emerald Cove Police District was a small one. Just him, two night shift senior constables, the new proby and the receptionist. They shared the space with a road safety expert and two water police officers who covered the wider coastal area and reported to the Police Area Command in the nearby Tweed Heads rather than to him.

It was an intimate and friendly post, and he liked it that way. No sense having too many officers in a place like the Cove. It was a waste of resources, especially when there were so many towns and cities under-staffed. He'd tried making that argument to the recruitment office in Sydney as well, but they hadn't bought it.

They were determined to replace his partner with someone new, whether he wanted them to or not. But he didn't have to like it, and there was nothing in the handbook that said he had to make it easy either.

He set the coffees down on the desk, plucked the now damp folder from between his lips and slumped into his chair. He opened the folder, scanned its contents.

It was a personnel file on the new recruit, and he had to say, even for a newbie, its contents were decid-edly spare on details. It didn't tell him much about his new partner, something that bothered him even more than the mere fact of being forced to take someone on right out of university. As if he had the time to bottle-feed a proby.

He sighed again and slammed the folder down on the desk. Then he distributed the remaining coffees to two other officers who'd wandered into the office soon after him. He chatted with each for a few moments before moving on.

When he returned to his desk, his own coffee in hand, there was a woman standing outside his door, her hands clasped in front of her perfectly pressed, sky blue and navy uniform.

He passed her without a word, sat behind his desk and sipped his coffee.

"Come in," he said.

She stepped inside, stood in front of the desk, her brown eyes flicking between his face, the back of his computer screen and the framed certificates and photographs on the wall, then coming to rest on his face again. Her eyes met his, flecks of green and gold lit up the brown, and her lips pressed a little tighter together as she studied him.

"You must be Constable Rebecca Mair. Correct?"

She nodded. "Yes, sir."

"Please, take a seat."

She slid into the chair opposite him. He'd expected her to be anxious, with sweaty palms, maybe nervous chatter...but instead she was calm, serene even. Her back was straight, hands resting on top of her thighs.

She was a petite woman. Obviously kept herself in good shape, but still. It wouldn't take much more than a stiff breeze to blow her over, and that was hardly what he needed out on the street when things turned bad. Who'd back him up? She wouldn't be able to do it. She looked more like a kindergarten teacher than a cop.

If he'd wanted someone to sing lullabies to the criminals he brought into the station, he could've asked Martha from the Foodstore to do that. The girl had a lovely voice. He recalled the Christmas she'd sung "Silent Night" at the Carols by Candlelight in the park a few years earlier. It'd brought tears to people's eyes. But he didn't need a fifteen-year-old girl singing lullabies; he needed a partner who could push a thug to the ground and run down a shoplifter.

He swallowed the things he wanted to say and instead opened her file and studied it as though it were the first time he'd seen it.

"So...Rebecca, you're from...Sydney?"

She nodded once. "Yes, sir."

"It doesn't say much in here, I'll be honest. But since you applied to join the force in Sydney, and trained there, I'm going to guess you're from there."

He posed it as a statement but hoped she'd divulge more information. She didn't. He studied her. She sat silently, not squirming, not shifting in her seat, no smile on her tanned face.

He inhaled a quick breath. "And this is your first posting?"

Another nod. "Yes, sir."

She wasn't a talker; he'd give her that. He liked a bit of quiet around the office. Still, he'd been hoping she'd give him more...fill out the details of her past so he could get some idea of who would be riding around town with him in his cruiser.

"Your desk is the one outside my door. Steph does up the shift schedule every Monday. You'll be riding with me, and I don't like smoking or gum chewing. Any questions?"

"No, sir."

"There's a stack of files on your desk, you can start by filing them in the grey cabinets against the wall."

"Yes, sir."

He watched her leave, irritation boiling in his gut. She was unreadable. Dewy-eyed, innocent, inexperienced and a complete mystery. If they ever did stumble across some real crime in Emerald Cove, she was going to get him killed. A shiver ran down his spine. He switched on his computer and leaned back in his chair while it booted up. His only option was to force her to leave of her own accord. Then maybe the head office would let him be, and stop insisting on assigning him a partner.

CHAPTER 17

MEG

*T*he unit smelled like bleach and lemon oil. Meg tucked a red curl behind one ear and scanned the living room with a sigh. Everything looked the same yet different. She'd moved things around as best she could after getting advice from an occupational therapist.

Thankfully, the building manager had allowed her to change her lease and take a bottom floor unit rather than the one they'd had. Brad's friend Jack had helped her move everything in one weekend. At least they didn't have much between the two of them, so it hadn't taken long. Then, Vicky had come over to help her unpack after work.

She'd had a small ramp installed from the front door down to the living room, and a railing in the shower. Had put all of the things he might need to reach in the lower cupboards in the kitchen and bathroom. She'd bought a book of suggestions about how to make their home wheelchair friendly and followed them as best she could. She hoped she hadn't missed anything obvious.

"It looks good, Meg," Vicky said as she arranged a bunch of fresh-picked flowers in a vase on the kitchen bench.

Meg turned to face her, hands pressed to her hips. "You think?"

"Absolutely. It's warm and inviting, he'll be happy here. You both will."

Meg's breath caught in her throat. Would either of them ever be happy again? She doubted it. Before she left Hawaii, Brad had barely looked at her, hadn't said more than a few words, hadn't even told her goodbye. She'd walked out of his hospital room and caught a taxi to the airport with a giant lump in her throat that hadn't gone away until well into the flight home when she'd distracted herself by watching a movie.

Even now, whenever she thought about him, she had to fight to keep the tears at bay. It wasn't even the accident; she'd come to terms with that, could live with his disability. The doctors had assured her that he could have a full life, and she believed them.

It was him. He'd pushed her away and didn't want anything more to do with her. She couldn't help wondering if maybe he never would.

"I hope Brad likes it," she said around a ball of grief that'd lodged itself in her throat, making her voice sound thick with tears.

Vicky wrapped an arm around her shoulders. "I'm sure he'll love it. After all, you're here, what more could a guy want?"

Meg shook her head. "You don't understand..."

"What? What is it?" Vicky's blue eyes studied hers, concern etched in the lines on her forehead.

Meg sighed. "He doesn't want…"

"What doesn't he want?" Vicky prompted.

"Me. He doesn't want me." Tears burst free, and Meg buried her head in Vicky's shoulder.

Vicky rubbed a circle on her back. "No, no, that's not true. Of course he wants you, he married you. I've never seen anyone more sickeningly in love. Trust me, *blurgh*, it was really disgusting for all of us to watch." She laughed softly. "It's going to be okay, Meg. He's had an accident, I'm sure he's angry about it, but he'll come around."

Meg couldn't help smiling through her tears. She wiped her eyes with her fingertips. "Really? Disgusting, huh?"

Vicky grinned. "Absolutely gross."

Meg rolled her eyes. "Well, in that case…"

"In all seriousness, honey, this is probably the hardest thing the two of you will ever have to face. But I believe in both of you, I believe in your love." Vicky pressed a hand to each of Meg's shoulders and looked her in the eye. "You can do this."

Meg nodded. "Okay, you're right. We can get through it… We *will* get through it."

"Good, now let's check the bedroom."

They found Vicky's childhood friend Sarah in the bedroom, putting fresh sheets on the bed. Meg remembered Sarah from when she was a kid. Sarah was the one all the girls Meg's own age admired from afar. She'd always been beautiful, long brown hair swinging down her back when she walked, lithe pale limbs, dark flashing eyes and a big smile with dimples at the sides. All the boys in town were in love with her, and she didn't seem to care.

Sarah was the volleyball star, the surfing champion, and finally, when she moved away to the big city to become an editor at a publishing house, Meg had dreamed that maybe someday when she grew up she'd do something just as glamorous. Of course, she hadn't had the money or grades to attend university. Instead, she'd left school early for a hairdressing apprentice-ship at a local salon and stayed in the Cove.

And now Sarah was back, standing in her bedroom with a smile on her face.

"Are these sheets okay, Meg?"

"Perfect," Meg replied. "Thank you so much for helping out, you really didn't have to."

"I'm happy to do it." Sarah smiled. "Besides, I could do with the company. It's a little...um...shall we say, quiet, out at the cottage with only a stray dog for company." She chuckled and continued smoothing the fitted sheet into place.

Vicky moved to help her, throwing the flat sheet over the top of the mattress. "Have you heard from Jeremy lately?"

Sarah's nose wrinkled. "Yes, he calls all the time. I can't seem to get away from him. I think I'm going to have to change my number."

"Really? It's that bad?" Vicky tucked the sheet under one corner of the mattress.

Meg checked the drawers to make sure all of Brad's clothes were folded neatly while they chatted.

"I don't know, maybe I'm being dramatic. I keep thinking he'll eventually stop calling, stop asking to come and visit. He wants to get back together, says he doesn't accept that things are over between us *just like that*. I told him it wasn't just like that, it was a gradual thing, only he didn't see it." Sarah lifted the corner of the mattress closest to her to tuck sheets under it.

"Who's Jeremy?" Meg interrupted.

Sarah and Vicky straightened. Sarah bit down on her lip. Vicky chuckled. "Jeremy Goodall. He's a dreamily good-looking, very talented and super rich and famous author from Sydney. And he's Sarah's former fiancé."

Sarah huffed. "You make him sound so perfect."

"Isn't he?" Vicky quipped with a wink.

"I suppose so, on paper. Only, he's not perfect for me."

"Oh, you were engaged...that's right. I think I remember reading something about it in the paper," Meg said.

Sarah's eyes widened. "It was in the newspaper?"

"Of course," Vicky replied. "Anything the famous editor Sarah Flannigan does is recorded for posterity in the Emerald Cove Gazette."

Sarah inhaled a sharp breath. "You're kidding."

"Nope." Vicky laughed.

Sarah shook her head. "This place is crazy."

"Nothing's changed," Meg replied with a smile.

She caught herself. Was that her first smile since the accident? Other than the fake ones she'd plastered to her face whenever she walked into Brad's room of course. She couldn't remember. It might've been. It felt strange to let it happen, to let her lips pull up at the corners that way and release a lightness into her heart. Familiar, yet somehow wrong. The smile faded.

They made their way back to the living room and sat on the couch. Vicky groaned, her face pale.

"You okay, Vicky?" Sarah asked.

"Yeah, I think so. Just not feeling great for some reason. I hope I'm not coming down with something."

"That's no good, let me know if I can get you anything," Meg added. "Water? Juice?"

"No, I'll be fine. I think I need to sit still for a few minutes."

Meg nodded, then exhaled a slow breath. "I guess we're done getting this place ready for Brad. Thank you so much for all of your help."

"You're most welcome," Vicky replied.

"No worries," Sarah said.

"What are you doing tonight?" Vicky asked.

Meg shrugged. "Going to bed early, I guess. I'm pretty wiped."

"But it's New Year's Eve... Come out with us." Vicky leaned forward, her eyes gleaming.

"Yeah, you should come," Sarah added. "Mum's having a party at the cafe, it should be pretty fun. There'll be live music, good food..."

"And we'll be there, so it's the place to be," Vicky added with a wink.

Meg grinned, though the expression was hesitant and felt foreign. "Okay. Count me in."

CHAPTER 18

SARAH

*T*he hum of conversation could be heard only when there was a break between songs. Sarah slid a tray of nachos and mini sausages in fresh-baked sourdough rolls onto a table, nodded at the call of thanks and hurried back to the kitchen.

Mum had hired extra waitstaff for the party, thank goodness. The place was packed to the rafters with people; most were locals, but there were a fair number of tourists as well. She'd agreed to help serve, though she felt bad for Vicky and Meg, who were seated in a corner, heads together, talking. She'd convinced them to come but now was ignoring them to take food to strangers.

She sighed and pushed through the kitchen doors. Standing inside the kitchen gave her a moment's respite from the noise.

"There you are," Mum said, pushing a plate of fried

chicken with chips towards her on the metal counter. "This one's for table eight."

The New Year's Eve menu gave partygoers a discounted three-course meal with a drink, to go along with the live music. So far, the chicken strips with chips seemed to be the crowd favourite.

"Thanks." Sarah set it on the black tray in her hands.

"How's it going out there?" Mum asked, wiping a line of sweat from her forehead with the back of her sleeve.

"It's packed. People are hungry and thirsty, and the music is great. Who's that singing?"

Mum smiled. "That's Crystal Waters. She waits tables most days but can sing like an angel as well. Isn't she great?"

Sarah nodded. "I love her music. I think the crowd agrees."

"Yes, she's very popular with the locals."

"She's got quite the stage name," Sarah replied with a laugh.

"It's not her real name, of course, but it's what she goes by. I'm not sure why…"

Sarah hurried back through the swinging doors and into the cafe. She waited tables, bussed the dirty dishes back to the kitchen and generally helped out for another two hours until her back ached and her feet throbbed.

Finally, she slumped into a seat across from Vicky and Meg with a groan. "I need a break. I'm not used to being on my feet so long. I've gotten soft in my old age."

Vicky chuckled. "Yes, you're so old."

"Didn't you used to work here years ago?" Meg asked.

Sarah nodded. "Yep. We all had to work at the cafe during our high school years. Family business, there was no way out of it, unfortunately."

"I don't know, I think it seems like a nice place to work...maybe not on New Year's Eve, but most of the time."

Sarah leaned forward, her gaze finding the full-time waiter on staff who was working that night. The rest of the group were temporary.

"See that guy over there?" She pointed him out as subtly as possible.

Meg and Vicky both looked.

"Do you mean the waiter with the floppy blond hair?" Vicky asked.

Sarah nodded. "His name is Thad. What do you think of him?"

Meg's brow furrowed. "What do you mean? On a scale or something?"

Sarah laughed. "No, his service - has he been doing a good job waiting tables?"

Vicky shrugged. "I asked him for a jug of lemonade about an hour ago, and I'm still waiting...so..."

"Really?" Sarah straightened in her seat. "Hmmm... I'm helping Mum deal with some issues here at the cafe, and from what I've seen of Thad so far, I'm not sure he's really helping things."

"He's a bit slow."

"And he was rude when we spoke to him," Meg added.

"He's spending a lot of time at that table of teenaged girls," Vicky mused.

Sarah crossed her arms over her chest. It wasn't a

crime to be a bad waiter, but if Mum was struggling to keep the doors open, every little bit of customer service, quality food and cost cutting mattered.

"So, what are we going to do about your love life?" Vicky asked, a glint in her eyes.

Sarah huffed. "What love life?"

"Exactly."

A picture of Mick McIntosh flashed into her mind the moment Vicky said the words "love life". Sarah's cheeks flushed with warmth. How ridiculous. She'd seen him one time when he came over to look at the cottage. The next day, she'd found his quote pushed under the front mat and decided to hire him to do the renovation since there weren't any other professional renovators in the area. She didn't understand why his face came to mind. He *was* good looking, and she had to admit she'd thought of him a few times since their brief encounter. But he wasn't her type - something she had reminded herself of more than once in the past few weeks.

Besides, he was probably married with children by this point in his life - weren't all men who lived in small country towns married in their early twenties? Not that she'd seen a ring on his finger, but that was probably because of his line of work. She'd read somewhere that men with physical jobs didn't wear jewellery for safety reasons.

Sarah cocked her head to one side. "I have a stray dog, Oscar, who visits every day, isn't that enough for now?"

Vicky chuckled. "Is he a cute dog?"

"Not in a classical way," Sarah replied. "He has his own style - dreadlocks, protruding ribs. He'd make quite the splash on a Paris runway."

They all laughed.

"I think we're going to get along just fine. Maybe I'll grow old at the cottage and become the crazy dog lady. All the strays will find out from Oscar about the bacon and leftovers."

"Is it bad that being the crazy dog lady sounds appealing to me right now?" Meg asked, her brows drawn low.

Vicky put an arm around Meg's shoulders. They all sat in silence a moment. Music pounded the air around them, Crystal's voice rising on a note that punctuated the humid night air. Sarah's heart ached for Meg and for Brad. She should appreciate what she had. It might not be everything she'd imagined for herself, but things could change in a moment.

She stood with a grunt. "Okay, break's over. I'll get you ladies that lemonade, and then it's back to work for me."

CHAPTER 19

MEG

*N*erves fluttered in Meg's stomach. She shifted her weight onto one foot, then the other, grasping the bunch of flowers more tightly in one hand.

Were flowers too much?

She wasn't sure what to bring to meet Brad at the airport. He didn't really eat chocolates or sweets, and she hated to have empty hands while she waited. So, she'd stopped and bought a bunch of flowers at the Foodstore on the way out of the Cove. Now that she looked at them, some of the daises sagged around the edges. The whole thing looked a little sad.

She inhaled a slow breath.

Why was she so nervous to see her own husband? It made no sense. It was Brad. She knew him better than she knew anyone else in the world. Or at least she'd thought she did, before the accident had changed him. She assumed it had changed him. If it hadn't...she couldn't bear the thought that perhaps she'd never known him.

A plane taxied across the tarmac and headed for the gate. Her breath caught in her throat. They were here. Finally. It felt like so long since she'd seen him. It was only two weeks but seemed like an eternity.

Would he be different? Would he be happy to see her?

She shifted her weight again, feeling a slight tremble in her knees that made them weaken.

It didn't take long for passengers to traipse out of the exit, satchels and handbags slung over weary shoulders.

Two children tumbled after their parents, shouting and squealing, no doubt grateful to be released from restrictive seat belts.

A knot formed in Meg's gut. She swallowed hard.

There they were. They'd stopped on the causeway. Brad was in a wheelchair, his parents behind him. A flight attendant pushed the chair and leaned down to pick something off the floor. They moved slowly, making their way towards her. Most of the passengers waited patiently behind them; a few strode past.

When they reached the exit, Meg stepped forward, a wide smile pressed to her face.

"Welcome home!" She leaned down to kiss Brad's cheek.

He didn't respond, only met her gaze briefly then looked away without a word.

Her throat tightened.

She turned to greet his parents, embracing them with genuine happiness. They looked older, more shrivelled somehow since when she'd left. Des had more grey in his hair, Sharon a few new lines around her eyes.

"I'm so glad to see you," Meg said, feeling her own eyes watering. "I missed you."

Sharon grinned. "It's good to be back. We can't wait to get home. We're heartily sick of hotel and hospital food, let me tell you."

"And that bed..." Des added with a grimace as he pushed one fist into the small of his back.

"It's really good to see you too, honey," Sharon added with a pat on Meg's arm.

"I hope the trip was okay?" Meg glanced at Brad who stared off into the distance, his shoulders hunched.

Sharon's lips pursed. She shook her head at Meg, a look of sorrow on her face. The lump in Meg's throat grew.

"It was fine," Des replied. "I've got indigestion though. I'd kill for a salad."

"First time I've ever heard that come from your lips," Sharon replied with a chuckle.

Meg swallowed around the lump. "Well, let's go and find your luggage so we can get out of here."

* * *

THE GARAGE WAS DARK, and shadows lingered in corners and crevices. Meg had never liked it much down there, all concrete and echoes, but today it gave her the shivers.

She set the last piece of luggage on the pavement and slammed the boot of the minivan shut. She'd had to trade her brand-new hatchback for a second-hand minivan with wheelchair access and a ramp. The previous owners had modified it to suit their son's needs, much to Meg's delight. Now, the sight of it made her stomach clench.

This was their life now. Her life and his.

It was still hard to swallow, though she was used to overcoming. She'd had to do enough of it in her childhood. She tilted her head up, pushed out her chin and grabbed the handles of two bags to wheel them after her.

Des picked up the remaining luggage, and Sharon pushed Brad in the chair as they made their way out of the garage and up the curving footpath to the front of the building.

Getting Brad's chair over the lip of the entrance was hard enough, but at least they didn't have to manoeuvre him up the staircase.

"I managed to get Gus to let us move our things to this unit on the ground floor," she said, leading the way. "I think it's going to work out well. I've added a shower rail and a ramp... I've moved everything I thought you might need into the lower cupboards. But if something's an issue, let me know and I'll fix it." She met Brad's gaze and saw anger lingering in his eyes. The same eyes that had looked at her with adoration only weeks earlier now simmered with hatred.

Meg pressed her lips together as she stopped at the front door to unlock it. So, he wasn't going to speak to her. She hadn't expected a kiss, but he could at least smile. Tears threatened, but she blinked them away.

"That all sounds wonderful," Sharon piped up.

"You've done a lot, Meggy," Des added.

Brad didn't say a thing.

"Hasn't she, Brad?" Des prodded. "She's done it all on her own, in only two weeks. That's pretty good."

Brad grunted. "Great."

Meg rolled her eyes at the closed door, then pushed it open, spinning to face the others with a smile. "Home sweet home!"

She put Brad's things away in their bedroom, while his parents got the kettle boiling. Meg joined them in the kitchen. She threw together a tossed salad with tuna and sourdough bread she'd bought the day before, and set it all on the table with glasses of mineral water.

"This looks amazing," Des said, his eyes gleaming.

"Perfect, just what we needed. I'm starving," Sharon added. "Aren't you hungry, love?" Sharon studied her son, who sat in the living room staring at the dark screen of the small television set in the corner.

He faced her, one eyebrow quirked. "I could eat."

They all sat at the small, round kitchen table and ate. Des and Sharon told Meg all about the last two weeks, what they did to celebrate the new year and the flight back to Brisbane. The chatter continued while she set out sliced mango and peaches for dessert, then they all cleaned up. All except Brad, who ate in silence, then wheeled himself back into the living room to switch on a game of cricket.

Sharon watched him, a worried look on her face until she noticed Meg's concern. She smiled and patted Meg's hand. "Don't worry, love. He'll come around. He's still in shock, that's what the doctor said. Grieving the loss of his legs." Sharon's voice choked on the words. She shook her head. "We're all still grieving, really."

Meg stared at the floor. "I don't think he wants to be here."

"Don't be silly, love. He's your husband, this is his home now."

"I know...but...he won't look at me or talk to me. I thought maybe things would be different after he'd had a couple of weeks to process...but it's worse. I don't know what to do."

Sharon's smile faded. "I know, we're all playing it by ear. But we have to stay positive. If I think too much about what he's lost..." She hesitated, her voice thick with emotion. "I can't do it. I can't think about what my baby has to give up, what he'll never do... It's too much for me. And for you, I'm sure. So, the two of us have to stick together. Okay?"

Meg nodded, unable to speak. She threw her arms around Sharon's neck and sobbed silently against her. She didn't want Brad to hear, hated the thought that he'd see her grief. It was the last thing he needed. She had to be strong for him, not the other way around.

She pulled away, dabbed quietly at her eyes with a tissue. "But you're going back to Brisbane," she whispered.

Sharon offered her a warm smile. "Yes, so the two of you can have some space. You'll need time alone to work this all out. We've found a physio close by, a doctor too. It's all set up, appointments, taxi for when you're at work, everything. But we're only a phone call away. Anything you need, you let us know. Okay?"

Meg wondered what it must've been like for Brad to grow up with so much love in his life. She couldn't imagine it, having a mother who doted, cared.

"I wish I'd had a mother like you," she sniffled.

Sharon's eyes glistened. "I always wished I'd had a daughter like you, and now I do." She kissed Meg's cheek. "You can do this, love. You're strong, and you love him. Those are two things I'm sure of, and if you've got that, you'll be able to do anything."

When Des and Sharon pulled away from the curb in front of their unit in a taxi, Meg turned to face the building with a ball of dread curled in her gut.

She knew Sharon was right. If they had some time alone together in their new home, maybe things would turn around. He'd have to talk to her; there was no one else.

Inside, Brad pulled the drapes shut over the living room windows. It was dark and smelled of tuna and the flowers she'd bought for Brad, that'd since found their way into a clear vase on the kitchen bench. Sharon's work, no doubt. She slid into an armchair, watching the cricket game for a few minutes.

"I thought we might go out later," she said.

His eyes narrowed, but he didn't respond otherwise.

"We could head through town, look around. I'm sure people will want to say hello."

He faced her with a scowl. "To look at the cripple in a wheelchair, you mean."

She gasped. "What? Brad! Don't say that. Everyone's been so worried about you. They ask about you all the time. I told them you were coming home..."

He huffed. "What do I care?"

"Okay, well, we don't have to do that. We could go to the beach..."

He faced her again, his scowl deepening. "I'm in a wheelchair, Meg. Get a grip on reality. I can't go in the sand, I can't go to the beach, I can't surf... I can't do any of the things I love, ever again!" As he spoke, his voice rose to a shout, and spittle flew from his lips.

Meg's heart leapt into her throat, and she found herself pushing away. A vision of her father shouting at her flitted across her mind's eye; in her memory his arm flew out, catching her young face and sending her across the room, crashing into the wall. She'd walked away from that life the first chance she got and never looked back. Now here she was, newly married, and her husband was yelling at her in the same way.

A shudder ran up her spine. "Please don't yell at me."

He rolled his eyes. "Why, Meg? Is it too much for your delicate nerves? Do you have any idea what it's like for me?"

"I know it's been hard for you." Her teeth ground together. "I understand that. But I really don't like it when you yell. You know how my father was, and it brings up all those bad memories."

He shook his head. "What do you expect? You force me to come back here, shove me in this ridiculous excuse for a home, right across from the beach…"

"What are you saying, Brad? I thought you wanted to live here. We picked the building together. We were so excited about living here. Looked forward to it for months…"

He issued a hollow laugh. "That was back when it meant something…when I could be a husband to you, when I could walk with you, hold your hand, when I could surf…" His voice trailed away, his head dropped and he pressed fingers to his eyes.

She hurried to his side, dropped to kneel by his chair and reached for his hand to press it between hers. "Brad, is that what you're so angry about? Because I don't care about any of that. I'm glad you're alive. Do you know how hard it was for me that day, not knowing whether you were dead or alive?"

He met her gaze, his eyes boring into hers. "I wish I'd died."

Her tears couldn't be held back then. They blurred her vision. "No, don't say that. You don't mean it. I couldn't cope with that..."

He looked away. "Face it, Meg. I'm not the man you married. You'd be better off without me, and I certainly don't want to be here." He tugged his hand from her grasp.

"But where would you go?"

"To Mum and Dad's. They have a bigger house, a swimming pool where I can do therapy. And it's not by the beach. They don't want me to, say I have to try to make things work here, with you. But I can't...I can't do this. I can't be married to you, can't be your husband. It's too much to cope with. I want to go home, be by myself. I don't want to be here. In fact, I'd rather be anywhere else in the world than right here." The words hissed from his mouth and felt like a stab to her heart.

Meg leapt to her feet. She backed away from Brad, her eyes wide. Then she turned and fled through the front door, down the steps in the direction of the beach. She ran across the sand, her lungs heaving as tears wet her cheeks. He didn't want to be married to her. Didn't love her after all. Why was she surprised? No one in her life ever had.

CHAPTER 20

MEG

*H*air lined the floor of the salon. Meg grabbed the long-handled broom and dustpan and swept it all away with a few brisk strokes. She set the dustpan against the wall, then spun to face Sarah with a smile.

"So, what are we going to do with your hair today?"

Sarah's nose wrinkled. "I don't think there is much you *can* do with it. It's long, straight and pretty hopeless, really."

"What? Don't say that, I love your hair. I'd kill for this straight, silky look."

"But I wish I had your curls!" Sarah objected.

Meg laughed. "Ah, the grass is always greener. Huh?"

"So, in answer to your question, let's do a trim, maybe a few layers."

"Perfect." Meg brushed the snarls from Sarah's hair while they talked.

It was funny for her to think of it now, but she'd been so intimidated by Sarah when she was younger. Sarah was the cool, older teen when she'd been a kid. Meg had looked up to her, admired her from afar - she was beautiful, sporty, talented and smart. She always seemed to know the right thing to say whenever someone was being teased, or acting unkind. Her retorts left the perpetrator speechless every time. Meg had always wished she could cut people down to size the way Sarah Flannigan had in high school.

Now, here they were, chatting like old friends. And it felt that way, most of the time. As if they'd always been friends. They'd certainly known each other a long time. She wondered why she'd ever been afraid of Sarah. Hanging out with Vicky and Sarah were the only times she laughed these days.

"So, when are you going to start renovations on the cottage?" Meg asked.

Sarah's lips pursed. "I want to start right away, but Mick McIntosh is my renovator, and apparently he's booked solid."

"Oh, Mick McIntosh, yeah, he's the best carpenter around here. He has a background in architecture, so everyone wants him on their job. They say he does beautiful work." *One of the many reasons people hired him.* Meg grinned to herself.

"So it seems. I can't wait to get started though. The cottage is quaint, but I'm sick of the leaking roof, the mouldy walls, the rotten porch... It'll be so much better to have everything fixed so I can relax and enjoy it."

"Definitely." Meg's scissors snipped the ends of Sarah's hair.

"He's starting in three days, at least I hope he is. I don't know how long it'll take. He was very vague about the details…"

Meg chuckled. "That's Mick for you. He's pretty easy on the eyes as well."

"I hadn't noticed," Sarah replied quickly.

"Oh, I'm sure you didn't." Meg winked at Sarah in the mirror.

Sarah's cheeks pinked, and Meg smiled with satisfaction.

"How are things going with Brad?" Sarah asked.

Meg's smile faded. She inhaled a long, slow breath. How could she tell the truth? It hurt even to think about the way Brad hardly spoke to her, sat in his chair staring at the television set in the darkened living room.

"Not great…"

"He hasn't improved?"

Meg shook her head. "I don't know what to do. He keeps those blasted curtains pulled over the windows all the time, sits in the dark and watches television or stares at the wall. The only time he does anything is when he goes to his physiotherapy sessions. I can't get him out of the house otherwise."

"I'm sorry, Meg."

Meg set the scissors on her tray and squeezed her eyes shut. "I wouldn't mind that so much if he spoke to me every now and then. He barely looks at me and mostly only grunts in response to questions. He doesn't want my help with anything, but of course I have to help him because he's new to all of this…" She rubbed both hands over her face. "I honestly have no idea what to do. I think our marriage might be over." Tears pricked her eyes, and her throat ached with the pain of sorrow.

Sarah rested a hand on her arm, and Meg slid into the seat beside her.

"There's no instruction manual for what you two are going through. No one can tell you the best way to grieve, to process everything that's happened. It's going to take some time. But I can see why you're concerned... It sounds like he could be depressed."

Meg's eyes widened. "Of course he's depressed, and I don't blame him... But I wonder sometimes if he blames me."

"Surely not, it wasn't your fault." Sarah's brow furrowed, her brown eyes glowing with compassion.

"No, it wasn't, but he's not thinking straight right now. And the other thing that bothers me - I'm a hair-dresser, I don't make a lot of money, and I didn't think I'd have to be the breadwinner of the family. But here we are... I'm the only one earning money and who knows for how long. What if he never gets a job, never contributes financially? What if we can't have chil-dren? I've always wanted to be a mum..." Her voice broke.

She hadn't shared these hidden, consuming fears with anyone before, and her chest groaned with the pain of releasing them into the world. It was hard for her to be vulnerable. Every time she was, she always regretted it, wished she could snatch back the words and shove them deep down into the darkest recesses of her heart all over again.

Sarah reached over to embrace her, her arms warm and inviting, her shoulder a strong place for Meg's head to land. "That's a lot of burdens to carry," she whispered. "No wonder you're feeling low."

Meg sniffled against Sarah's shirt. "I'm not usually like this… I don't cry very often, definitely not at work in front of people."

Sarah chuckled soft and low. "Well, if there was ever a time for it, this is it. Meggy, I don't know what the future holds, but I do know nothing stays the same. You love Brad, he's a bright, driven, strong man, I can't imagine he'll let this thing win. But right now, he's hurting, he's dealing with an unimaginable loss, and he isn't coping very well with that. I think he might need to talk to someone."

Meg pulled away, reached for a tissue on the second level of her hairdressing tray and blew her nose into it. She got another and dabbed her eyes dry. "Talk to someone…heck, if he would talk to anyone at all, that'd be a win. And now he says he's not going back to university. They gave him a semester off, said he could take his time going back… He was studying business there part-time while he surfed. But he doesn't want to go back, says he's going to withdraw."

Sarah shook her head. "I don't have any answers for you, but I'm here for you whenever you need this shoulder." She patted the one still damp with Meg's tears.

Meg laughed through a blur of moisture. "Thanks. You're a good friend. I'm sorry for all the drama."

"Never apologise for drama." Sarah winked. "My social life now revolves around the degustation schedule of a mangy dog. I can listen to any drama you need to get off your chest." She hesitated, patted Meg's arm. "Remember, he loves you. You know that. The rest of it…

well, it doesn't seem like the boy I remember. He always had a big smile plastered across his face, would fly down the street on his bike, standing high on the pedals, feet flashing as they went around. Nothing seemed impossible for him. Do you remember that time he climbed the tree that hangs over the river? That big old fig tree?"

Meg blew her nose again, nodded.

"No one would do it, because the tree branch looked like it was rotting, but he decided he wasn't going to let that stop him. The river was so full that day, rushing by, and he climbed out on the branch and did a little dance for all of us. We laughed so hard, then when it broke and he fell into the river, we all held our breaths until his head pushed through the surface and he grinned. He was always doing stuff like that. He's a fighter, he's brave, and we have to believe that part of him will win through in the end. Right?"

Meg smiled. "I'd forgotten about that story. I had the biggest crush on him, even then."

Sarah smiled. "That's adorable."

"So, let's get your hair shampooed," Meg replied, jumping to her feet and shoving the tissues she'd used into the nearest rubbish bin. "Otherwise we'll take all day and my other customers will start to complain." She pushed a smile onto her face. It helped to get things off her chest, to talk about them. But in the end, she still had to go home at the close of business to face her husband in their darkened unit. She still had to smile, be cheerful and chatter, expecting nothing more than the occasional grunt or sarcastic comment in response. And she still had to face the possibility that her marriage may well be ended before it'd truly had a chance to begin.

CHAPTER 21

SARAH

*S*arah switched off her hair dryer and fluffed her hair around her shoulders with one hand, twisting this way and that in the mirror to survey her handiwork. The knock at the door startled her, though it shouldn't have. She was expecting it.

Her heart leapt into her throat, then she reminded herself it was only Mick. He said he'd be coming early to begin renovations, which suited her fine because she was heading to the airport.

She set her hairbrush on the bathroom sink and hurried to open the door.

"Good morning, Mick," she said with a wide smile.

His hair had been pushed back away from his face, in a perfectly mussed yet stylish kind of way. She wasn't sure how he managed to pull off a look that screamed *I just rolled out of bed*, but he did somehow. It suited him.

His green eyes looked paler than usual in the cool morning light. He grinned.

"You ready for this?"

Her heart skipped a beat at the look in his eyes. She frowned. "Huh?"

"Your house is going to be a construction zone for weeks. I hope you know what you're getting yourself into."

She sighed with relief. *Oh, that.* "Yeah, I know. I'm not really looking forward to it, though I'm excited to see the finished product."

"And you're on board for the new master suite?"

She nodded, her imagination running over the plan he'd laid out for her weeks earlier when she'd signed the contract to have him renovate the cottage. He'd suggested adding a large master bedroom with an en suite bathroom and walk-in wardrobe, and she'd jumped at the idea. It was exactly what she needed. And it'd have bifold glass doors that would lead onto an extended porch, to look directly out over the ocean from her bed. She couldn't wait.

She handed Mick a key she'd had made for him so he could let himself and his workers in and out of the cottage when she wasn't there.

"Here's your key. I'm on my mobile if you need anything, call me anytime." It sounded like she was asking for a date, and her cheeks burned at the thought. He must get this kind of attention from women all the time.

He didn't seem to notice her discomfort. "Sure, have a great trip. How long are you gone for again?"

"Only two days, I'll be back on Thursday."

He nodded. "Great. So, we'll be knocking down

walls today. By the time you get back, we should have all of the demo done."

She bit down on her lip, glanced around the cottage one last time. She'd put everything into a back room, her life packed away in boxes yet again. Anything that remained was draped in drop cloths.

"Okay, please be careful. I really love having a roof over my head. I'd hate to see this place disintegrate, but I have a feeling that's a distinct possibility."

He chuckled, raised a hand to his head in a mock salute. "Don't worry about a thing, Sassy, I'll take care of it."

The sound of her childhood nickname on Mick's lips almost made her legs buckle. She hadn't been called Sassy in so long she'd almost forgotten about it. Coming from him, it made her forget herself for a moment and consider throwing herself into his arms.

She cleared her throat. "Uh...great. Well, I trust you. I'll see you on Thursday. Oh, and please feed the dog. You may not see him, he's pretty shy, but if you could leave food in his bowl on the back deck, or somewhere close by, that'd be great."

He nodded. "No worries, I'll take care of it."

She tugged her suitcase through the doorway, brushing past Mick so that for a moment she was pressed up against his muscular chest. Her breath caught in her throat until she'd moved past him and turned to wave awkwardly.

"Uh...okay. Bye."

He raised a hand. "See ya."

She made it to the car before the embarrassment hit. What was wrong with her? She wasn't a teenager anymore. She was a professional woman, an adult. So why had her confidence drained the moment she opened the door and saw his wrinkled work shirt and torn shorts, his tanned legs and heavy work boots?

She issued a heavy sigh and started the engine. As she pulled out of the driveway, she passed a truck filled with labourers, its bed laden with toolboxes, ladders and more, coming the other direction. She issued a quick wave, then slowed to study her rear-view mirror. The paint-chipped, weary cottage almost winked at her under the rising sun. Its stained walls, leaky roof and weed-strangled garden brought a lump to her throat. It would never look the same again, and as much as that brought her relief, it also raised up feelings of nostalgia. She'd only lived there a few weeks, but already it felt like home. Still, homes shouldn't leak or emit foul odours.

She stepped on the accelerator and turned onto the main road in the direction of the Gold Coast Airport. It was time to switch her thoughts to work. She'd been so distracted lately with everything that was going on in the Cove, with Oscar and the cottage, not to mention her mother's cafe. She'd allowed the quality of her work to slip, which wasn't something she was accustomed to doing.

It was harder maintaining her focus from a distance than she'd ever thought it would be.

And besides, a trip to the office in Sydney would very likely mean seeing Jeremy.

Her heart lurched at the thought. Perhaps she could avoid him. She had meetings lined up for most of the time she'd be there; maybe no one would tell him about her visit, and she could sneak away without him knowing.

She grimaced.

It was comforting to imagine, but she knew there wasn't a chance of that happening.

CHAPTER 22

CINDY

*H*er feet ached, and the evening was only just beginning. Cindy wasn't sure she'd manage the evening shifts at the cafe for much longer. They were too hard on her. And she was definitely cancelling the annual New Year's Eve party. She'd done it forever, the same way her parents had - though she'd taken it to the next level with live music and flyers handed out to the tourists in the area. But after the latest celebration, she'd taken three days in bed to recover.

She was almost sixty-one and felt far too old to host a party for two hundred, especially when she had to bring in a team of inexperienced waitstaff to help her do it. She'd ended up doing most of the work herself. She was grateful Sarah had spent the evening helping out. And even though they'd been busy all night long, the takings from the night didn't match up to the outgoing food from the kitchen, something she hadn't been able to figure out in the weeks since.

She lowered herself into a chair in the cafe's spacious kitchen and kicked off her shoes to rub each foot for a moment. Happy hour was about to begin, another tradition at the Emerald Cafe, although a much more recent addition to the calendar.

She and her long-time friend, Diana Jones, had sat down twenty years earlier and agreed that if Diana would promote the cafe to her guests, Cindy would throw a happy hour every weekday evening that would allow vacationers staying at the Seaside Manor Bed and Breakfast to buy half-priced drinks and appetisers. It'd always been a big hit with the guests, but after checking over her receipts the past few months, Cindy wasn't sure it was viable for her any longer.

Guests had to provide a room key to get access to the discount, but for some reason, it seemed the promotion wasn't generating the same kind of revenue as it had in past years. Maybe it would have to go the way of the recently departed New Year's Eve party.

She slipped her feet back into her shoes as Thad wandered into the kitchen.

"Good afternoon, Thad."

He nodded, smiled. "How're you, Cindy?"

"Fine, thanks. Ready for happy hour?" she asked.

He shrugged. "I guess." His thick Norwegian accent smoothed out the words, giving them an enticing lilt.

She knew the customers liked Thad, at least the young women did, but sometimes it was difficult to get him motivated to do the work he should - and whatever he left undone, she ended up having to do herself. That was part of being the boss, she supposed.

"Well, let's get out there and take orders, then."

He wandered back through the doors, tying a black apron around his waist as he did.

Cindy followed and watched for a while as guests flooded through the doors. During happy hour, Crystal manned the bar until her set, then played her guitar and sang while Cindy took over mixing drinks. Thad was their only waiter, so between the three of them, they did their best to cope.

With a quick inhale, Cindy hurried to join Thad in taking orders. The cook had his hands full keeping up with the food orders, and Crystal was run off her feet behind the bar. Every time Cindy looked up from what she was doing, someone was flashing a room key at Crystal.

Cindy decided to have a word with Diana next time they met for tea - was the bed and breakfast booked solid? She couldn't remember a time when it'd housed as many guests as it had lately. Were they doing something different? Maybe some advertising in the city? Whatever it was, she was grateful for the business. Perhaps things would turn around after all.

While Crystal set up her guitar and microphone, Cindy slipped behind the bar to take drink orders. The room keys kept coming, and before the night was over, her feet ached, a strange pain was shooting through her right hip and into her lower back, and she could barely walk.

Thad and Crystal cleaned up, though if she was being completely honest, she noticed Crystal did most of the work while Thad lounged around, whispering into his mobile phone. Cindy simply couldn't stay on her feet any longer to help them. And besides, she had to count the cash and balance the till.

"I'm heading home, Cindy," Crystal called with a wave.

Cindy waved goodbye. "You okay to get home by yourself?"

Crystal nodded. "Of course, Emerald Cove is the safest place in the world. You should try Bangkok sometime."

Cindy chuckled. Crystal had lived there during her childhood, though Cindy had never visited the place herself. "Fair point. I'll see you Monday."

When she checked, she found Thad had already left, so Cindy settled back in her office chair to count the money that was piled in the till, along with credit card and EFTPOS receipts from the night's service.

By the time she was done, she was even more confused than she had been before she started. It didn't make sense. Given the number of guests who'd filed in through the cafe's doors, and the hundreds of drinks she and Crystal had served from the bar, there should've been thousands of dollars more than was accounted for in the till. She cocked her head to one side, tapping a fingernail against the top of the desk.

With a sigh, she straightened and stretched out her back. She grimaced, leaned over to touch her toes and found that she could barely reach halfway anymore. Gone were the days of her girlhood when she could lie down on her legs in her ballet tights, and then leap in the air to kick her legs out and lay her head back like a gazelle. She shook her head and reached for her purse, then carried the till to the safe to lock up for the night.

It didn't make any sense, but perhaps she'd calculated wrong. She'd count it again in the morning before carrying the cash to the bank. And if she still couldn't figure it out, she'd have to ask Sarah for help...again. Because something wasn't right at the cafe, and she had no idea what it was. But if she didn't figure it out soon, the mortgage Andrew had raised against the business would mean she'd have to sell everything and close up shop. And the thought of that brought an ache to her chest.

CHAPTER 23

REBECCA

"*D*on't touch my radio." Franklin's voice was abrupt and cold. Rebecca crossed her arms over her chest and peered out the passenger window of the police cruiser.

"Yes, sir." There was a hint of sass in her voice, though she tried to hide it as best she could. She knew going into police work she'd have to submit to authority, whether pleasant or painful, but it was beginning to make her skin crawl. She bit down on a further retort and pressed her lips tight together instead.

She'd worked at the Emerald Cove Police Station for almost three weeks now, and her boss had given her nothing but the cold shoulder the entire time. It was troubling to her that she'd yet to figure out if he was simply a jerk or if his bad attitude was particularly aimed in her direction. Given the fact that everyone else in the office seemed to worship at his feet, she had to go with the latter, though she couldn't imagine what she'd done in the brief time she'd lived in the Cove to tick him off so badly.

Neighbourhoods of small, square fibro houses flitted by the window. A dog barked up against a chain-link fence, straining at its tether to get at a trio of children who were riding past on their bicycles as fast as they could, standing on the pedals to pump past the animal with wide eyes and puffing chests.

She smiled at the sight, as it prompted a memory from her own childhood of sprinting past the neighbour's house every week to get to the local park, a dog nipping at her heels. It only ever followed her to the next intersection, then stopped to bark at her as she crossed the street. She'd spin back when she reached the other side, breath heaving in and out of her lungs, to study the animal with narrowed eyes. Then continue on her way, while it trotted back to its yard.

"When we get there, I want you to be particularly careful." Franklin interrupted her reverie and jolted her back to the present.

She nodded. "Okay."

"Domestic incidents are unpredictable, so be on your toes. Got it?"

"I've got it."

His mood seemed particularly curly today, his words almost a snarl from tight lips. She tried to think back over the morning to see if she'd done anything to trigger the foul temper he was in, but nothing sprang to mind. Apparently, her mere presence irritated him to no end. Well, there wasn't much she could do about that. Not yet, anyway. She had to be in Emerald Cove for now, had to keep her head down, do her time as a new recruit and stay out of trouble. Leaving wasn't an option.

She rested an elbow on the windowsill as the car jolted over a pothole, then pressed her hand to her forehead like a visor under which she could study her boss's profile without him knowing. She did it every now and then, trying to figure out the man she spent so many hours of each day seated beside. So far, she'd come up with next to nothing, other than a cryptic comment made by Steph - calling Franklin the *Lone Ranger*. Perhaps that's all it was - he preferred to ride solo. But from what she'd been told at the state headquarters, they were intent on giving him a partner, whether it was her or someone else. Franklin Russell wouldn't be riding the beat alone.

So, why couldn't he simply accept that and give her a break?

She sighed against the window, dropping her arms to her side. The car pulled up to the curb. She checked herself in the mirror, felt her gun, taser, cuffs... Everything was accounted for, all in place. She was ready.

They crossed the road side by side, she followed him through a broken gate and up a set of rotting timber stairs to knock on a paint-chipped timber door.

"Maybe no one's home," she muttered.

He huffed. "Give it a minute. Jeesh. Got an appointment at the hair salon or something?"

Rebecca bit down on her lip and stared at the grubby half-circle window at the top of the door, anger burning in her gut. He had no respect for her; that was clear enough. She didn't ask for much, didn't expect him to like her, but had hoped he'd at least treat her with a little respect. Not that she'd ever won anyone's respect in her short life so far, but joining the force had been a new start for her. A chance to make something of herself. And she'd foolishly believed being a recruit, having done her Associate Degree in Policing Practice, and being placed in a New South Wales police station as a new recruit meant she *was* someone. That she deserved a little respect. It seemed Franklin was intent on proving those hopes wrong.

A shadow passed by the window, completely obscured by grime and dust, only darkening it for a moment, and her entire body tensed.

"Someone's home," she whispered.

"Go around back, Constable," Franklin ordered. "I don't want anyone leaving this house without my say-so."

With one hand on her gun holster, Rebecca jogged down the stairs and through the yard. Tufts of grass decorated the dirt here and there; a kid's bike lay on its side, rusted with both tyres flat. There was just enough space between the house and the fence for her to pass through, and she soon found herself in a backyard littered with trash and dotted with clusters of tall weeds.

Rebecca tripped on a fallen rubbish bin, announcing her presence with a loud clatter. She swore beneath her breath and caught herself, just as the screen door flung open. A man rushed down the stairs, glanced in her direction and ran in the other.

"Stop! Police!" she shouted, regaining her balance in time to sprint after him.

He was at least six feet tall, which meant he had almost a foot of height on her, and at least fifty kilograms. He wore a stained, white singlet over the top of a pair of football shorts. A beer belly protruded above the waistband of the green shorts, and a long, dark blue tattoo of a dragon with a red eye curled over his shoulder and down his forearm.

When he found himself facing the chain-link fence, with no option but to leap over it, he stopped and spun on his heel to face her with a sneer.

"There's no way out. Just stay where you are, and link your hands together behind your head," she said as she undid the snap on her holster, ready to draw her weapon, her eyes fixed on the man's face.

He barely hesitated before charging, knocking her flat on her back before she'd had a chance to react.

The wind whooshed from her lungs, and she lay on her back in the dirt, her hand still on her holster, her eyes blinking in the glare of sunlight overhead.

Memories pecked at her like a flock of angry seagulls. A punch to the face, a kick to the gut, seeing her own blood spurt from a burst lip, hearing the crack of her bones breaking. Panic flooded her, eyes widening as her hands fluttered in front of her face as if trying to grab at something that wasn't there.

No, no, it was happening again. But it couldn't, she wasn't there any longer, she'd moved, she was in Emerald Cove. Safe. It was okay. She'd only had the wind knocked out of her, nothing she couldn't handle.

She talked to herself, ran words through her mind, all the usual ways of calming herself down, reassuring herself she was okay. She'd learned them over the years; it was the only way she'd been able to survive until she could get away, finally, and start again - a new life, a new home, a new chance at finding peace if there was any to be had in this world, something she still wasn't entirely convinced of.

She gasped for air but couldn't fill her lungs. In the distance, she heard a muffled shout, then the sound of footsteps running away, a door slamming, crying from inside the house.

Still, she couldn't breathe. She sat up, her lips fish-like, as slowly her lungs filled with oxygen.

She leaned forward, gulping in great, big breaths, as dizziness sent a wave of nausea through her gut. She hadn't expected that. For some reason, she'd thought he'd listen to her, do as she asked. It was her first real confrontation with a perpetrator on the job, and she'd failed.

With a grunt, she scrambled to her feet, then stood with her hands on her hips for a moment to get her bearings as her head swam. Sobbing from the house caught her ear, reminding her of the possible victims inside, and she hurried in, her gun out of its holster and pointed down.

When she was sure the house was clear, she knelt beside a woman on the floor. Two boys huddled in a corner, one sobbing and the other sucking his thumb. The woman cried silently now, her legs tucked up beneath her chin, tears streaking her cheeks.

"Are you okay?" Rebecca asked, returning the gun to her holster.

The woman didn't respond.

"Are you hurt?"

Rebecca used her radio to call for an ambulance, then checked on the boys. By the time she'd done that, she was about to try again with the woman when she heard footsteps outside. She peered through the window by the front door and saw Franklin bent at the waist, puffing hard. The man wasn't with him.

He straightened, saw her and pushed through the front door.

"Have you secured the premises?"

She nodded. "Yes, sir. A woman and two boys inside, she appears to be injured but I'm not sure how badly. I've called for an ambulance, should be here in fifteen."

She watched with surprise as Franklin squatted beside the woman, talking gently to her until she stopped sobbing and answered his questions. Rebecca did what she could to draw the boys out of the corner and, when the ambulance arrived, helped them into the vehicle beside their mother, who the paramedics laid out on a stretcher.

By now, the woman's face was swollen and purple, with large, angry lumps on her lower lip and above one eye.

The ambulance pulled away from the curb, lights flashing but without the siren. Rebecca watched it go, then headed for the house to help Franklin lock it up.

She found him out the back, studying the fence line, hands pressed to his narrow hips. A muscle in his jaw clenched when he saw her, and his nostrils flared.

"Something wrong, Sarge?"

His lips pursed. "You tell me, Constable Mair."

"I let him get away, I know that…"

"You're darn right you did. I can't begin to tell you how dangerous your actions were today, to the victims, to me and to yourself. Do you know what might've happened if things had run a different course?"

She swallowed. She hadn't thought about that, had simply been grateful her injuries weren't any worse.

"No, sir."

"If he'd had a weapon of some kind, you'd be dead, and the rest of us might be as well."

Her heart fell. "I'm sorry, Sarge... He caught me by surprise."

"Exactly. That's what happened, you were caught off guard. Because you aren't ready for this. I'm sorry to be the one to have to break it to you, Constable, but you're not cut out for this job. You're not police material, that's a simple fact. And because of that, we could've had a tragic situation on our hands today."

Her eyes widened. She swallowed around a lump growing in her throat.

"I'm sorry... I'm doing my best, but I'll improve, get better..."

He shook his head, glowering. "No, you won't. Because as I said, you're not cop material. And besides, I don't need a partner, I don't want one either. I had a partner, he's gone, and he can't be replaced. It's as simple as that." The fire dimmed in his eyes as fast as it had sparked.

He looked away, sighed, then strode for the side of the house and disappeared from view. She heard his voice echo back to her. "Well, are you coming or do you need an embossed invitation, Mair?"

CHAPTER 24

SARAH

"*I*'m happy to run through the schedule with you," Sarah said.

Across from her, a trio of young, up-and-coming editors nodded almost in unison.

"Thanks, that would be great. We'll have to transition the memoir you're holding onto as well..." One of the firm's top editors, Pauline Gates, didn't look up from the notes she was scratching out on her iPad.

Sarah frowned. "What? I'm only one third of the way through that manuscript."

Pauline eyed her. "I thought you were going on some sort of sabbatical. A sea change, getting away from it all?" A titter spread throughout the room.

"No. I'm working from home. I'm keeping the same workload as I had, you know that." Anger boiled in Sarah's gut. She'd always had a problem with Pauline's jealousy; she should have expected her to take the opportunity to dig the knife in.

Pauline raised her hands, as if in surrender. She offered a warm smile. "Never mind then, I must have misunderstood. Although we never hear from you, so you can't really blame us."

It was true. She'd been missing in action lately, and it wasn't like her. But there were so many things in the Cove to distract her from her work. She'd have to focus more on her career if she was going to keep hold of it.

As soon as the meeting was over, Sarah gathered her papers together, folded her laptop beneath her arm and strode through the office. Greenmount Publishing hummed with activity and buzzed with excitement. She'd always loved working there, and she missed being there physically, as much as she hated to admit it.

Katrina Rousseau fell into step beside her, a manila folder clutched to her chest.

"You showed her," Katrina said, grinning.

Sarah shrugged. "I don't know about that, I'm not very good at confrontation. I always think of a killer retort hours after the fact." She chuckled. "Anyway, she's harmless enough. Beverley won't let her have too long a leash."

Sarah took a seat at her desk, setting her laptop back into place beside the large monitor. A potted plant sat on the end of the desk. Its leaves had shrivelled to a dark brown and lay dead over the edges of the black pot. It'd been her plant, and obviously no one had watered it after she left.

"What happened to my plant?"

Katrina pressed one hand to a hip and studied

Sarah with pursed lips. "Forget about the plant, Sarah. You've got bigger things to worry about. Since you left, Pauline has taken over everything you were a part of. She has more influence than ever. And she's been telling everyone that you're stepping away, that you aren't coming back and you're transitioning to a more manageable workload." Katrina used her hands to make air quotes around the last, emphasising the words with a bob of her head.

Sarah's brow furrowed. She hadn't realised things had gotten so bad in the office. She should have anticipated that Pauline would move to fill the space she created when she relocated to the Cove.

"I haven't left," she said.

Katrina shrugged. "You know what I mean."

"I haven't left, I'm still part of the company, I'm in the same role, and I'm not going anywhere."

Beverley's head appeared above the cubicle partition where Sarah sat. Sarah pressed a hand to her chest, startled. "Oh, hi, Beverley. You surprised me. When did you get in?"

Beverly tipped her head back and laughed. Her laugh always sounded like a waterfall trickling over smooth rocks. "I'm sorry about that. I wanted to pop by and tell you that I'd love to catch up before you leave. Okay?"

Sarah nodded. "Yes, of course."

Beverley came around the end of the cubicle and perched on the edge of Sarah's desk, a charcoal skirt pulled taut across her narrow hips. "Have I told you I've taken up horse riding?" she asked.

Sarah blinked. "No. Horse riding? Really?"

Beverley was always taking on new hobbies, almost as if on a quest to discover the meaning of life.

Inevitably she ended up getting hurt, overextending or simply giving up. Her career had been a driving force in her life; she'd never married or had children. And if asked, she'd say she made the right choice. Sarah admired her for knowing what she wanted. Still, there was a manic quality to the way Beverley lived her life that Sarah couldn't quite appreciate.

"Oh yes, I love it. It's my passion. I go three mornings a week. Don't I, Katrina?"

Katrina's lips widened into a smile. "Yes, of course, you love it."

Katrina and Sarah exchanged a look behind Beverley's back that almost made Sarah laugh out loud. She loved Beverley, loved her boss's enthusiasm for life. But it was a well-played joke around the office that she changed hobbies as often as she did boyfriends. And she was passionately dedicated to both, for as long as they lasted.

"Just this morning, I took Alpine for a ride, and we made it over a jump that I have been too scared to try for months. It was a huge victory, we all celebrated." Beverley's eyes sparked. "We had coffee at this darling little place just down the road from the riding club, and I splurged on a scone."

Sarah arched an eyebrow. "It must have been a big celebration, for you to eat carbohydrates."

Beverley laughed. "You know it."

"I'm considering getting back into surfing," Sarah said.

Beverley clapped her hands together once. "Surfing, oh, that would be marvellous. I've always wanted to try that."

"Maybe it can be your next hobby?" Katrina interjected.

Beverley's brow furrowed. "Next? You think I'll give up horse riding, don't you? Well, not this time. I think horse riding is what I've been searching for all along. I have finally found a relationship I can commit to." She chuckled. "Anyway, Sarah, make sure you come to my office for a chat before you leave today. We have a few things we need to talk about. And I feel like I never see you anymore. It's crazy."

Sarah swallowed. This wasn't going as well as she hoped it would. "Yes, of course, Beverley. I won't forget. And you know I'm only a phone call away."

Beverley stood, straightened her skirt and smoothed it into place with perfectly manicured hands. "Of course you are, I seem to forget that. Out of sight, out of mind, you know how it is."

As Beverley walked away, Sarah's heart fell. She had spent her twenties building a career, forgoing a social life, turning down the chance to build a solid personal life, believing that one day the time would come that her career would be rock solid and she'd find the man of her dreams, settle down and start a family. She'd never imagined that the career she had worked so hard to develop could so easily be undermined. Although, perhaps she'd been naïve, walking away from the epicentre of publishing to live in a small beachside town.

Her friends had warned it wouldn't work, but she hadn't listened to them. She believed she could manage it, that she could be the one person who'd prove everyone else wrong. The technology existed to work remotely, so why not use it? Now she wasn't so sure... about anything.

"That went well," Katrina said.

Sarah sighed. "Did you hear that?"

Katrina shook her head. "What?"

"I think it was the sound of my career dying."

* * *

LATER, on her way to Beverley's office to talk to her boss about a breakout book series by an up-and-coming author she wanted to sign, she was so focused on the task ahead of her that at first she didn't notice the group of junior editors clustered around a table in the conference room. With the first manuscript of the series pressed to her chest, arms wrapped protectively around it, she studied the group.

What were they doing in there? She slowed her pace but kept walking, straining to see if she could hear anything they were saying.

She heard the words "Some kind of cottage," and "She can't expect..."

One of the editors looked up and caught her staring. The woman's cheeks flushed pink.

Sarah's gut clenched. Were they talking about her? She hated office politics. Always had. It wasn't something she'd ever wanted to be part of. She'd avoided it as much as she could while she lived in Sydney, and now she was the subject of the gossip. She hated thinking about all of them huddled together talking about her, her life choices, her home.

What did they think it would achieve anyway?

She pressed the end of one finger to her mouth and absently chewed her fingernail. Distracted, she ran into something hard. And tall. Her nose smacked into a firm chest; the manuscript flew from her hands and fluttered to the ground, sheets of paper flying in every direction.

"Where are you going in such a hurry?" a masculine voice asked'.

Her gaze travelled up a wide chest, over designer stubble and rested on two bright, blue eyes.

"Jeremy! What a surprise."

He sniggered. "I'll bet. If you'd known I was going to be here, you'd have hidden in the ladies'."

Her face burned. "No, definitely not, I'm glad to see you. You look good." Her heart beat against her rib cage. Why hadn't anyone told her that her ex-fiancé would be in the office today? Surely that was a juicy piece of gossip that was too hard for them to pass up. They'd discussed Richard the mail guy's hair plugs for ten full minutes; they couldn't mention that Jeremy would be visiting?

"How long are you in the city?" A dimple played in one cheek, and she was reminded again how charming Jeremy could be when he wanted.

"I'm here until tomorrow. Right now, I have to go - there's something I need to discuss with Beverley. Sorry I don't have time for a better catch-up." She quickly gathered together all of the papers from the manuscript she had dropped when she collided with him.

He moved to help, his face so close to hers she could almost feel his breath on her skin. He was good at this part. He knew how to make a woman swoon. But it wasn't going to work this time. She was immune to his charms.

"Thank you, but you don't have to help. Really, I'm fine."

He chuckled. "It's the least I could do. Although you probably should learn to watch where you're going. What were you looking at anyway?"

She picked up the last piece of paper, pressed the mess of sheets to her chest and straightened, her cheeks flushed. He shadowed her movements, pressing his hands to his hips.

"Nothing." She couldn't tell him she was listening in on the office gossip about herself. It was embarrassing.

"I'm not sure I believe you, but I'll let it go this time. You always were easier to read than one of my books." He chuckled. He was in a good mood today or at least doing a good job of pretending.

But she wasn't in the mood to deal with him.

"Let's have coffee," he said suddenly. "We need a better catch-up than this. I want to hear all about Emerald Cove and how things are going."

It was exactly what she'd been hoping to avoid. She knew he wanted a chance for the two of them to talk; he'd been calling on and off since she moved to the Cove. She'd been avoiding his calls for just as long. But she knew she couldn't dodge him forever.

"Okay, coffee."

He grinned. "Great, I'll text you the details."

* * *

CINDY

The scent of freshly baked muffins wafted out from beneath the red-and-white-striped cloth that covered a basket hanging from her arm. Cindy puffed a little as she crossed the street with a quick glance to the right and left.

The muffins were Diana's favourite, and Cindy hoped they would help her broach the subject of happy hour at the cafe. She and Diana Jones had been friends for as long as she could remember. Diana and her husband had bought the bed and breakfast when they were in their thirties and had become neighbours. They'd all celebrated with a bottle of champagne.

Cindy visited the Manor regularly, glad to have a neighbour she could call on, since she had three young children and didn't get out often. Diana had hoped for a family of her own, but she and Rupert had never been able to fall pregnant, and so she'd helped Cindy to raise her kids.

To Cindy's children, she was Auntie Diana. And Diana had taken to the role with gusto. There'd been sleepovers at Seaside Manor, birthday parties in its expansive gardens, and once when Adele was thirteen, she'd run to Diana to cry on her shoulder about a boy she liked who didn't like her back. The memory still sparked a little pang of jealousy in Cindy's chest.

Diana and Rupert were part of their family, and so when Diana had first floated the idea of a collaboration with the cafe - a happy hour for guests - Cindy had jumped at the idea. Now she wasn't sure it was something she could, or should, continue to offer. Although she hated to give it up.

The building rose like a majestic old lady from the patchy verge. Cindy passed through a white, timber-slatted gate, pulling it shut behind her, even as the scent of pink climbing roses greeted her. They'd bloomed late this year, and already the petals curled at the edges and fell to the footpath at her feet. She leaned forward to inhale the scent and startled when a bee buzzed from inside the flower, almost colliding with her nose.

With a chuckle, she continued on her way, patting the handle of the wicker basket that swung from her arm. Diana had done a wonderful job of building a cottage-style garden using Australian native plants, like kangaroo paw, wattles and grey myrtle, mixed with clusters of roses, gardenias and hydrangeas. Her garden was the envy of every green thumb in the Cove, and Cindy often peered over the fence to see what Diana was doing, perhaps to learn a tip she could adapt to her own failed efforts to grow roses. Cindy's garden didn't compare with Diana's. Although she liked to potter around weeding, watering and occasionally planting, she preferred something hardy and maintenance free with her busy lifestyle.

She knocked on the door and waited. This time of day was when Diana stopped work to drink a cup of tea, after a busy morning cooking, serving breakfast to guests, cleaning rooms and making beds.

Diana answered the door, kissed Cindy's cheek and ushered her inside.

"Perfect timing," she said. "You're just in time for tea. Would you like a scone with jam and cream? I was about to go to the kitchen for one myself."

Cindy peeled back the red-and-white-striped cloth that covered her basket. "I made cheesy muffins, those ones you like."

Diana's brown eyes widened, and the creases across her forehead deepened. "Perfect! I'll get us some plates. Grab a seat in my office, I'll be right back."

Diana took the basket and hurried towards the kitchen, her sensible heels clacking on the hardwood timber floor as she went. Cindy let herself into the office and sat in one of the two navy velvet occasional chairs in the corner.

Diana soon returned, this time with a tray that she set on a small, round table between the two chairs. She fell back into her chair with a sigh. "I've had the most horrendous morning."

Cindy poured tea from a teapot into matching china cups. "Oh dear. What happened?"

Diana inhaled slowly, pressed a hand to her forehead. "Never mind, I don't want to get into all of that. Suffice it to say that the next time a family of six comes to stay, I'm going to ask to take their temperatures at the door. Vomit and Turkish rugs don't mix well."

Cindy's eyebrows shot towards the ceiling. "That sounds dreadful. Here, have a cup of tea." She handed one of the cups to Diana, who took it with another sigh.

"Thank you. And thanks for the muffins, it's as if you knew I'd need a pick-me-up today."

"Well, aren't we getting a little old for all this...?" Cindy tutted.

Diana took a bite of muffin and spoke around her mouthful. "Has something happened?"

"Oh no, I'm only talking about the cafe and the ridiculous New Year's Eve party."

Diana frowned. "Everyone I've spoken to says it was a raging success. They loved it."

Cindy set a muffin on a plate and held it in her lap. "I know, it went perfectly well, I suppose. Only... I do think I'm getting a bit old to be hosting parties with live bands until the wee hours. I honestly didn't think I'd still be working in the cafe at my age, I'd hoped one of the kids might take it over. I suppose I should be grateful they've found other things to occupy themselves, I'm not sure I'd want to wish it on them now."

Diana shook her head. "I sure know what you mean. I'm so tired all of the time. And Rupert's next to no help at all now he's done his shoulder. He sits in our room, watching the television most of the time or playing on that ridiculous iPad I bought him at Christmas. How I regret that gift!" She humphed. "Never mind, I'm not sure what else to do. We haven't saved quite enough to retire, and I'd hate to give the place up to strangers - there's no telling what they might do with it."

Cindy chewed thoughtfully, then swallowed, savouring the flavour of cheeses and herbs as they slid across her tongue. "I know what you mean, and I'm a little relieved to hear you say it - because I'm hoping you'll understand my predicament..."

Diana set down her plate on the table and leaned forward, her brow furrowed. "What is it? What do you mean?"

"You know how I mentioned that Andrew had left me in a bit of a bind?"

Diana nodded.

"Well, I wasn't being entirely forthright. You see, it seems he mortgaged the cafe without me knowing..."

"What?" Diana's eyes widened, and she reached for Cindy's hand to squeeze it. "Oh no, I'm so sorry, honey."

Cindy shook her head, tears pricking her eyes. It was easy to keep her emotions squared away when she was alone, or busy at the cafe, but with Diana looking at her that way, everything she'd squashed came rushing to the surface. "I'm okay...at least, I think I will be. That's why Sarah came back to the Cove - she's here to help me find a way out of the mess I'm in."

"I wondered about that... It did seem strange, with everything she'd built in the city, for her to come home all of a sudden, that way. Well, you let me know if there's anything I can do."

"Now that you mention it," Cindy began with a smile as she blinked back the tears. "That's why I'm here. One of the things Sarah is doing is looking through my accounts to see where I can cut expenses. I'm afraid I might lose the cafe and even the house if things keep going as they are...and so we're trying to figure out why the cafe is haemorrhaging money so badly, given we've got plenty of business."

Diana's eyes narrowed. "Hmm... That *is* a quandary."

"And," Cindy continued, finding her confidence grow as she went. "I noticed at happy hour, there seemed to be an awful lot of guests cashing in on the half-priced drinks and appetisers with their room keys. I hoped we might talk about making a change..."

"Making a change?" Diana's nose twitched. "I'm fine with that...but first, let's talk about what's going on. I'd like to get to the bottom of it, because it doesn't sound...well, what exactly is going on?"

Cindy explained what she'd witnessed and how she'd counted the takings at the end of the night and checked them again that morning when she'd opened up for the day. That somehow, the money wasn't adding up, and the growing popularity of the bed and breakfast was getting a bit much for the small cafe to manage.

Diana leapt to her feet and slid into her office chair. She flicked on the computer monitor and began typing. "You're saying this was yesterday?"

Cindy dipped her head in agreement. "Yes, that's right."

"But we only had ten guests last night, the family of

six who stretched my washing machine's capabilities all night long, two single men and a couple."

Cindy's heart thudded. "What?"

"That's right, and I guarantee you the family didn't go to happy hour." Diana chuckled. "Oh heavens above, I'm glad they checked out early this morning."

"But...I..."

"And I really don't know why you're talking about our growing popularity... We've been under-booked for months now. As I said, I've been thinking about what we'll do with the place when I'm not up for taking care of everything on my own any longer. To be honest with you, I couldn't manage having the place booked solid these days."

Cindy leaned back in her chair, one finger pressed to her lips. What Diana was saying didn't make any sense. She'd seen the guests with their room keys; she'd served them herself.

"Well then, if that's the case," she muttered, "I believe I have another issue on my hands entirely."

CHAPTER 25

SARAH

*S*arah's fingers drummed on the outside of her coffee mug. It was just like Jeremy to insist she meet him for coffee, then make her wait. She'd put up with his games for far too long. At first, she'd given him grace - he was a writer after all. She'd been an editor long enough to know that there were plenty of writers who lost track of time or got so caught up in themselves and what was going on inside their heads that they forgot everyone around them. That was what she'd told herself so many times when he'd left her alone at restaurants or been an hour late to pick her up - he was creative, a thinker, it wasn't his fault. But over the years, she'd begun to wonder if perhaps it wasn't his way of showing her exactly where she stood.

She inhaled a long, slow breath to calm her nerves.

Why was she so fidgety today? Perhaps it was the

coffee. She was already on her fourth cup for the day and didn't usually drink more than one in the morning. That was what happened when everyone wanted to catch up - they'd meet over coffee, discuss office politics over coffee; it was the thing to do. In an office full of women, no one wanted to eat; they only drank - caffeine, black or skim, no sugar.

She'd gotten used to it while she lived there; now it grated a little.

Finally, she saw him picking his way through the tightly packed round tables and coffee-drinking professionals to where she sat. She stood to kiss his cheek, while he kissed hers, the scent of his aftershave reminding her of everything they'd shared, his strong arms around her, his lips against hers. She bit down on her lip as she sat and reached for the cup to give her hands something to hold.

"It's good to see you, Jer."

He grinned, that dimple taunting her again. "You too, Sarah. If it's possible, I think you got even more beautiful in the time since I saw you last."

She ducked her head, her cheeks flaming. Had he always been so obvious?

"I'm sorry I haven't had a chance to call you back..." she began.

He interrupted. "You mean, you're sorry you've been dodging my calls?"

She issued an uncomfortable laugh.

He waved a hand at their waitress, placed his order, then focused his blue eyes once again on her face.

"Yes, sorry about that."

He cocked his head to one side, reached for her hand. "Why is that? Why aren't you talking to me? I thought everything was fine, we had a good thing going, we were going to spend the rest of our lives together." He swore beneath his breath, the sound like a hiss. "What happened? I have a right to know."

Sarah extracted her hand from his, took a sip of the now tepid coffee. "We weren't right together. That's all. I figured it out a little late, I know that. I shouldn't have agreed to get married, but you proposed in front of all of our friends... I didn't want to embarrass you."

His eyes darkened. "You agreed to marry me so I wouldn't be embarrassed?" Jeremy combed fingers through his hair, setting the almost-black mass on end. "Wow, that's cold, even for you, Sarah."

Her heart pounded against her rib cage, and sweat trickled down her spine. "I'm sorry... Wait, what do you mean - even for me?"

He shrugged. "You know what I mean."

"No, I really don't. You think I'm cold?" Anger boiled in her stomach, making her hands shake. She pressed them harder against the coffee mug.

He made a harsh sound in his throat. "You walked away from your fiancé without an explanation, without looking back. I'd say that's pretty cold. And it tracks with your record. You never think of me, of my feelings. It's always about you, what you want."

His words cut her to the core. That wasn't what'd happened. She'd tried to work things out with him, to talk about the issues in their relationship. The way he told it, she was no better than her father. It couldn't be true. She wasn't like him; she wouldn't walk away with no explanation. Jeremy hadn't listened to her as usual, hadn't taken her concerns seriously. Although in fairness, she'd never confronted him about the infidelity. She'd been too broken-hearted to try. Perhaps she was more like her father than she'd realised, but she wasn't going to let him make himself out as the victim, not now and not ever.

"That's not even remotely true," she hissed, then tempered her voice, noticing the stares they were drawing. She straightened, took a calming breath. "Please don't say that, we shouldn't say things we'll regret."

"Fine, you're right. Here's what I came here to say: I want you to move back to Sydney. I know you gave up your unit, but you can move in with me - I've been asking you to do that for years anyway, and it's the right thing, the next step since we'll be married soon anyway."

Sarah's eyebrows drew low across her eyes. She held her breath. Was he serious? How could he be so deluded to think she'd do that?

"Jeremy, I gave back the ring, we broke up - we're not getting married. And I am definitely not moving in with you, I made myself pretty clear on that subject the last ten times you asked me."

He eyed her, his face red. "I don't get it - plenty of women would love to move in with me, to marry me. Didn't you see the *Sydney Post*? I'm the most eligible bachelor in the city..."

She pressed her lips together to keep from laughing in his face. The list had been put together by a PR group hired by the publishing company to promote his newest release. That he'd bought it only made her resolve stronger.

"Then you shouldn't have any trouble replacing me," she said, rising to her feet and slinging the strap of her handbag over one shoulder. "In fact, you certainly didn't seem to have any difficulty with that while we were together."

He stood too, his face incredulous. "What do you mean by that? You can't leave yet, I haven't even got my coffee. We have to talk about this, Sarah."

She drew a deep breath, faced him. "I don't want to marry you, Jer. I'm sorry it worked out this way, I'm sorry I didn't figure things out sooner. I hope you'll forgive me and someday we can be friends, but I'm not moving back to Sydney. I like it in Emerald Cove - I'm with my family, my friends, it feels like home to me. I've missed that, without even realising it, for so long now. It'll probably be the end of my career, but suddenly I don't care." She issued a hollow laugh. "But I'm not cold, it does upset me to walk away, and you have to know why I did it. I'm not stupid, Jer, even if I do take a while to catch on. I didn't want to hurt you, just as I'm sure you had no intention of hurting me - but here we are. I wish things hadn't ended this way...but you'll recover from this and do better than ever, I know you will. I wish you all the best."

He stared at her, eyes wide, unbelieving. "So, that's it?"

"That's it."

"I'll call you later, and we can discuss..."

"No, Jer - please don't call me. No more late-night phone calls. Okay? No more calling over and over, hoping I'll pick up. It's time to move on. I'll always care about you in a way, but it's over."

He pressed hands to his narrow hips, gaped. "But I..."

"I'll see you around, Jer. Oh, and I think I should probably give your books to Pauline to edit from this point on - might make things a little less awkward for us both at Greenmount."

"Pauline? No, she's not you. I need you." His voice resonated with emotion, raspy. "You're my editor."

Sarah put a hand on his shoulder, stood on tiptoe to kiss his stubbled cheek. "Not anymore, Jer. Goodbye."

CHAPTER 26

SARAH

*T*he key slipped from her fingers and Sarah sighed before bending to retrieve it as her purse swung around and clocked her in the back of the head.

She straightened with a grimace and rubbed fingers where the purse's silver buckle had connected with her scalp. Then, she pushed her key into the lock on the cottage's front door. It swung open before she'd had the chance to turn the key, and she studied it with a frown.

There weren't any workmen's trucks in her drive; she'd assumed everyone had gone home for the day. She'd have to talk to Mick about making sure to lock up before they left. It seemed like it would be a natural thing to do, but this was the Cove after all.

She glanced over her shoulder, hoping for a glimpse of the dog, but there wasn't much to see in the dull light of a humid dusk. The sea breeze blew strong over the cliff top, pummelling the cottage and sweeping stray strands of her hair into her face. She pushed them back with a grunt, lugged her bags into the cottage, then rammed the door shut with her behind.

The light in the living room was on, as was the one in the kitchen. Adrenaline burst into her veins, accelerating her heart rate. Was someone there?

She set her keys and purse on the floor beside her luggage and stepped forward, careful to keep her movements quiet. She peered into the kitchen - it was empty. Then, into every corner of the living room. All that remained was the bedroom and bathroom, and she clenched her hands into fists as she faced them. There was no one else to do it. If she was going to live alone, she'd have to face an empty cottage and night-time noises alone.

It was different than living by herself in the city, with neighbours on every side, upstairs and down-stairs, and a passcode to get through the glass security doors in the building's lobby. Out here, there was nothing but space, the ocean breeze, trees and bushes, hundreds of noisy birds and the occasional possum or bilby. The cottage was blanketed in the kind of quiet that would take her a long time to get used to.

Something out the back caught her eye. She stared, then strode to the deck. It'd been removed; there was nothing there but a few divots in the sandy soil where pylons had been. And beyond it, the back end of Mick's truck.

With a sigh of relief, she pressed both hands to her forehead. Mick was still there. Somewhere. The adren-aline faded, and she slumped onto the sheet-covered couch, scrubbing her hands over her face. One glance around the cottage revealed several walls had been torn down, there was plaster and dust everywhere, a hole in the ceiling reached from the wall to halfway across the living room, and a third of the kitchen cabinets had been removed.

The cottage was a disaster zone. Instead of unpacking, she might simply take her luggage and head over to Mum's. It didn't make sense to stay here when she couldn't even boil water for a cup of tea since she'd packed up all her things and the jug was in a box in her bedroom.

"I thought I heard someone come in." Mick emerged from the bedroom, a pencil stuck behind one ear and measuring tape in his hand. "I was measuring the bathroom. You're going to love the new one. Much bigger."

Sarah smiled. "I can't wait. I thought there was a murderer running loose in the house or something until I spotted your truck out the back."

He chuckled, reaching for a notepad on the kitchen bench. "Sorry about that. I should've shouted out or something."

"You probably would've given me a heart attack."

"Did you just get in?" he asked.

She nodded. "Flew into the Gold Coast Airport about two hours ago, then drove here. I'm exhausted."

"Good trip?"

She shrugged. "Define good."

He grinned, set the notepad back on the bench. "Okay, did you achieve what you set out to achieve?"

"I think so. I wanted to pitch a series to my boss, and she agreed to take it on. So, I guess that was good."

"Congratulations."

"Thanks," she replied. "I think I'm going to head over to Mum's. I can't really face this place the way it is right now."

He chuckled. "I think that's probably a good idea."

"How's the dog?"

His eyes narrowed. "What dog?"

Sarah leapt to her feet, heart fluttering. "What do you mean, what dog? Oscar!"

He laughed. "I'm joking. The dog is fine. In fact, he's asleep in your bedroom on an old rug as we speak."

Sarah's brow furrowed. "What? He's in the cottage?"

"Yep. Hey, listen, are you sure you want the oak for the floorboards?"

"Hold on," she interrupted. "I'm still stuck on the dog being inside. He never comes inside."

"He did for me." Mick pressed hands to his hips. "He's gentle as a lamb. I gave him a bath because…well, phew!" He waved a hand in front of his nose.

"He let you bathe him? Now, this I've got to see." She strode to the bedroom and peeked around the doorframe. There he was, curled in a heap on a rug she'd used to sop up drips on the floor. His feet twitched, he was running in his dreams. His fur was soft, clean, less matted. His ribs weren't as pronounced as they had been.

She muttered beneath her breath, "Of course, I leave town for a couple of nights, and you suddenly become domesticated. That's the thanks I get, huh?"

"What's that?" Mick called from the kitchen.

"Nothing," she replied as she walked back towards him. "Just that the dog is a complete pain in my rear end. I've been trying to get him to come inside for a bath for weeks. If I turned on the hose outside, he ran for the hills. Now, suddenly he's powder fresh and sleeping in my room. I'm feeling a little rejected." She laughed. "But I'm glad the two of you hit it off."

He took a swig of water from a bottle. "Don't worry, I'm sure he'll get used to you."

"Gee, thanks."

"So, are you hungry?" he asked.

"Starving," she replied before she'd thought about it.

"I'm heading home, was going to stop somewhere to grab some food. Would you like to join me?"

* * *

THEY DROPPED Oscar off at her mother's house before they found a restaurant. Petal the Pomeranian launched a yapping assault for the first full five minutes, but calmed down when Oscar didn't react and trotted around the house with her head high giving him a tour of the place. He ambled after her, his nose to the ground. Sarah continued to marvel at how meek the dog had become while she was gone. He padded into her mother's like he'd been there a hundred times before and immediately slumped down onto the bed Sarah had bought for him but he'd never used. She set it in the kitchen so he could be close to Mum. Though it seemed Mum wasn't sure it was such a good idea at first, she had warmed to him and was feeding him slices of cold sausage before Mick and Sarah walked out the door.

"Your mum's good with dogs," Mick remarked, once they were seated in his truck and driving down the street away from the house.

"Yes, she's always loved them. Although I was sure she'd object to having a stray in the house - but she's full of surprises these days."

"Oh?"

Sarah shook her head. "Never mind, it's a long, long and very boring story."

"I've got all night," he said.

She felt a tingle in her chest. He was calm, steady - like a rock. Didn't seem to mind the way she'd rattled on for the entire journey into town - that would've driven Jeremy crazy.

"Get to the point," he'd often admonish her. "I haven't got all day."

Well, it seemed Mick had all night, though she wasn't sure what that was supposed to mean. Perhaps he was only being friendly; it was a saying after all. He wasn't interested in her; he was a friendly guy. And after her recent breakup with Jeremy, she wasn't interested in any kind of romantic relationship.

They ate at the only Mexican restaurant in town, El Torito's. Mick chose the restaurant, and Sarah was delighted since Mexican food was a favourite and she'd discovered El Torito's on one of her first nights back in the Cove. It was a reasonably new establishment, and she'd found it to be delicious, with a magnificent view of the ocean from an elevated balcony.

They sat outside on the balcony and watched the sun set over jewelled waves. Seagulls cawed and fought for the prime position on the balcony railing as close as they dared to the diners. They squawked, dancing with wings half raised until they were pushed off by another bird, then glided into the fading light.

After they ordered their meal, they talked together about what they'd each done with their lives since high school, the cottage, their town. The conversation was warm, easy, familiar. It amazed Sarah how quickly she'd fallen back into a comfortable familiarity with this town and the people who lived there. She had known them years ago and hadn't spent much time at the Cove, no more than a few days here or there, since. But it didn't seem to matter, to them or to her.

It was as if no time had passed at all. Mick had been a schoolmate, years seven to twelve; she had fond memories of surfing the same waves, learning in the same classrooms, laughing over an awkward ballroom dance routine in PE class. But they'd never been close friends. The strange thing was it didn't seem to matter. She felt connected to him, like they'd shared something important that linked them. It was a feeling that'd been missing during her time in Sydney, of being grounded, belonging.

"So, why did you give up architecture?" she asked, after he'd told a funny story about a client from years earlier.

He bit a corn chip, chewed thoughtfully. "I guess I lost my passion for it when my wife left."

Her mouth would've fallen open, but she bit her lip instead. He'd been married? She hadn't expected that. She'd asked around and discovered he was single, but no one had mentioned an ex-wife.

"You were married?"

He nodded, chewing. "Yeah, it didn't last long. Only about five years."

"Five years seems like a long time to me."

"I guess...although I thought it'd be forever, so five years is a drop in the bucket." His lips pursed. "She had an affair with my best mate. So, it was over, just like that, and I didn't have much of a say in the matter. They were in love, I discovered. Had been for a long time. I didn't wait around to find out more. I sold the house, packed up my stuff, closed down my architecture practice and headed for home."

"Wow. I'm so sorry that happened. It must've been heart-breaking." Sarah's throat ached for him. That her father had recently done something similar awoke a pain inside that worked its way from her gut until it constricted her throat.

"Thanks, it was a while ago now. Four years, actually. When I left Canberra, I was gutted. I thought I wouldn't recover. I lost my best friend as well as my wife, and the business I'd spent the past two years building... It was rough. But since I've been back, I've discovered that I love renovating old buildings, bringing aged structures back to life. The old stuff is so much more beautiful, more interesting, than anything modern architects and designers are doing."

Sarah nodded. "I agree. I love old buildings too."

"And I missed the Cove while I was gone. Canberra's a pretty town, but it's full of politicians, lobbyists and public servants - they all wear suits and flounce around the place like they're doing something special. All I want to do is work with my hands, build things... and then go for a surf."

Sarah laughed. "I can't imagine you flouncing...so it was probably a good call. And I know what you mean. I didn't even realise I missed the Cove until I got back here. I haven't started surfing again, but the ocean's calling my name."

"You've got to do it...get out there. There's nothing quite like it. In fact, you should come out with me sometime. It'll be fun. Like old times."

They'd surfed side by side many times during their teenaged years, along with the rest of their group of friends. Mick had been two years ahead of her in school, so she hadn't spent much time with him other than out on the waves.

She offered a half smile. Could she still surf? It'd been so long since she'd tried she was certain she'd overbalance and land nose first on her board, or plunge into the ocean with her rear in the air.

"Okay, I'll try to dig up my old surfboard at Mum's."

"You'll do it?"

"Yeah, I'm in."

CHAPTER 27

SARAH

*T*he hum of traffic behind her, Sarah walked through the automatic glass doors into the Foodstore. She waved hello to the checkout operators. Sylvia had worked at the grocery store for as long as Sarah could remember. Her hair was entirely grey now, but otherwise she still looked the same.

"Good morning, Syl!" she called.

Sylvia grinned, revealing tobacco-stained teeth. "Mornin', sweetheart, how's that cottage of yours coming along?"

Sarah rolled her eyes. "Slowly. I'm living in a construction zone, and even when I leave, I can still hear hammering and sawing in my head."

"Ah well, it'll be worth it in the end, love."

Sarah shook her head. "I sure hope so. Gonna grab some groceries, see you in a bit."

Sylvia returned her attention to the customer at

her checkout, and Sarah pulled a shopping trolley from a line of them and pushed it ahead down an aisle. The trolley leaned to one side and kept trying to knock into the displays and rows of cans that lined the aisle.

Sarah grimaced and leaned harder on the trolley. She hadn't been exercising as much lately as she usually did. Her core had suffered and gotten a little pudgier than she liked it to be, but never mind, pushing the trolley while shopping was all the workout her stomach muscles would need that day.

"Is that Sarah Flannigan?" A woman's voice stopped Sarah in her tracks. She spun to face the speaker.

"Oh, hi, Mrs Bunyan."

Her old Physical Education teacher stood, hands on athletic hips, all long, tanned legs and rippling muscular arms.

"Well, I heard you were back, but it's good to see you in person."

Sarah had always enjoyed PE classes at school, especially when Mrs Bunyan had taken them all surfing. She'd been a fun teacher, and one Sarah had learned a lot from about self-discipline and teamwork.

"Is it true you left your editing job? Because that seemed like a really great career..."

Sarah's eyes narrowed. "No...I'm still working for Greenmount Publishing, just from home now rather than in the Sydney office."

"Oh, that's good to hear. I'd hate for you to give up on all that potential. You were a gifted student."

"Thanks." Sarah smiled, her cheeks warming.

"When's the next Jeremy Goodall thriller coming out? I sure love those books." Mrs Bunyan's interrogation was interrupted by Marg from the deli section.

"Now you leave Sarah alone, Mandy!" she called across the store.

Mrs Bunyan's brow furrowed with irritation, and she waved a hand in Marg's direction. "Oh shush, you old hag."

"What did you call me?" Marg's voice deepened. "She doesn't need you asking her a million questions about her life. Let her shop for her groceries."

Mrs Bunyan turned her back on Marg. "Is it true you were dating Jeremy Goodall? He seems like such a nice fellow...good looking too...and of course, his books are amazing." Her eyes glowed, and she leaned forward, awaiting Sarah's response.

Marg appeared at Mrs Bunyan's side. "What are you asking her about? Let her be... My goodness!"

Sarah chewed the inside of her cheek. She hated confrontation.

"Oh wow, look at the time..."

"Now you've upset the girl," Mrs Bunyan said, slapping Marg on the shoulder.

Marg's eyes widened, her blue hair almost seeming to quiver with rage. She faced Sarah, pushed a smile to her pink-painted lips. "You'll have to excuse my sister, she's always been nosier than was good for her."

Sarah had forgotten they were sisters. She sighed with relief. "Oh yeah, don't worry about it. I don't mind."

"Everyone's so curious about you, what you're doing here, why you moved back, what you're going to do next, when we might see that handsome Jeremy fellow in town..." Marg's smile grew wider as she and Mrs Bunyan both stared at Sarah now, waiting for answers.

"Well...um...I'm not working on Jeremy's books anymore. So, I'm sorry I can't help you on that one."

"Is it because you broke up?" Marg asked.

Sarah's lips pursed, sweat beading across her forehead. She understood how people must've felt during the Spanish Inquisition. "Uh...well, that's part of it. We're no longer engaged."

"I told you so." Mrs Bunyan turned to face her sister.

Marg frowned. "I know you did, but it's not like I didn't guess anyway. He's nowhere to be seen. It's pretty obvious, don't act like you've got some kind of inside scoop."

While they argued, Sarah crept away, pushing her trolley ahead of her. She grabbed the few items she needed as quickly as she could and headed for the checkout. As much as she loved this town, it was more than a little crazy at times. Too few residents, with too much time on their hands for idle gossip. It was still so bizarre to her that anyone would be interested in her life and what she was doing, whom she was dating and how her career was progressing.

She was in such a hurry to leave the Foodstore that she almost ploughed directly into Vicky and Meg as she left.

"Whoa! Where's the fire?" Vicky asked, blocking the trolley with both hands so that it didn't run her down.

Sarah sighed with relief. "I'm so glad to see the two of you. Marg and Mrs Bunyan were asking me all kinds of intrusive questions. They cornered me in the canned foods aisle, and I didn't think I was going to be able to get out of there."

Meg laughed. "You still call her Mrs Bunyan?"

"Yeah, of course. What do you call her?" Sarah huffed.

"Mandy - we haven't been in high school in over a decade." Vicky chuckled. "We were about to grab a coffee, come with us."

Sarah eyed her groceries. She hadn't bought anything that needed refrigeration. "Okay, let's go."

* * *

THE THREE OF them found a table at the Emerald Cafe that had a view of the beach in the distance through a grove of banksia trees and clumps of wispy spinifex grasses.

With her groceries in cloth bags by her feet, Sarah relaxed into one of the colourful, high-backed chairs that dotted the outdoor area. As Thad walked out with a tray of food, she caught a glimpse of her mother in the kitchen through the swinging door. The door swung shut again, and Sarah turned her attention to her friends.

"I love your mum's cafe. It's got such a great view and some of the best food in town," Meg said as she took a sip of the green smoothie Crystal had brought to their table a few minutes earlier.

"Yeah, me too. I had to work here this afternoon, anyway, so I thought we might as well have our coffees here." Sarah shrugged. "Besides, I think I'm becoming addicted to the coffee - it's so smooth and divine."

Vicky chuckled. "You could be her PR manager."

"Yeah, well, she needs one, that's for sure."

"Are things that bad?" Vicky asked, her brows knitting together above wide blue eyes. Her straight, mousy brown hair was tucked behind her ears.

"They are... Dad left the cafe in pretty bad shape financially. I'm helping Mum. I have a few things to figure out, but I've basically narrowed down the things that are costing the cafe the most money. Now, I have to talk to Mum about it - and I don't think she's going to like it."

Sarah had never enjoyed confronting her mother - some kind of hang-up from childhood where she always wanted Mum to be pleased with her. She'd been the good child, the girl who did well in school, didn't get into trouble, made good choices and was easy to get along with...well, most of the time anyway. It made the difficult conversation she had to raise with her mother about the fate of the cafe even more challenging.

"Enough about all of that, though. It'll work itself out. Tell me what's going on with the two of you."

Meg stared at the table.

Vicky cocked her head to one side. "I'm okay in most respects, still not feeling great. I don't know what's going on with me, but I think it's probably just a food intolerance or something."

"You should see someone," Sarah suggested.

"I know. I will... I'm a procrastinator. I hate going to the doctor."

"I know what you mean," Meg added.

"Things improving with Brad, at all?" Sarah asked.

Meg shook her head. "Not really. He's talking a little bit more but doesn't say anything unless he absolutely has to. He's as angry as ever, though, and still taking it out on me. Thankfully, he seems willing to go to his appointments, so I'm trying to focus on that as a positive. But I'm having to work extra shifts at the salon to pay for all of the appointments - doctors' visits, physiotherapy, the medical debt from the hospital in Hawaii that wasn't covered by our insurance, rent... The list just goes on and on. It's pretty overwhelming, actually. Apparently, he'll get some kind of payout from his superannuation disability insurance, but if they agree to do it, we won't see it for a while yet. There's so much paperwork, red tape...ugh."

Meg pressed both hands to her forehead. "I'm holding it all together, and I think I could manage, if only he didn't snap at me, glower at me and basically live as a hermit in the dark." She sighed, combing her fingers through her red curls, which glowed like they were on fire beneath the rays of the morning sun.

Sarah pressed a hand over Meg's where it rested on the table. "I'm sure it will get better. You'll both be okay... It'll take some time, that's all."

Meg's eyes glistened. "Thanks. I know that's true, but it's hard to hold onto right now. If he would only... ah...well, there's nothing more I can do about it. I can't control him any more than I can control the waves. Right?"

Vicky and Sarah both nodded in agreement.

They chatted about other things for a few minutes, until they each drained the coffee cups dry, then embraced. Sarah watched her friends leave. She inhaled a slow breath, shaking her head as she did. No matter what was going on in her life, she couldn't imagine suffering the way Meg and Brad were.

"There's my girl," Mum said, enveloping her in a hug. "Are you here to see me?"

"I thought I'd do some more work on your accounts...and I need to talk to you." Sarah picked up her grocery bags, one in each hand.

"In that case, come on through to my office. We're about to start the lunch rush, but I can spare a few minutes."

Once she was seated in the small office, Sarah took a few moments to gather her thoughts. It was a strange position, giving her mother advice. Most of her life, their roles had been reversed, and she wasn't sure how to begin.

The tiny space was crammed with things - a small, old timber desk and matching chair with an embroidered seat cushion, a dented filing cabinet, a bookshelf housing cookbooks from decades past, and framed photographs that hung on the walls and dotted every empty surface.

Mum settled onto her embroidered chair. "So, what did you want to talk about, sweetheart?"

Sarah swallowed. "We need to discuss happy hour. I know it's an arrangement you've had with Auntie Diana forever, but…"

Mum waved a hand. "Oh yeah, happy hour. I know."

"Really? You already know? Know what?"

"That it's a problem. I've spoken to Diana about it."

Sarah chewed her lip. "Um…okay. What exactly did you discuss? Because I'm not sure what the problem is, only that you're losing a lot of money on it. I'd have to be here taking note of everything that's going on to figure out why."

Mum arched an eyebrow. "Well, let's see. I've noticed lately that happy hour has been very well attended…more than usual. And when I spoke to Diana about it, she said the B&B hasn't been full, in fact bookings are down. So, we know people are taking advantage of the offer, we just don't know how they're doing it. I'm assuming word's gotten out about how good Crystal's music is, there've been a lot of people cheering and dancing, they love her."

"She is very good," Sarah admitted.

"Yes, she is, and she's a darling girl. Besides that, I think the food here is pretty well liked, and the half-priced drinks are drawing diners in as well."

"I'm sure you're right. But that doesn't explain why it's not boosting revenue the way it should be."

"I know," Mum replied, her lips pursed. "I was hoping you'd help me figure that one out. We've got to make a change, one way or the other. I hate to give up our connection to Diana's business, but…"

"You may not have a choice," Sarah finished, crossing one leg over the other.

"I may not have a choice," Mum echoed her words with a sad smile. "But I'm glad you're here with me."

"So am I," Sarah replied. "I never thought I'd be glad to be living back in the Cove - I used to believe it would be a sign of failure. But I'm here, and it feels like home."

CHAPTER 28

FRANKLIN

*T*elephones around the small police station had been ringing all day. The water police who shared their office space had made a drug bust the day before, and journalists from all over the country were calling to get their hands on the story.

Franklin sat in his office, tapping at his keyboard, filing a report of his own. So much of what he did was paperwork. He'd resented it when he started out, but he was used to it now and had been through enough trials to know that good work in the office often meant the difference between a conviction and a criminal being let loose on society again.

His new constable strode across the office, a cup of coffee in her hands. She sat at her desk and clicked the mouse to wake up her computer monitor. Her desk was in full view of Franklin's office and flanked by other, empty workstations only utilised whenever visitors from other locations needed a place to hot-desk.

The sight of her sent a mild stab of guilt through his chest. He regretted the way he'd yelled at her two weeks earlier, though he'd yet to mention it to her. He was the boss; he didn't need to apologise. At least, that was what he'd been taught by his father back when he was younger and his dad could remember what day of the week it was.

Something beeped in the break room. She stood and walked out of sight. He could do with a cup of coffee himself. He yawned, stretched his arms over his head and stood to follow her.

"Good afternoon, Constable," he said as he walked into the small kitchen with two round dining tables and matching chairs that served as the office break room.

"Good afternoon, sir."

She pulled a bag of popcorn from the microwave. The scent of popcorn and butter soon filled the small space, making his stomach grumble.

He didn't have to apologise, but he shouldn't have gone off on her the way he had. After all, she was only a proby. She didn't know any better. It was his job to teach her, a job he didn't want and certainly didn't need. Even though Emerald Cove was quiet for much of the year, there were only a few of them on the job, and it kept all of them busy enough that anything extra, like holding the hand of a new recruit, meant longer hours he didn't want.

Still, it wasn't strictly her fault. She wasn't needed, he didn't want her as a partner, but she hadn't asked for the posting - at least that was what he'd been told.

He poured coffee into a mug, then opened the

refrigerator to search out the milk. "Are you settling into the Cove okay?" he asked in a gruff voice.

He hated small talk, didn't have any desire to form a connection with her, but he was curious enough to make the effort.

She poured the popcorn into a bowl, faced him with a smile. "I guess so."

"Is it what you'd hoped?"

She cocked her head to one side. "I don't know... It's quiet, which is good. But..."

"What?"

"Everyone seems to know each other. They're not really looking for friendships." Her cheeks coloured, and she looked away, she seemed to regret opening up to him.

He shrugged. "Yeah, that's what it's like living in a small town. Everyone's friendly, no one wants to be a friend. To them, you're an outsider, just like the tourists that file through here day after day during the summer months."

She placed a piece of popcorn in her mouth and chewed, leaning against the bench behind her. "So, how long does that last?"

He chuckled. "You mean until you're a local?"

She nodded.

"About thirty years," he replied.

She gaped. "Thirty years?"

"They don't want to invest in a friendship if they don't think you're gonna stay." He laughed as he headed out of the kitchen, then stopped at the door and spun to face her. "So, did you ask to be stationed here, or was it dumb luck?"

She frowned. "I asked for somewhere quiet, I guess

they figured this was as good a place as any. And you needed a partner...so..."

His nostrils flared as anger surged. "Actually, I didn't need one—" He stopped himself with a quick breath. He'd already decided not to go there again; it wouldn't achieve anything. "Never mind."

Her face clouded. "I'm sorry, I didn't know...about your old partner, I mean. I looked it up... Anyway, I'm sorry."

Heat spread through his chest. He didn't want to talk about it, certainly not with some first-year-out-of-training proby cop who wouldn't stick around anyway. "Yeah, well...thanks." He gritted his teeth. "Where were you before this?"

It was blunt, but he had never asked before and was suddenly curious. The recruitment office hadn't told him, and he couldn't remember seeing anything in her file.

"Around...you know, here and there. I was in Sydney, obviously, to do the training. And before that, I moved around, mostly in New South Wales."

His eyes narrowed. He'd interviewed enough liars to know one when he saw one. But why would she lie? Her gaze flitted to his face and away again. She was nervous too, her knuckles white as she grasped the popcorn bowl. He'd been curious about her past, who she was; now he was intrigued.

He headed back to his office and slid behind the desk, immediately tapping on his keyboard to search for anything that might come up involving a Rebecca Mair.

Nothing.

That was odd. Most people who reached their late twenties, like Rebecca, had some kind of digital footprint online - a Facebook page, a Twitter account, Instagram or a newspaper article about their role on the local debating team. Some kind of evidence that they existed. But not Rebecca.

He scratched his chin with one hand, reached for his phone with the other and made a call.

"Hey, Mack, how are you? It's Franklin Russell from Emerald Cove here."

Mack went through the training process with Franklin years ago, and they'd kept in touch. Mack worked in recruitment now and was usually a rich source of information for Franklin whenever he wanted to know what was going on in the head office.

"Frank! Great to hear your voice. How's it going up there? Living the dream, living the dream!" He chuckled, his deep voice booming.

Franklin grinned. "It's idyllic. Listen, I have a quick question for you - you guys sent me a new recruit, Rebecca Mair. She's been here a few weeks, but her personnel file is on the light side, and I really don't know that much about her. Can you fill me in?"

There was a pause; Mack coughed. "Uh, let me see, Rebecca Mair." Another pause. "Oh yeah, I remember her. Sweet girl. Got potential, I think. There's really not much else to tell. She wanted a quiet posting, we gave her to you. End of story."

"Yeah, that's pretty much what she said as well," Franklin replied, his eyes narrowing. What were the chances he'd hear the same story in almost the exact same words from two different people? "Nothing else you can tell me?"

"Nope. Nada," Mack replied.

"Okay, great, thanks for your time. I'll give you a call soon, and we can catch up."

"Sounds great. See ya."

He hung up the phone, pressed his chin into his hands and studied his computer screen. Something was fishy about his new constable, and he was going to find out what it was. Then, he'd send her back to where she came from.

* * *

SARAH

The sand was warm beneath her feet. A wave curled lazily to shore, bubbling and frothing as it tumbled up the beach. Cold water tickled her toes, and she scrunched them up in response.

Sarah adjusted her hold on the surfboard under her arm. Her wet suit was a little tight, but since she hadn't worn it in almost a decade, she figured that was to be expected. Although, a little tight was probably an understatement; she could barely breathe. It'd faded a little as well and felt stiff. She only hoped it wouldn't split while she was surfing.

"Ready?" Mick asked, jogging up beside her.

She faced him with a nod. He set his surfboard on the beach, then tugged up the wet suit that lay loose about his waist. His tanned muscles flexed as he slipped each arm into the suit.

"It's cold," she complained.

He chuckled. "No, it's not, it's beautiful. Perfect. You can't call this cold, it's the hottest part of summer. You seem to have gone soft living in the city, Sassy. Are you a city girl now?"

She studied the waves; they were big but not

dumping. "I'm not soft... I'm cautious. And yeah, I guess I am a city girl."

He laughed. "Okay, let's see some surfing then. We've got to find the country girl inside you and dig her out, she's buried in there somewhere."

The first wave smacked her in the face, making her gasp. The cold of it woke her up as the sun crept over the horizon and blinded her with its golden reach the moment her head peeked over the crest. She squinted at the horizon, her arms digging through the water, taking her into the face of the next wave, this time with a smile.

She duck dived, feeling the water rush over her, churning, pummelling, the cold no longer such a shock. When she burst into the sunlight this time, she was already laughing.

Why had she stayed away so long? Muscle memory had her pulling long strokes through the water, faster and faster, diving beneath the waves and coming up again with a shake of the head to dislodge the biggest drips that would run into her eyes if she let them.

She felt alive. Awake. Fierce.

Mick had reached the calm before her, behind the set. The place where they'd sit up on their boards and wait for the perfect wave. He pushed himself into a sitting position, crossed his arms over his chest and grinned.

"There she is. You found her. The country girl is back."

Sarah giggled, reliving her teenage years. The first duck dive had sent her back fifteen years in an instant. She was young, carefree and had saltwater dripping into her eyes.

She sat on her board beside Mick and offered a half

smile. "Feels good to be out here again. Thanks for inviting me."

"No worries," he replied.

She caught the first wave. It wasn't as easy to spring to her feet and balance on the board as it had been years earlier, but she managed it and stayed up for a few seconds before ploughing headfirst into the water. The tug of the leg rope around her ankle, the bubbles of air floating skyward from her mouth. It all rang a nostalgic bell in her head.

When she reached the back of the break, Mick was riding a wave almost to shore. She caught glimpses of him whenever he rode high, then he was gone again. Sarah squeezed her eyes shut and inhaled a deep, salty breath. The air was fresh and invigorated her. The water, a clear azure colour, sparkled beneath the rising sun. In the distance, she saw a family splashing at the water's edge, the children laughing, squealing and chasing each other into the waves.

After an hour, she was exhausted. Every part of her body felt bone-tired in the way that signalled sore muscles would soon follow. She stumbled up the beach, dropped her board in the sand and fell onto her rear end, puffing hard. Mick followed her, irritatingly even-breathed.

"That was great," he said. "See, it's just like riding a bike - you've still got the moves."

She laughed between gasps for air. "Yeah, only I think I'm about to keel over and die. Ugh."

Sarah peeled the top of her wet suit down, grateful to get the restrictive material off her chest and stomach. She gulped great mouthfuls of breath. "Ah, that's better."

"Definitely." He smiled, his eyes sparkling.

She punched him softly in the shoulder. "It was too tight, I couldn't breathe."

He laughed. "Well, please don't let me get in the way of you stripping down. I'm all for freedom of breathing. It's very important."

She rolled her eyes. "Okay. You know, I'm officially your boss, so you should watch yourself."

"Oh yeah? Hmm... That's true. I didn't look at it that way. Okay, I quit."

Sarah's brow furrowed. "You can't quit. My cottage has no walls and is a complete disaster zone. I need a kitchen, I miss cooking and being able to breathe without sneezing."

Mick shook his head. "I suppose it would be rotten to leave you in the lurch like that."

"Yes, it would. Although I wouldn't blame you. How you can see anything good coming out of that mess and clutter of broken palings and rotting timber is beyond me."

His eyes narrowed, and a smile played around the corners of his mouth. "That's the beauty of it. I love seeing everything come together, the way destruction becomes creation. It's a pretty great thing to be able to use your hands to build something."

She watched him, marvelling at the way his voice soothed her, his words touched her. "That's how I feel about editing. I see a raw manuscript with a great story, but the writing needs work and there are passages that repeat themselves and poor grammar - and I work on it, stitch the bones of it together in a way that highlights the story without all those distractions, and the final product is a beautiful piece of art."

"Wow, I never thought of it like that."

"Yeah, well, most people don't even realise what an

editor does. The writer gets all the glory, but that's fine with me. I feel the satisfaction of making something special, whether anyone else gives me credit for it or not."

He grinned. "I'd better get to work, my boss is a real pain in the…"

"Hey!" She slapped him again. "You watch yourself."

He winked. "Come on, Sassy, let's go."

"I can't stand up," she complained, shifting her seat in the sand.

He chuckled and reached out both hands to pull her to her feet. The strength of his arms caught her off guard, and she found herself smack up against his bare chest. He stared down at her, his eyes full of an intensity she'd never seen before. He usually wore more of a sleepy expression, as though he'd only woken minutes earlier and run his fingers through his hair. But not now. Now his eyes were like embers as they locked on hers.

"Sorry… I…" she began.

He released her hands and pressed his to either side of her face, then lowered his lips to hers. The taste of salt hit her tongue as his lips caressed hers, sending a zing of electricity through her body and setting her legs trembling. Her hands rested on his chest; she could feel his heart pounding beneath her palms. She'd felt the electricity between them, the tension, the attraction building every time they saw each other, but she still hadn't expected the kiss. It took her by surprise and stole the breath from her lungs.

When he pulled away, she wanted more. Her lips missed his the moment they were gone.

Her eyes flitted open, and she found him staring at her with a half smile on his lips.

"I've wanted to do that for a long time."

She released the breath caught in her lungs. "It's only been a few weeks…"

"No, it's been twenty years, actually." He caressed her cheek with his hand, then let it fall to his side.

Her eyes widened. "Really?"

"Yeah, of course. You didn't know I had a huge crush on you?"

She shook her head. "No. You were two years older than me. Besides, I couldn't have waded through all the girls who were hanging around you in time to catch your attention if I'd wanted to." He was the surfer, the laid-back, bleached-blond, board-shorts-hanging-low, tanned surfer whose gentle charm had always attracted the girls of Emerald Cove, even with the skinny legs and braces on his too-big teeth. She was younger, a nerd and too busy with her studies and sports to notice much of anything.

"Never mind, the wait was worth it," he said.

They wandered back to their cars, and he slid his hand over hers, entwining their fingers. Feet dug toes first into the sand, and by the time they reached the car park, sweat was trickling down Sarah's temples and spine.

They loaded up the surfboards. Mick helped Sarah strap hers to the roof of her car, then he pinned her against the car to kiss her again, one hand on either side, pressed to the metal. There was no way out, and this time, the passion behind the kiss left her gasping for air.

As she drove from the parking lot, he waved good-bye. Her heart thudded against her rib cage. What'd just happened? Her contractor had kissed her. What was she thinking? He was renovating the cottage, and now it'd be awkward between them. Not to mention the fact that she wasn't ready for anything even remotely romantic. She ran her tongue over her lips, still tingling from his touch, and a smile tickled the corners.

CHAPTER 29

MEG

*A*s she pulled the keys from her purse, Meg rolled her head from one side to the other, stretching out the kinks in her neck. She yawned wide and wriggled her toes in the black flats that'd stopped being comfortable about four hours earlier. A day on her feet at the salon had left her drained, her stomach clenched with hunger, and she had the beginnings of a headache in the base of her skull from not stopping often enough to drink water. She always intended to drink more water, just found some days too busy and ended up with a pounding in her head that nothing could fix other than an early bedtime.

The door swung open, and she was greeted once again by darkness. Brad left it to her to switch on the lights when she got home at night. No doubt he'd be seated in front of the television set as usual, and she'd have to start on dinner instead of sitting with her feet up for a few minutes of rest.

With a sigh, she stepped inside, then hesitated, her eyebrows drawn low. It was silent. No noise from the television set, no running water. Not even the sound of a breath. The only thing she could hear was the crash of waves across the road behind her as they slapped at the shore.

"Brad?" she called, moving into the unit and switching on the hall light. "Brad, I'm home. Where are you?"

She walked through the small space, flicking on lights, calling out. When she reached the bedroom, a gasp escaped her throat. The bed was made, a miracle in itself, and Brad's bedside table had been cleared of medications. When she opened the dresser drawers, she found his completely empty. His clothes, toiletries, even his magazine collection - all gone.

Her throat tightened as her head spun. Where was he? What had he done?

She ran to the kitchen. "Brad! Where are you?" Shouting now. No response. He was gone. The television set sat dark in the corner, the curtains still shut over the windows, the way he always left them.

"Brad," she whispered as she fell onto the couch. She sat, hunched over, as tears pooled in the corners of her eyes. Her vision blurred, and she blinked a few times to clear them. There must be an explanation, but first she had to find him.

That was when she saw the note. A single sheet of paper, from her own stationery kit, folded on the coffee table. She leaned forward and read her name on the outside.

It was in Brad's handwriting. The sight of it sent a chill down her spine. She grabbed it and began to read.

Dear Meg,

I know you'll be upset to see that I'm gone, but I believe it's for the best.

I haven't been happy here, and having me around isn't helping you either. It's too much for you to deal with - paying for everything, taking care of me, driving me to appointments. I can see how tired you are and how hard it is on you.

I've gone to stay with Mum and Dad until we can get our marriage annulled. Our marriage never really had the chance to become real.

You deserve better than this - better than me and what I can offer. When you married me, you made a vow to spend your life with a whole man, someone who could take care of you. That's not me anymore.

Honestly, I don't know who I am now. The accident took everything from me, and I don't know what I want from this life.

I need time to figure things out, but the one thing I do know is I don't want to be married. I have to do this on my own from now on.

I hope you'll understand and not hate me too much, although I don't blame you if you despise me.

Please don't call me. I need some space, it's too hard to talk to you, and I can't face it. Not yet anyway. Hopefully someday.

Don't let the pain of this hold you back. You should find someone else to share your life with and live out your dreams, even if I can't.

I'm so sorry for any pain I've caused you. Please forgive me.

Brad

THE LETTER FELL from her grasp and drifted to the cream carpet below. Tears fell silently down her cheeks, and her mouth hung open.

How could he do this to her? To them?

He wouldn't even try, hadn't given them a chance to make things work. He couldn't have loved her as much as she loved him if it was so easy for him to give up on their life together. She'd have fought with every ounce of strength she had to keep what they had, to protect their love.

As the tears continued to cascade down her cheeks, Meg dropped to her side, hugged a cushion to her chest and tucked her legs up beneath it. She stared at the curtained windows, the darkness of them making her heart ache. He'd blocked out their view of the beach, the waves and sand he'd loved so much, and now he'd blocked out their love, throwing it away like it meant nothing more to him than a worn wet suit or a broken surfboard.

Her chest ached, and her throat tightened so hard she thought she'd choke. And as her eyes drifted shut, images of Brad smiling as he ran into the surf with a board beneath his arm flashed before her mind's eye. Then another memory, his lips on hers, his arms around her waist, a look of love in his eyes, pushed a groan from her gut and through clenched teeth.

CHAPTER 30

SARAH

*S*arah shoved a pair of dirty underwear into the makeshift hamper in her closet. A cardboard box couldn't really be called a hamper, but it was all she had to work with at that moment, and with Mick coming over to check on the progress the painters were making at the cottage, she was doing her best to tidy up.

They'd hardly spoken since the kiss on the beach.

Her heart skipped a beat as she ran through the moment again in her mind. Then, she tossed a shirt into the overflowing box and shoved the closet door shut.

The cottage was a disaster zone. The walls were up, the new kitchen was in - hallelujah! - and the deck was complete, but there were drop cloths everywhere, dust covering every surface, and she'd been going crazy every time she needed something and had to search for it.

As a result, she was wearing a pair of too-tight shorts, an oversized shirt - she had no idea where it came from - and her hair was pulled into a messy ponytail, since she'd yet to locate her hairbrush and the bathroom was currently occupied by a burly tiler with a propensity to burst into song at inopportune moments. Not to mention her mood. She was in a tizzy, and she knew it. She had to calm down before Mick walked in and saw her like this. He'd think it was because of him, which it most certainly was not. It was the cottage. She was a neat freak, and the bomb crater she was living in gave her the jitters. That was all.

Besides, she'd only recently ended an engagement. It wasn't the right time for her to be starting something new with Mick. It wasn't sensible, and she'd decided to be sensible. Or perhaps she was always sensible, and it was time to shake things up in her life? She wasn't sure. Either way, it didn't make sense to dive into a new relationship, regardless of how appealing Mick was and how comfortable she felt around him. Well, most of the time. Perhaps not when he was wearing half a wet suit around his muscular waist and dripping wet with seawater. She wasn't particularly comfortable then.

With a quick breath, she hurried out to the living room. One of the walls had been half painted; two others were complete. A light grey, with a feature wall of charcoal behind where the television would be hung. She loved the way it looked. It was coming together the way she'd pictured it in her mind - only better. The painter had left behind a short stepladder and an open bucket of grey paint with the paintbrush balanced on top.

She frowned, bit down on her lip. Where was he?

Perhaps he'd gone to use the bathroom, although she could hear the tiler singing Italian opera at the top of his lungs, so it didn't seem likely. She scanned the room, hands pressed to her hips, then peered outside. No sign of him. Another painter was outside, balanced on a ladder against the wall, painting the outside of the cottage a light shade of grey that complemented the internal walls.

It irritated her to see a wall half done. With a grunt, she picked up the brush, climbed the stepladder and got to work. After a few strokes, she had forgotten all about the painter and was lost in the work. Painting was such a calming pastime. Really no need to think, plan or strategise. Simply stroke the brush up, then down again.

"You're good at that." Mick's voice startled her.

She spun about, then awkwardly stepped down the ladder just as Oscar rushed in from the back deck. They reached Mick at almost the same time, Oscar's tail wagging along with his body in a frenzied welcome. In his headlong rush, he crossed Sarah's path. She tripped, fell over his back and landed on her hands and knees at Mick's feet.

"Whoa! Are you okay?"

He helped her to her feet. Sarah wanted to dig a hole directly through the floorboards and crawl into it. Her knees were raw, she'd jolted something in her left shoulder, and her pride had taken a definite hit.

"Uh...yeah, thanks. Watch where you're wagging, Oscar."

The dog licked her face, then shimmied against Mick's leg. It was hard to believe the transformation. His coat was no longer matted or patchy, but a healthy reddish brown. His ribs barely showed, and his eyes sparkled with health. He'd also taken to showing signs of affection with great enthusiasm, generally involving a long, wet tongue on her face or legs.

"Ugh." She wiped the dog slobber from her cheek.

"That was very graceful," he said.

She laughed. "I'm nothing if not swan-like."

"You know my occupational health and safety insurance doesn't cover you. You're not supposed to be painting. And where's my guy?" His brow furrowed, but a smile teased the corners of his lips.

She shook her head. "I don't know what happened to him, but I saw that half-finished wall and couldn't help myself."

"Tell you what, I'm going to have a quick chat with the painters, then how about we take a walk on the beach?"

She dipped her head in agreement, considered changing, then realised all her clothes were dirty and stuffed in a box in the closet, and headed for the porch.

A steep, winding path led from the top of the bluff where the cottage was perched down to a small, wild-looking, private beach. Black rocks were scattered in piles across the sand like they'd been dumped there by the waves. Seagulls strutted and cawed along the sand, and small waves crashed against the shore.

They walked side by side in silence for a few moments. Sarah wondered if he'd take her hand, then decided she didn't want him to. She wasn't ready to take that step; she still hadn't decided if she should ignore the professional boundary that existed between them.

"Everything okay?" he asked.

She pushed her hands into the pockets of her too-tight shorts. "Yeah, fine. Messy, but fine. I can't wait to get the cottage done and have my own personal space again. But otherwise all good. Work is better since I visited Sydney. I'll probably have to do that every now and then, so they don't forget my face."

"Sounds like a good idea."

She stopped, faced him. "I think we should talk about what happened on the beach…"

He squinted against the bright sunlight. "Uh huh. You mean the kiss?"

She nodded.

"Well, it was a great kiss…" he began with a smirk.

She sighed. "I didn't mean that…"

"I know. Look, I'm not sure where this thing is going. But I like you. I wanted to kiss you…so I did."

She inhaled a slow breath. Were things really that simple for him? They weren't for her. There was so much to think about, so many things to consider. "Okay, but I don't think it's a good idea."

"Kissing?"

"Us. A relationship."

"Oh. Why not?"

She shrugged. "I was engaged back in Sydney, I'm not sure if you know that. But I was, and I broke it off before I moved here. It wasn't very long ago, the wound is still pretty raw… I'm not ready to start something new. And besides, you're my contractor. It wouldn't be…professional."

"Well, I'm nothing if not professional." He grinned, mimicking her words from earlier.

She shook her head. "I'm trying to be serious here."

He crossed his arms over his chest. "Fine, let's be serious. I hear you, you're not ready. That's okay with me. I'm not in any hurry. When you're ready, you let me know. As far as being professional - I'm renovating your house, we don't have an ongoing working relationship, and it's Emerald Cove, not the Hague. I think it'll be okay."

"You make it sound so easy."

He shrugged. "It might not be easy, but it's pretty simple. If we like each other, we should see where this thing might go."

"That doesn't ever scare you?" she asked.

"Not really."

"Even after everything with your wife?" Sarah bit down on her tongue. What was she thinking bringing that up? It was insensitive. "Sorry, I shouldn't have said that."

"No, it's fine. If I didn't want to talk about it, I wouldn't have told you. I don't have anything to hide, Sarah. I'm not afraid of starting something with you because I know you, I care about you, I know you care about me, and I think we might share something special. If we can only give ourselves a chance."

He reached for her hand, threaded his fingers through hers, then lifted it to his lips to kiss her softly.

"Mick…" she objected but didn't pull away.

He smiled, released her hand. "Take your time. I'll be here."

Then he turned and headed for the path that would take them back to the cottage. Sarah stood watching him, her heart hammering in her chest, sweat trickling down her back and a frown on her face. He was exasperating. She'd set up all the arguments in her head before they spoke. She'd seen it all so clearly. And yet he'd completely confused the matter with his calm, matter-of-fact response. Her lips pursed. How utterly irritating.

CHAPTER 31

MEG

Four days later, Meg sat in the same spot on the couch, a piece of paper laid out on the coffee table, a pen poised in one hand. She chewed on her lip, staring blankly ahead of her. What should she write? What to say to a husband who'd abandoned her before they'd even had a chance to experience marriage?

He'd asked her not to call, and so far, she'd respected his wishes. She knew him well enough to understand that pushing him now, when he'd made up his mind, wouldn't get her anywhere. He needed time, and she'd give it to him. But how much time was too much?

She pressed the pen to the paper and wrote an opening line. Then, with a frown, she crossed it out, crumpled up the sheet of paper and threw it into the small wire wastepaper basket she'd set on the floor beside her. A dozen paper balls already rested in the bottom of the basket.

A knock on the front door interrupted her thoughts. As she pulled another sheet of paper from her stationery kit, she called out, "Come in!"

Vicky opened the door and peered inside. "So now you're inviting strangers into your unlocked home without checking who's out here?"

Meg grimaced. "No one locks their doors in the Cove, you know that. And besides, as miserable as I am, I'd welcome the company of a thief or serial killer. Just so long as they put me out of my misery quickly."

Vicky came in and sat on the couch beside Meg, hugging her with one arm. "Oh, come on, it's not so bad. You've still got your health."

Meg glared at her. "Really? Thanks, that's so comforting."

Vicky chuckled. "Come on, lighten up, it was a joke. It's exactly the kind of thing my grandmother used to say to me when I was a kid and the boy I liked didn't know I existed."

Meg grunted. "Well, the boy I love doesn't seem to know I exist anymore, so I guess it fits."

"Yes, he does, he's going through something - the pain is too much for him right now. I know him pretty well, don't forget, and I can see things from a different perspective to you. He always retreats when things are tough. Don't you remember during our final exams in year twelve, no one saw him for a month? And when his uncle died, he disappeared for ages, didn't surface again until he'd dealt with the grief? He'll work through this, I'm sure of it."

"I wish I could be so certain," Meg grumbled. "Did you bring the wine?"

Vicky tugged a bottle of chardonnay from her oversized purse. "Voila! And I brought a DVD... Can you believe it? And no, I don't have a time machine, just have access to my parents' basement. It's like traveling back in time when you walk down the staircase, let me tell you." She giggled. "So, in honour of broken hearts, I borrowed their copy of *The Holiday*."

"A romance? No, I can't handle a romance right now," Meg complained.

"But you love Kate Winslet."

"Yes...I do. I love Kate Winslet."

"So, come on," Vicky urged, bumping her shoulder against Meg's. "Let's watch Kate Winslet falling in love. We can order a pizza and drink chardonnay. It'll be great - just what the doctor ordered."

"Fine. And thank you. I really appreciate you coming over here. I know you could be doing something far more interesting with your evening than sitting here and cheering me up." Meg leaned her head on Vicky's shoulder, grateful she had such a good friend. She didn't have any family support, so her friendships were all she had now that Brad had abandoned her. He'd been her family; now he was gone. And he hadn't thought twice about how that might affect her.

She'd called her mother the day after Brad left to tell her what was going on, and Mum had basically accused her of not keeping herself pretty enough, told her that she needed to put in more of an effort, wear makeup, work out daily and so on, if she wanted to keep a man in her life. Meg had hung up in disgust, then cried into a tub of ice cream for an hour afterwards.

Vicky stroked her hair. "It's going to be okay. And I

assure you, there's nowhere else in the world I'd rather be right now. Okay, maybe on a date with Ryan Reynolds. But since he's married, I'll have to settle for spending the evening with my very best friend."

Meg couldn't help laughing, even as tears blurred her vision. "Ryan Reynolds? Really? Isn't he a little old for you?"

"Never. Blasphemer." She giggled. "I'll order a pizza, and you can finish writing your sappy journal entry or whatever it is you're struggling over." She glanced at the wastepaper basket. "And wasting reams of paper on."

Meg swallowed. "I'm writing a letter to Brad."

"Wow, people still do that?"

Meg crossed her eyes at Vicky. "Shut up."

Vicky laughed. "Sorry, I didn't even realise you could do that. You have heard of email, right? Plus, they have these nifty new things we call telephones."

Meg crossed her legs and leaned back on the couch. "He asked me not to call him."

"Oh wow, I'm sorry. That's rough." Vicky's lips pursed.

"Yeah, it's so hard. All I want to do is call him and talk to him. Probably yell at him a little…" She laughed. "Maybe he's right after all. We probably both need a little time to cool off."

Vicky shrugged. "So a letter…huh?"

"Yeah, only I have no idea what to write. I want to be loving and patient, but all I can think to write is how angry with him I am right now." She sighed. "So, that's why I keep starting over."

Vicky patted Meg's leg. "Okay, well, I'll leave you to do that while I order the food and get the DVD ready."

"Thanks."

Meg reached for the pen and began to write as Vicky retreated to the kitchen to call the only pizza place in town that delivered.

She scrawled a few words, leaned back to think, then continued writing. She wanted him to know she loved him, and if he thought that a divorce or annulment was best, she wouldn't stand in his way, although she didn't agree it was best. He had to know she didn't have any desire to live her life with someone else. Regardless of what'd happened, he was still her husband and they could build a wonderful life together if he'd only try. Then she signed her name, with love and a few kisses, and folded the paper, setting it on the coffee table to mail the next day. Maybe he wouldn't read it. He might tear it up, and it could make things worse between them. All she knew was that she had to send it; what happened next was up to him.

CHAPTER 32

MEG

*I*t'd been over a month - more like six weeks, actually - since Brad left. Was that enough time to decide on their future?

Meg studied the symmetrical patterns on the wallpaper at the solicitor's office in Brisbane. She'd driven the two hours north for an appointment with a solicitor she'd found online who seemed to have good reviews. Although, how you could get five stars for taking a marriage apart she couldn't understand.

She planned to ask some questions, telling herself she didn't have to commit to anything yet. It was important that she found out what their options were. Could they even get an annulment?

She'd sent the letter to Brad over a month ago and heard back from him. He hadn't written about anything of substance, just chatter really, about his life in Brisbane, the appointments, the physical therapy, his routine and newly made friends.

No matter how many questions she asked, he never responded with an explanation for what he'd done, what he was doing to destroy their marriage. Fury churned in her gut. How could he abandon her this way, after everything they'd been through together? And to not call her to talk it through... It wasn't fair.

She hadn't broken his rules, the boundaries he'd set. Well, not really. She'd called the house and spoken to his mother a couple of times, just to make sure he was okay. Sharon said he was doing fine, improving with his strength training, even learning to swim on his own in their pool. Then, Meg had hung up the phone and cried herself to sleep on her side of their bed, her back to the empty space where Brad should've been.

"Meg Taylor?" asked a woman dressed in a pinstripe suit, with black-rimmed glasses perched on the end of her nose.

Meg stood, fixing the purse strap into place on her shoulder. "Yes?"

"Come with me, please."

She followed the woman into an office decorated with dark timber furniture, ice blue draperies and dozens of framed certificates and photographs lining the walls.

The woman faced her, holding out a hand to shake Meg's. "I'm Victoria Sanders, one of the solicitors here. Pleased to meet you, won't you take a seat?"

"It's a pleasure to meet you as well." Meg sat in a chair that faced an imposing hardwood desk.

Victoria sat behind it, leaned on her elbows. "So, tell me a bit about your situation."

Meg inhaled a sharp breath. "I need to know

whether or not my husband and I can get an annulment."

She explained the situation, feeling a lump grow in her throat, larger with every minute that passed. She couldn't believe where she was. They'd been married a few days; for her, it was a dream come true. She'd never bought into the Disney princess mirage. To her, happy endings only happened on the screen. She'd seen with her own two eyes how relationships involved yelling, fighting, throwing things, and someone walking out on someone else. When Brad came along, she'd been overwhelmed by his kindness, gentle nature and thoughtfulness. She hadn't known men like him could exist, let alone that someone as wonderful as him could love her. Perhaps, after all, the fairy tale could become reality. She'd been so wrong.

When the accident happened, everything since had been a nightmare.

"I can definitely help you with that," Victoria said, once Meg had finished telling her story. "I'll get the paperwork started for the annulment right away, if you like. I don't think you'll have any trouble convincing a magistrate to approve it."

Meg's breath caught in her throat. Could it really be that easy to end a marriage?

"Okay, thanks."

She left the office in a haze. Her body was numb, and she stared straight ahead, arms wrapped around herself in a kind of hug. There was a small, neatly manicured park in front of the office building. She slumped onto a park bench and stared out at the cityscape ahead of her. The skyline was dotted with skyscrapers. Some reaching to the clouds, all shiny silver and tinted glass windows, others short and squat with retro concrete gargoyles leering from parapets.

A noisy miner flitted about in the branches of a lilly pilly bush behind the bench, chattering as if to scold her.

"No need for you to scold," she muttered. "I'm well aware of how pathetic I am."

Her stomach growled with hunger. She hadn't eaten a thing all day and had barely had a gulp of water. Still, even with the hunger pangs, she couldn't bring herself to eat. Her heart hurt too much. Was this how their relationship would end, in an expensively decorated office in the city surrounded by ringing telephones, plaid wallpaper and strangers?

She tugged Brad's last letter to her from a pocket and laid it on her lap, smoothing out the wrinkles with the palm of her hand.

I don't know if I can make it across the pool, but Tim says we're going to try tomorrow. Wish me luck.

He could write to her about therapy sessions but not his feelings. He was only about a fifteen-minute drive away from where she sat. She wondered what he was doing.

I enjoy reading your letters. They give me something to look forward to.

Her hands trembled where they held the edges of the paper, making the letters blur on the page. Was it an opening? An admission that should give her some hope? She couldn't say. And what did she hope for now anyway? What kind of life would it be to share a home with a man so angry, so full of hatred that he couldn't offer her a kind word?

I'm sorry for how everything has turned out. Perhaps after the annulment, we can be friends.

The last paragraph sucked up any hope she'd had and crushed it. Friends? A tear trickled down her cheek.

It was time for her to move on with her life and let Brad Taylor go once and for all. After all, happy endings weren't real life. She'd forgotten that for a time, but now she knew it to be true. She stood with a sigh, stuffed the letter back in her pocket and hunched her shoulders. Then strode towards the parking lot.

She had to get back to the Cove; her boss had let her have the morning off, but she had a long afternoon shift ahead of her, and she'd have to drive quick to get back in time. There wasn't anyone else she could rely on in this life but herself. Her own two hands were the only ones that'd rescue her, provide and protect. She'd remember that from now on.

CHAPTER 33

CINDY

*T*he chairs were stacked upside down on each round table. The floor shone in places where the water from the mop had not yet dried. The silver benches in the kitchen gleamed. It was time to go home.

Cindy waved goodbye to the staff, then pulled the cafe door shut behind her. With a loud sigh, she trudged towards her car, slid into it and leaned her head back on the head rest.

She was tired.

No, tired didn't do it justice. She was exhausted.

Ever since she'd uncovered the desolate state Andrew had left her finances in, she had laid off most of the staff at the cafe and was doing almost everything herself. She hadn't wanted to complain to anyone about it, hadn't even told Sarah what she'd done. She thought if she cut costs here and there, the cafe would recover, she'd pay back the debts Andrew had left behind, and life could go back to some semblance of normal.

But it wasn't working.

At least, that was what Sarah had told her over a cup of coffee earlier that day.

Occupied with her own work commitments, Sarah hadn't had time to spend at the cafe lately, and Cindy was too busy running the place and filling in for the staff she'd let go to give it more attention either. As a result, neither one of them had any more an idea of what was causing the cafe's financial woes than they had weeks earlier when they discussed the issues with offering happy hour to bed and breakfast guests.

So, Cindy had asked Sarah to stop by that morning to give them a chance to talk about what they should do. Sarah had spoken to the bank on Cindy's behalf earlier in the week, and Cindy was looking forward to her daughter relaying a message that went something along the lines of: great work, Mum, you've paid down the debt, and the bank is going to reward you by forgiving the rest of it! Well, perhaps that wasn't it exactly, but she'd thought it would be good news. She'd been working so hard to cut costs and get things in order.

But it hadn't been good news. In fact, it was the opposite. The bank was threatening to foreclose on the house unless she increased her payments to more than double what she'd been managing, since, according to them, she'd been late on repayments for so long she still wasn't caught up.

Cindy rubbed both hands over her face, her throat aching. It wasn't her fault; how could they hold it against her? But according to Sarah, that argument wouldn't work so there was no point in making it.

Her house.

She could lose the home she'd spent decades raising a family in, that she'd decorated with her own two hands.

It wasn't so much the building but the betrayal. She'd always assumed she and Andrew would downsize one day. The kids had moved out, they were getting older, and the current house was simply too big, not to mention the gardens.

Still, it shouldn't be this way. If the bank took the place, what would she do then? She wouldn't even have a deposit to buy something else. She'd be starting over again in her sixties, alone and broke. A chuckle erupted from her stomach, travelled up her throat and broke free from between her lips. Her eyebrows arched high. It was too much, unbelievable. The girl who had always had everything she'd ever wanted, had grown into a well-to-do woman, and was respected in her hometown would end her life as a beggar on the streets.

Perhaps she was being overly dramatic. But asking one of her children if she could occupy their guest room was almost as bad as begging, to her way of thinking.

She'd faced the challenge with a resolute jut of the chin, taken it all without many tears. But this was too much.

Tears pooled in her eyes. She jabbed at them with the back of her hand, but they were quickly replaced by more. The chuckle turned into a wail, and she buried her face in her hands, her entire body shaking.

All of a sudden, she raised her eyes to stare at the

purse on the passenger seat. She tugged her mobile phone free, dialled and set it against her ear.

"Heeeellllooooo," Andrew said, his voice chipper.

Cindy's nostrils flared. "How dare you!"

Andrew hesitated before answering. "Cindy? Baby, is that you?"

"Don't you call me baby. You don't ever get to call me baby again. Do you hear me?" She was shaking with rage; her free hand clenched the steering wheel, knuckles white.

"What's going on? Are you okay, Cindy?" His voice sharpened with concern. "Has something happened?"

"Happened? Do you mean other than my philandering husband walking out on me after forty years of marriage?"

He didn't respond.

She couldn't stop now. Anger surged like molten lava through her veins, burning as it went. "How about that same rotten husband leaving me with so many debts I can't possibly repay them? What were you thinking, Andrew? I mean fine, have an affair, leave me for a younger woman - congratulations on finding someone even more simple-minded than yourself, by the way..." She'd never spoken to him like this before, never talked to anyone the way she was shouting at him now. It felt good. And as they tumbled from her mouth, the words she spoke emboldened her to go on. "But why would you mortgage the business my parents left me? I might lose it, you know, our home as well. Did you even think about that?"

She could hear the deep breath he drew before answering. It satisfied her a little to know she'd made him feel uncomfortable, hesitant. He was Andrew Flannigan, always ready with the right words to say, a vivacious, charming, extroverted wordsmith. But now he was stuck for words, only his breathing letting her know he hadn't hung up yet.

"Hold on a minute, Cindy. Let me explain—"

"You'd better have a great set of reasons…"

"I didn't mean to do it. There, how's that?"

She shook her head, eyebrows furrowed. "That's not good enough. You didn't mean to leave me, or you didn't mean to destroy our finances?"

"Either…both. I mean, we didn't have a good marriage. You know that. We weren't connecting, we hadn't in years. You had your work, your friends, your activities, and I wasn't a part of that. We lived separate lives, Cindy."

Her lips pursed, and she grunted out a burst of angry laughter. "Oh, please, that's no excuse. You could've tried harder."

"I know that, I'm not blaming you."

"I hope not. It wasn't me who gave up on us."

"I'm sorry, Cindy, but I couldn't stay any longer, I just couldn't. Especially when I realised the state of our finances was so bad. I knew you'd find out, that you'd hate me, probably leave me anyway. I couldn't stand to see that look on your face…"

"You could've talked to me about it," she said, trying to control her voice.

"No, you wouldn't have listened. And what could I say?"

"Whatever it was would've been better than nothing. It was cowardly, stupid and about a dozen other things I can't think of right now. I'm so angry with you, Andrew!"

"I'm angry too!"

"What do you have to be angry about?" Cindy asked, incredulous.

"Well, things didn't exactly work out the way I'd planned," he said, his voice rising in pitch. "I wanted to retire, maybe buy a fishing boat and have some fun. But by the time I retired, there was nothing left. No money, no business equity...no intimacy...nothing."

She shook her head in disbelief. "That was *your* doing."

"Look, if you called to yell at me, I've got better things to do." His voice shook with repressed emotion.

"Fine, I guess I'll take care of everything myself. Like I always do!"

She hung up the phone, wishing not for the first time that it was an old-fashioned rotary phone so she could've slammed it down and at least echoed in his ears. Instead, she tossed it across the car and winced as it *thwacked* against the opposite door and bounced onto the passenger seat.

On the drive home, she turned up the radio, blasting the music as loud as she could manage without damaging her eardrums. She pulled into the driveway and saw Athol climbing out of his parked car ahead of her. She switched off the engine, glanced in the rear-view mirror to smooth back her hair and climbed out with a smile.

"Athol, how lovely to see you. I hope you haven't been waiting for me." Her face and neck were pocked with red blotches; she'd seen the evidence of that in her reflection but hoped he wouldn't notice in the dull light. She took steadying breaths to calm her nerves. There was no sense in letting Andrew ruin what was left of her evening; he'd already done enough damage to her life.

He grinned, kissed her cheek. "Nope. Just got here. I thought I'd swing by after work to see you."

"I'm glad you did." She reached for her purse and slung it over her shoulder. "Come on inside, I'll make us both a cup of tea."

"Thanks, that sounds perfect."

"Or maybe even a glass of whiskey."

"Even better," he said with a grin.

CHAPTER 34

REBECCA

The sand shifted beneath her feet as she made her way up the beach. Each footstep away from the harder sand slowed her pace, but she pushed forward, running as fast as she could. She was puffing hard, her arms pumping by her sides and sweat streaking her face, back. Bare skin glistened beneath the afternoon sun.

Rebecca glanced up ahead and spotted the boxing gym across the street. She stopped at the road to check for traffic, then sprinted over the asphalt, the hard surface a relief after her beach run.

A pelican wandered along the footpath and leapt out of her way as she ran by, wings flapping. She grinned and called out an apology, but continued on her way.

After four months as a resident, Emerald Cove was

growing on her. At first, it'd seemed so foreign, so strange after the hum and buzz of city life. The busy tourist season was over, and everything had slowed down to the pace of a snail. Most restaurants weren't even open for dinner these days, and Rebecca was surprised to find that she liked it. Liked the slower pace, enjoyed the fact that wherever she went, locals had begun to recognise her face and called out her name in greeting.

Still, it wasn't her home, and she had to remember that. She might have to move on at any moment; she couldn't get attached. That was what she'd promised herself all those months ago - no more attachments, nothing holding her back. She was starting afresh, and she'd take nothing with her on the way.

She stepped inside the gym, slowed her pace and wove through the small group of boxers to the front of the room.

"Good afternoon, Bec," said a woman with gnarled tree branches for arms.

"Hi, Sam. Did you have a good day?"

"It's getting better by the moment," Sam replied with a wink. "Grab your gloves, we're about to get started."

They warmed up with some jabs, intermingled with a minute on the skipping rope, lunges and a few more jabs in the air. Finally, it was time to box. Rebecca partnered up with Sam. She always went for the instructor when it came time to find a sparring partner; she wanted to challenge herself, to be pushed to be the best she could be.

Sam grunted as she caught each of Rebecca's punches, the two of them switching out holding the pads or wearing the gloves. They took turns as Sam called out the routine to the rest of the group. Rebecca listened, but her mind was intent on one thing - she needed to learn how to defend herself, how to kill if it came to that. She wasn't going to be pushed around again, not by anyone, no matter how big they might be.

They took a break as Rebecca gasped for breath, her arms aching, her legs tired.

"You're getting better, stronger," Sam said, swigging water from a bottle, her skin glistening with sweat. "You gave me some hard hits today."

"Thanks, I've been working at it."

"Yeah, you have. But don't overdo it. Okay? You're pushing yourself, and that's great - I worry you're pushing too hard sometimes. You've got to give your body a chance to recover, have a break every now and then."

Rebecca jogged in place, leaning her head to one side, then the other to stretch out the stiffness in her neck. Her hands pumped up and down at her sides, still wearing the padded gloves.

"Yeah, okay." She knew she should do it, and perhaps she'd have a day off over the weekend. She wasn't working any shifts this weekend for the first time in months. Usually Franklin gave her the shifts no one else wanted - the cost of being the new recruit, he'd told her when she asked about it.

Well, he could punish her, haze her, push her and needle her all day long. She wasn't going to break, and she wasn't going anywhere. She'd come to the Cove for a reason, and nothing he did would change that. Everything he dished up, she'd have to put up with, since she had nowhere else to go. So while she was there, she might as well build up her strength for the inevitable.

The break over, she took her turn punching the pads again.

"Whoa!" Sam said, stepping back. "Not so hard, Rocky."

Rebecca offered a half smile. "Sorry. I might try the bag for a while."

Sam nodded, waved her away.

Rebecca loved punching the bag. It never complained she hit too hard, never gave up, never got tired of what she dished out. She bounced on her toes, punching, ducking, weaving. She imagined an assailant coming at her, and she'd dodge to one side. They'd throw a kick at her shin, and she'd dance out of the way, then jab, uppercut, hard right to the middle of the bag. Now again. And again.

As she worked, images flashed through her mind's eye. Blood spurting. Bones broken. A hit to her nose that made her see stars. A punch to the gut that stole her breath. Then a journey to the hospital, all flashing lights, white walls and pain, until it faded to darkness.

She stepped back from the bag, undid her gloves and pulled them off, then unwrapped the tape from her hands. They stank of stale sweat. One glance around the room revealed she'd been left in semi-darkness, the other boxers long gone. With a deep breath, she set the gloves in the box with the others, balled the tape to carry back home and wash, and headed out. She jogged across the street, now lit up by overhead lights, and headed down to the sand for the long trek home.

She was strong now. Stronger than she'd ever been. She'd never let herself be weak and vulnerable again. Never let someone hurt her that way, not if she could help it. She picked up the pace, lowered her head and clenched her fists at her sides as she ran.

CHAPTER 35

MEG

"*D*id you hear about Martha's formal fiasco?" Tracy asked, her blunt black fringe almost entirely obscuring her dark eyes.

Meg shook her head as she swept the cut strands of hair from the floor into a dustpan.

"Apparently, the boy she was supposed to go with had an asthma attack in the limousine on the way to the RSL club. Poor girl thought he was going to die in her arms." Tracy chuckled as she combed the knots out of a woman's hair. The woman winced in the mirror, but Tracy didn't seem to notice.

"Wow, that would've been scary for her. I hope the driver helped."

"Yeah, he called for an ambulance. Plenty of drama, that's for sure. Poor girl missed most of her own formal."

"What a shame." Meg found it difficult to concentrate on the daily dose of gossip she heard in the salon these days. Although, it gave her a distraction from thinking about her own life for a few hours at least.

The bell over the door rang just as Meg was tipping the hair clippings into a rubbish bin. She glanced up to see Vicky walk through the door, her straight brown hair tied in a loose knot on top of her head.

"Vicky, how lovely to see you," Meg said, genuine affection almost bringing tears to her eyes.

She held it together most of the time, but seeing her friend made her want to burst into tears. She inhaled a slow breath. She couldn't fall apart at work; it was hard enough to get through each workday without giving her colleagues something more to talk about.

"Did you want a cut or a colour or both today?" she said as she ushered Vicky into one of the swivel chairs that were dotted along the wall of the salon facing tall, rectangular mirrors.

Vicky studied her reflection, poked at the shadows beneath her eyes and tugged at her hair. "Ugh. Do I really look like that?"

Meg laughed. "Everyone says that when they sit down. I don't think the florescent lights and massive mirrors are very flattering. You look as beautiful as always."

Vicky grimaced. "Not sure that's as reassuring as you meant it to be." She patted Meg's hand where it rested on her shoulder. "I'd love a cut and a few highlights, please."

"Perfect. How are you going?" Meg slipped a cape around Vicky's thin shoulders, snapping it together in the back.

"I'm okay. I went to see my GP this week. They're running tests but so far have no idea what's wrong with me. Maybe it's nothing. I don't know, I really don't feel great. Not terrible, but not good either. It seems to be getting worse as well."

Meg pushed her eyebrows together. "Really? Oh wow, I'm sorry to hear that. I hope they work it all out soon."

"Me too."

"What's wrong? I mean, what feels bad?" Meg set to work brushing Vicky's hair in long, smooth strokes.

"I'm kind of achy, and my ankles are a little swollen. Plus, I feel tired all the time, and there's this rash..." She lowered her voice, glanced around the salon. "It sounds terrible, I know, but I've got a little red dotty rash across my stomach. The doc said not to worry, it's probably viral, definitely not contagious he said, but still...ugh."

Meg shook her head. "I'm sure it's nothing, like the doctor said - probably a virus."

"Yeah, I guess. How about you? How's things?"

Meg's lips pursed, and she tugged scissors from her tidy tray and began snipping Vicky's straight brown hair, tidying up the ends.

"I'm okay, I suppose. I feel a little better, haven't been crying as much lately." She chuckled. "I sound pathetic."

"Not at all. You're grieving, as anyone would in your situation." Vicky patted Meg's hand again.

Meg shook her head slowly. "I know. I'm still getting letters from Brad, which is good, I think. He talks about his parents' dogs a lot." She laughed; it seemed so bizarre, but perhaps it was all he was willing to share with her for now. "And he gives me blow-by-blow descriptions of all of his physical therapy sessions, how he's progressing and so on. Seems like he's really improving - he's built some upper body strength, is able to do a lot of things around the house on his own now, can swim laps in their home pool."

"That's amazing, Meg. I'm so glad he's getting better. He must be feeling more mentally healthy as well, with all of that going on."

Meg shrugged. "Seems like it, I guess. He still won't talk to me on the phone or see me in person, it's only letters back and forth, which is frustrating in one way, but kind of romantic in another. Don't you think?"

"Absolutely," Vicky agreed. "It's very romantic and probably a good way to give him space but keep up the connection."

"Yeah. Maybe you're right - but whenever I bring it up, he's still adamant about the annulment. He doesn't want to be married to me any longer. I've got the paperwork at home, ready to go, but I haven't been able to sign it..." Meg pressed her lips together, unable to go on. The thought of losing Brad didn't bring her to tears so much anymore, but it filled her heart with an aching dread and swamped her with a fatigue that made her want to go to bed and sleep for a decade.

She set the scissors on the tray again, rubbed a hand over her face. It was hard to talk about, but Vicky was the only person she'd been able to confide in about everything that was going on in her life.

Vicky spun in her chair to face Meg, her hair damp from the water Meg had sprayed it with. She grabbed Meg's hands and squeezed them. "Don't sign the papers if you're not sure. Wait. There's no rush. If you're not ready to give up on him, then don't."

Meg's throat closed over, and she blinked back the tears she'd thought were already spent. "Okay."

CHAPTER 36

SARAH

"*A*re you sure you want to do this?" Sarah asked as she tugged a black knit cap down over her hair, then tucked the length of it up into a bun held in place by the cap.

"Yeah, of course. Let's do this thing." Mick's eyes glinted in the dull light that emanated from the cafe's outdoor seating several feet away.

They were hidden by the set of bushes that lined one side of the cafe, could peer through the branches to see what was going on inside, but in their dark clothing, Sarah assumed they wouldn't be seen by anyone.

She crouched low and pushed aside some branches. "So, what we're looking for is...well, anything really. Anything that looks a bit strange. I really don't know how it might play out. It could be nothing. But Mum and I can't figure out how we're losing so much money during happy hour unless someone is stealing it. And I can't imagine any of the staff letting a customer behind the bar to do it, so it has to be a staff member. Something Mum is refusing to face, I might add."

Mick chuckled softly. "I understand, I wouldn't want any of my guys to turn out to be crooks. You spend all day, every day with them, it starts to feel a bit like family."

Sarah cocked her head to one side, studying him. "We've got to figure this out, or Mum might lose everything."

He held up a thumb. "Got it. Don't worry, I'm sure we'll get to the bottom of it. After all, we are dressed as super spies, so really, what could possibly go wrong?"

She ignored his sarcasm and patted the backpack on the ground in front of her. "Have you got your camera?"

"My phone," he said with a nod.

"But that won't pick up much in the dark," she objected.

"I'll use a flash."

"Great, Sherlock, that won't give you away at all. Very spy-like."

He bumped a shoulder against hers. "Hey, no need for sarcasm. I'll pretend I'm a tourist."

She giggled at that, then the giggle grew until she had to clamp a hand over her mouth. He watched with amusement, one eyebrow arched.

"What's so funny?"

She gasped for breath. "A tourist all dressed in black taking photos in the dark." She burst into another giggle as she pressed her backpack to her face to stifle the sound. This time, he giggled as well. She kept imagining the scenario and bursting into a fresh round of laughter until finally she was spent and her stomach ached.

"Fine, I'm not very good at the undercover stuff, but I'm all you've got, Miss Flannigan."

She nodded. "Ain't that the truth. Okay. I'll stay on Thad. You watch Crystal."

He grinned and gave a mock salute. "Yes, ma'am."

She poked out her tongue, then turned to watch Thad, who was behind the bar mixing drinks for the throng of thirsty customers.

"Good turnout tonight," she mused.

Mick grunted in response. "A little too good. From what your mum said, the B&B hasn't been doing this kind of business."

"Not in a while, at least," Sarah agreed. "Hold on, Thad's on the move. I'm going to follow him. You stay here and keep an eye on Crystal."

"Ten-four," he replied.

She rolled her eyes, wishing he could see how unimpressed she was in the darkness. Still, he was pretty cute in his black shirt and black knit hat, even if he was wearing board shorts and sandals to complete the outfit.

She bent low and loped after Thad, who strode from the cafe and headed down the road to the main street where most of the tourists who visited Emerald Cove spent their evenings.

When she caught up, she found him handing out flyers, taking money and pointing tourists towards the cafe. She stopped a young couple with a wave.

"Hey, what's that guy selling?" she asked.

The man grinned. "He sold us this card, said if we go to the cafe down the road and show it at the bar, we get half-priced drinks and food, plus live music. Pretty good deal. Only cost us thirty bucks."

"Thanks," she said, anger already sparking in her gut.

He was selling room keys to tourists. That was how so many were coming to the cafe and the takings were too low for the number of customers. Thad was stealing from her mother. Dad had done it, now Thad was doing it. Anger made her cheeks burn.

She jogged back to the cafe and told Mick what she'd seen.

"Well done, Sassy. You figured it out."

She frowned. "Yeah, but he's been stealing from Mum, for who knows how long."

"And now you know what the problem is you can fix it. In my books, that's a pretty great result."

She grinned. "Yeah?"

He slipped his arms around her waist and pulled her close. His breath was hot on her cheek as his lips found their way to her skin. "Yeah," he whispered.

The excitement of the night had her feeling carefree, adventurous. Like she could do anything, be anyone. It wasn't like her to stake out businesses, stalk criminals, all dressed in black, or follow thieves through the dark of night. Perhaps she was a different person than she'd believed all along. Maybe she could dive into relationships with her eyes squeezed shut, not overthinking the consequences, instead letting the moment, the attraction, the passion carry her forward. Maybe she could be someone else, not the always-sensible, ever-responsible Sarah Flannigan, but someone who let their heart lead the way.

She let her eyes drift shut as a shudder of anticipation worked from her toes to the top of her head, and when his lips found hers, she kissed him back then stood on tiptoe for more.

CHAPTER 37

FRANKLIN

*T*he coffee had grown cold waiting. Franklin swished the contents of the cup around, watching the tan liquid growing more tepid with each swirl. He grimaced and set the cup down as a tall man with a stomach protruding over a pair of blue board shorts and beneath a too-tight t-shirt with a surfboard on it strode into the cafe.

Franklin stood to shake his hand. "Mack, it's good to see you. It's been too long."

Mack grinned, squeezing his hand until Franklin thought the bones might break. "You too, Frank, how long? A year? More?"

"I think it's been about that. Last time I came to Sydney for that meeting of senior officers…"

"Oh yeah, that's right."

Mack waved a hand at the cafe's only waitress then

sat across from him. She hurried over, wiping her hands on her apron, then took his order and left.

"How's the family?" Franklin asked.

Mack's head bobbed up and down as he spoke, almost as if he was agreeing with everything as it came from his mouth. "Great. Just great. We love it up here. We're staying at Coolangatta, and the surf's fantastic. My girls love the beach, and the weather of course. Can't beat it. Right?"

"How long do you have?" Franklin asked.

"We're only here for a week, unfortunately. Wish it was longer, but you know how it is. Can't afford more than that on my salary." Mack laughed, patting his rotund belly as it jiggled.

"I hear you," Franklin replied.

They exchanged small talk for fifteen minutes before Franklin felt comfortable broaching the subject he'd called Mack to discuss. It made him squirm in his seat a little to ask the question, but he convinced himself it was for the safety of his team. If he and his crew didn't know who they were working alongside, it put all of them at risk.

"So, I wanted to ask you about Rebecca Mair again…" he began.

Mack's eyes narrowed. "Oh yeah, your new recruit. How's she going?"

Franklin shrugged. "Fine, I guess. I wish she was about six-four and one hundred kilograms, but I guess you can't always get everything you're looking for in the one recruit. She's pleasant enough to work with and seems to have a bit of a knack for reading people."

"Good, good," Mack replied, taking a last swig of his almost empty coffee cup.

"I was hoping…now we're face-to-face…you might

have a little more you can tell me about her. She's tight-lipped about her past, there's nothing in her file. I don't know where she came from, who she is really... why she's a cop. She won't open up to me, and I'm old-fashioned enough to believe I should get to know my partner if we're going to work together so closely."

Mack's smile faded. "If she doesn't want to talk about it..."

"I get that." Franklin swallowed his frustration. "Only, I don't feel comfortable around her. And you know what that can mean for a partnership."

"Dangerous, is what it is," Mack muttered. He shook his head. "Look, I pulled her file when I spoke to you on the phone. There's stuff in there I could tell you, but it's marked confidential. You know me, I'd usually tell you anything you want to know, but not when it's stamped like that. I can't budge on this one, Frank."

Franklin's lips pursed. He pushed back from the table with a sigh, crossed one leg over the other. "Okay, I guess that's that then."

Mack leaned forward. "I will tell you this - give her a chance. She deserves that. There's nothing in the file that means you can't trust her, there's no reason not to. I'm telling you that as a friend. I'm also asking you not to be too hard on her. Show her the ropes. No one's better to do that than you. She could be a good cop. But not if you don't give her a chance."

Franklin inhaled a sharp breath. "Well, if you say so."

Mack gave a quick nod. "I do."

"Fine."

They said their goodbyes, and Franklin marched to his cruiser, his head spinning with questions. He hadn't gotten the answers he'd been looking for. Everything Mack said had only increased his curiosity. What would be so confidential that Mack couldn't talk about it, the same guy who leaked the entire promotions list two years earlier? He'd been lucky they didn't discover it was him.

Franklin slid into the cruiser, started the engine and sat staring out at the beach across the street. Dark clouds gathered on the horizon, swirling and churning as they made their way towards the shore. A brisk wind whipped the curling waves, frothing the edges into white bubbles.

Give her a chance.

That was what Mack had asked. Why? Give her a chance - what was that about? And since when did Mack ask him to give a break to a new recruit? Mack was the one in their graduating class voted most likely to razz on probies.

There was more to Rebecca Mair than he knew - it'd been a feeling before, something buried deep in his intuition. It'd sat in the back of his mind, itching but without any defined shape. Something was there, but maybe it was all in his imagination. But now there was no question in his mind about it: Rebecca Mair was hiding something.

CHAPTER 38

FRANKLIN

*B*ack at the office, Franklin climbed from the cruiser and stood for a moment staring at the station. Inside, he knew he'd find people buzzing with activity, phones ringing, keyboards clicking. His shift was about to begin, so there'd be a changeover, and soon he'd be out in the car with his partner. She'd sit silently, staring out the window while the radio played. Beside her, he'd be wondering.

With a grunt, he slammed the car door shut and strode into the station. He waved hello to Stephanie, her auburn hair piled into a high bun. She waved back, the phone pressed to one ear.

He pressed his ID badge to the scanner on the wall, and the door buzzed open. He made his way directly to the small gym behind the offices. She was always there before her shift, working out in a way that seemed almost demented. Franklin was as concerned with his physical fitness as the next officer, but since her encounter with the perp who'd knocked her down, she'd taken to working out as if her life depended on it. And perhaps it did.

He ducked into the gym and walked down the short hall, the scent of damp socks and sweat tickling his nose as he turned the corner.

She was there, like he'd known she would be. Hands taped, she was hitting the swinging bag. Hard. Muscles bunched in her shoulders. Beneath the small crop top, her stomach was defined, hard. Her arms were still small, but hard, rounded muscles flexed beneath her creamy skin.

His lips pressed into a straight line as he watched her for a few moments. She'd transformed from a soft, pale woman into something hard, fit, determined. Almost a different person to the one who'd walked into the office four months earlier.

Just as she looked up and caught his eye, he spun on his heel and left, his jaw clenching.

CHAPTER 39

MEG

a crow cawed overhead, perched on a telephone line. It turned its head to the side, peered at Meg out of one black eye and cawed again. The sound of the bird's call echoed an aggravating echo through the valley behind her. A valley full of suburban homes dotted in amongst a blanket of greenery - palm trees, poinciana, jacaranda and bushy lilly pillies shaped into hedgerows.

The grass on the lawn at her feet was patchy green and brown together, like an unfinished quilt. It hadn't rained much lately, although it'd threatened plenty of times. Still, winter was around the corner and generally dry in Brisbane. She knew as much from the times she'd visited her mother during a short stint when she lived there right after the divorce. Although, she could count those times on one hand. Mum wasn't very interested in visits from her daughter or really anything at all to do with Meg, though she'd never admit that. She always claimed she was a good mother, said it over and over, trying to convince herself if no one else. Meg knew the truth. After all, she'd been raised by the woman.

With a sigh, she tented a hand over her face and started up the long, pebble-stone concrete driveway to the single-level red brick house. There was a cool breeze, but not cold enough to warrant a coat. She rubbed both palms down the front of her jeans; sweat broke out, refusing to be dried on the thin denim.

She raised a fist to knock on the timber door, waited a few moments then knocked again. The door swung open even as her hand poised for another try.

"Hello? Oh, Meg! You're here." Sharon swooped out and wrapped Meg up in her arms.

Meg blinked back tears. She didn't have a mother who cared enough to be there for her during the hardest moments of her life. But from the first time Brad had brought her home and introduced her to his parents, Sharon and Des had welcomed her into their home and their family. They'd been warm, kind and completely accepting, and it'd taken her by surprise. Then, she'd transitioned to an awkward phase, always waiting for them to change, for the masks to come down and the real Sharon and Des to appear. But it'd never happened. They'd continued to love her, much to her constant amazement. Now, she found she missed them. Missed having someone she could talk to, rely on, embrace.

"Oh, honey, I'm so glad to see you." Sharon wrapped one arm around Meg's waist and ushered her into the house.

The cool of the tiled entryway washed over her,

along with the scent of vanilla with a touch of cinnamon from a nearby unlit candle nestled in a bed of sea glass on a small table set against the wall.

"I'm sorry I didn't call," Meg said, her lower lip quivering. "I wanted to see you, to see Brad. I've been reading his letters, but I miss him - all of you really. Miss seeing you."

Sharon shut the door behind them and led her into the kitchen. "Of course, love. You don't have to call. We're family, you can drop in any time you like. Now, Brad's out in the backyard swimming his laps. He'll be out there a few more minutes, I'd imagine. But that just gives us more time to catch up." She cupped both hands to Meg's face, her eyes glistening. "I'm so sorry for everything - the way things have turned out. How are you coping?"

Meg slid into a chair at the kitchen table with a shake of her head. "I don't know. I guess I'm okay, but it's hard. I thought I'd be married, living with the love of my life - I knew it was a fairy tale, but I was naïve enough to believe it might actually happen." She scrubbed both hands over her face. "I'm sorry, I know that's insensitive. It's not like I have to deal with being paralysed - Brad's been through so much more than I have."

"You don't have to apologise to me, love. We've all had to deal with more than we can bear."

Sharon skated around the kitchen, setting a kettle to boil and extracting a cake from a floral cake tin to set on a plate with familiar, deft movements.

"How…how is he?"

Sharon hesitated, offering a warm smile as she carried the cake to the table and set it in front of Meg. "He's much better than he was. Hawaii…well, it was awful. You know what he was like. He's coming to terms with what happened. At least, it seems that way. He won't talk to us about it much, but he's less angry, more determined..."

She poured them two cups of tea and carried them to the table, then sat across from Meg. "I don't want to say too much... He should tell you himself."

Meg sipped the tea, grimaced. It scalded her tongue, and she set it down again with a quick breath over the burned flesh to cool it.

"Too hot?" Sharon asked.

Meg only nodded, her tongue extended between her lips. "Burned my tongue," she said around it.

Sharon laughed, covered her mouth. "Sorry, I didn't mean to laugh, you just look so cute. I'll grab you some water."

Meg chuckled as well, then gulped the cold water down, feeling it soothe her tongue as it glided down her throat. "Ah, that's better. Thank you."

Sharon sat again and held the tea between her hands, watching Meg.

"It's like a metaphor for my relationship with Brad," she said with a shake of her head. "I rushed in and got burned."

Sharon reached out and patted her arm. "He didn't mean to hurt you... You know that, right?"

Meg nodded. "Of course, I know he didn't. And I feel selfish even saying anything about it after what he's been through. But I'm angry... I mean, we said vows to each other, and I meant those vows." Tears thickened her throat; her voice caught before she went on. "I mean, I promised to be by his side through sickness and health, and when that time came along, when the worst happened, he didn't give me a chance to keep those vows. He stole that from me." She couldn't hold back the sob that shook her entire body from head to toe. Tears trickled slowly down her cheeks. "I wanted to be there, I wanted to hold him, to kiss him, to tell him it would all be okay. But he didn't let me."

Another sob. Now her nose was running as well. She hadn't planned this. She'd come to Brisbane with the idea that she'd be cool, calm and open to a discussion. She wanted to talk to Brad, face-to-face, to find out if he truly wanted to get an annulment or if it was only the pain talking. Now, she was humiliating herself in front of his mother and couldn't seem to stop. The tears kept falling. She'd held them in for so much of the past months, ever since the accident, held it all together - she'd had to be strong for Brad, then for herself when everything balanced precariously on her narrow shoulders.

She'd always had to be strong. But Sharon's kindness had dislodged the plug that'd been holding her emotions at bay, and now they were tumbling out like eggs dropped from a carton - no matter how she tried, she couldn't catch them all before they hit the ground and smashed wide open.

Sharon moved to hug her from behind, then sat next to her and reached for her hand. "Oh, honey, it's not your fault."

Meg nodded but couldn't respond. Sharon tugged a dozen tissues from a nearby Kleenex box and handed them to Meg.

"Thank you." Meg wiped her cheeks dry, then blew her nose.

The back door opened, and Brad wheeled inside, up a small ramp that'd been added to the outside, and down another one on the inside. He stared in surprise at Meg, water dripping into his eyes from newly shorn hair. She hadn't ever seen him wear his hair so short before. It was darker and accentuated his light green eyes.

His brow furrowed. "Meg? What's wrong? What's going on?"

For a moment, she saw concern flit across his features, then he buried it beneath a scowl.

"Nothing's wrong. I came over to say hi, see how you're going."

He shrugged, wiped his hair dry with the towel draped around his shoulders. She caught a glimpse of the watch she'd given him for Christmas on his left wrist. "Fine. I'm fine. I'm going to get dressed."

He wheeled his chair down the hall and out of sight.

Meg pursed her lips. At least he'd been civil, and he was wearing the watch. For a moment there, he almost looked pleased to see her. But perhaps she was only imagining things.

When he returned, he was dressed in a blue t-shirt and jeans. His hair was spiked on end as if he'd run the towel over it and left it that way. He looked strong, healthy and tanned. He looked like the Brad she'd fallen in love with instead of the man who sat in the dark, shrinking from life while he watched television or barked at her.

He was himself again.

Relief coursed through her veins, and her throat ached. She'd go home and cry into a pillow, but for now, she had to seem happy, at ease, see if she could get him talking.

They sat on the back veranda together. Sharon made them each another cup of tea and sliced the cake to set on two plates. So far, Meg hadn't touched hers. Brad ate his slice in two bites, then picked up the crumbs with the end of one thumb.

"I love cinnamon teacake, it's my favourite," he said.

She smiled. "I remember."

He grinned for a single moment, then the smile faded as though he remembered he wasn't supposed to show it to her. "Yeah, of course. So, what are you doing up here in Brisbane?"

She shrugged. "We've been writing to each other for a while, I thought we should see each other face-to-face."

He nodded, watching her closely. "Okay."

"It seems like your physiotherapy is going well."

"Yeah, I'm enjoying swimming again. It's different for me now, of course…but I can manage it, so I'm happy with that. Helps build my upper body strength too."

"That's great, Brad. You love the water, so I'm glad you're able to get back out in it."

He inhaled a slow breath. "I guess so." Then, his eyes lit up. "I've decided to go back to uni."

Meg's eyes widened. "Really? That's wonderful. Are you going to study business?"

"No. I've decided to change to engineering. I've always loved designing things, and I'm good at maths. I think it'll be a better option for me…now."

Meg wanted to reach for his hand, wanted to kiss his lips, do something to show him how excited she was, how happy it made her to hear he wasn't giving up on life. Instead, she pushed her hands under her thighs, sitting on them to keep them from straying over to his.

"That's a great idea. I'm so happy for you."

His eyes sparkled, and he seemed happy to chat for now. Meg was delighted and launched into a series of funny stories about hairdressing clients she'd had since he'd been gone. He laughed out loud, a sound she hadn't heard in so long it made her heart sing.

Finally, it was time to go. She had an afternoon shift at the salon, and it was a two-hour drive home.

"I wish I could stay longer," she said, standing and reaching for her purse.

He nodded, wheeled closer. "Thanks for coming. It was good to catch up."

She set a hand on his shoulder and on an impulse leaned down to press her lips to his. The kiss was warm, friendly and familiar. When her eyes blinked open, she found him staring at her with a tortured expression.

"Don't…"

"What? Why not? You're my husband."

"Not for much longer," he replied. "Don't start things up again between us. You're better off without me."

She straightened, pressing her hands to her hips as anger surged in her gut. "Better off? Is that what you're telling yourself? Because it's selfish, that's what it is."

His eyes narrowed. "Selfish?"

"Yes, selfish. Why do you get to decide what's best for me? It's not up to you. That's my call."

He huffed. "I don't know how many times I have to tell you the same thing before you finally get it - I don't want to be married to you! I don't love you anymore, not like that." Brad's mouth was set in a line, his eyes hard.

Meg gaped. She wouldn't let herself cry, not in front of him. How could he be so callous, so uncaring?

"Fine, I'm leaving. Have a nice life."

She stormed through the back door and passed by Sharon in the kitchen.

"Meg…? Meg, where are you going?" Sharon ran after her along the hall and pulled her by the arm before she reached the front door.

Meg spun on her, eyes flashing. "He is…he's just mean. He's mean!" She didn't know what to say, words wouldn't come. She sputtered with fury.

Tears threatened, but she swallowed them, instead pressing her lips together and breathing deep.

"What did he say, honey?" Sharon's eyebrows pulled low over her green eyes. Eyes just like Brad's.

"It doesn't matter. Thank you for having me, the cake was lovely. I'll call you later." She hugged Sharon, kissed her cheek.

"I love you, honey," Sharon whispered against her hair.

Meg's eyes flooded. She blinked hard.

With a nod, she fled, running down the driveway as fast as she could in her patent leather flats. She threw the car into drive and hit the accelerator, the back end fishtailing as she sped away from the curb. Tears blinded her, and so she let them fall, wetting her cheeks as she drove.

CHAPTER 40

CINDY

*T*he jingle of the bell over the cafe's front door as the last of the staff left for the evening filled Cindy with relief. She sighed. Another night over, one more new staff member trained. Daniel still needed some help with this and that, but he was reasonably well versed in how to wait and bus tables now, giving Cindy back some of the space she needed to manage the place.

She expertly counted through the cash on hand, added up the credit card receipts, then got out her calculator to peck away at the numbers with one finger. Sarah wouldn't be pleased. She'd been banging on lately about transferring everything to the computer, but Cindy had told her she could only manage one massive change at a time. Replacing Thad and changing happy hour was about all she could deal with for the moment. Maybe when things settled down again, she could bring the cafe into the current century.

With a satisfied sigh, she leaned back in her chair. A smile flitted across her face. They'd made a profit. A decent-sized one too - with everything they'd brought in this week, they had enough to make the payment on the loan at the bank.

She wouldn't lose the cafe or her home. At least not this month, anyway.

Cindy packed up her things, grabbed her purse and locked the money in the safe before locking up the cafe. She turned to head towards her car, startled by a figure standing in the darkness.

"It's just me," Andrew said.

Her heart thudded back into place. "For heaven's sakes, you scared the blue out of my jeans."

He chuckled. "Sorry, I didn't think about that. I was waiting for you to lock up so we could talk."

She strode past him, her hand in her purse trying out every object it found as she searched for her keys. Hairbrush, no. Change purse, no. Reusable shopping bag, no.

Finally, her fingers closed around the set of keys, and they jangled in her purse. She pulled them free and held them tight.

"Wait, please, Cindy. Talk to me. Just for a moment. I didn't want to do this on the phone."

She spun to face him, her heart hammering against her rib cage. "The phone? The phone would've been nicer. You left without even talking to me. There was a note. That's it. A note. Do you know how that made me feel, Andrew? After so many years of marriage, you left a note to tell me you'd found someone else and weren't coming home."

He jammed his hands into the pockets of his pants. At least he had the decency to look sheepish, maybe even a little repentant. Although, she was certain that had more to do with the fact she was yelling at him than that he was actually sorry for what he'd done. She wasn't convinced he knew how to be sorry, since that would require him to think of someone else's feelings.

"I am sorry for that. I know you probably don't believe me, but I am."

He could always read her like a book.

She inhaled a slow breath, waited for her pulse to slow a little and pushed a smile onto her face. "Never mind. What's done is done."

"I want to see you. You and the kids. Maybe I could come over to the house sometime…"

Her eyes narrowed. "No. Definitely not."

"They're my kids too," he objected, his voice rising.

She huffed. "They're grown adults, Andrew. If you want to see them, you can call them. It has nothing to do with me."

"And it's my house…"

Her eyes flashed. "Not anymore, it's not. You gave up the right to call it your home when you walked out and left me with the bills to pay all alone."

"I didn't know what else to do. And I was in love…"

She rolled her eyes. "In love?" She huffed. "You were in love. That's wonderful. To me, the worst of it is the debts. You didn't love me anymore? Fine, leave - run off with your secretary. I never liked the woman, and she deserves you. But why did you have to leave me with all this debt? That was a low blow, even for you, Andrew. I should be thinking about retirement, not working double shifts to pay for a mortgage I didn't even know about."

"I didn't mean for it to happen. It just did. I lost control..."

She leaned against her car door, crossed her legs at the ankle. "I'm listening - I'm ready for an explanation. You've hinted at a few things, but I think I deserve the whole story. Where did all our money go, Andrew? Did you buy yourself an island somewhere or maybe a secret yacht for you and your girlfriend? Huh? What did you do that required so much of our life savings?"

Cindy couldn't believe the way she was talking. She'd never spoken to anyone in her life with that kind of attitude. It was clear Andrew was as shocked as she was by her combination of confidence and anger as she lounged against the car.

"I...uh. Well, give me a minute to explain."

"I'm all ears," she said.

"The business was going downhill for years before I closed it for good."

"Why didn't you tell me?" she shrieked, her voice getting louder by the minute. "We could've done something about it."

He shrugged. "I was embarrassed. You've always been so successful at business, and you've never really respected me. But you thought I was good at my job, if nothing else, and so I stuck at it. I wanted to prove to myself, and to you, that I could do it. If I'd told you, you would've hated me."

She frowned. Was that really how he felt? He'd never let her know he cared at all what she thought.

"I wouldn't have hated you. Whatever gave you that idea?"

"Oh, it's nothing you did, really. I always knew I wasn't good enough for you. I tried to live up to your standards, but you're so perfect, Cindy - no one can be as perfect as you. No one."

Cindy's brow furrowed deeper still. "That's not fair. You can't put that on me. I didn't push you. I never criticised you."

"Yeah, but you judged me," he said with a sniff.

She couldn't argue with that. He'd given her so many reasons to judge, and she'd tried not to do it, but the anger had boiled up within every time he let her down, and she couldn't seem to help it. Maybe she had been too hard on him, but that was still no excuse.

"I thought I could fix it, that I could turn things around. So, I borrowed from the bank. It was a small loan at first, meant to float the business for a few months until I could turn a profit on an investment I made. But then, that didn't work, and it seemed wrong not to keep trying after I'd borrowed all that money, so I borrowed more..." His voice broke, and his head dropped until he was staring at the pavement. "I'm sorry I let you down, Cindy." His shoulders slumped.

She studied him, pity stirring in her heart. "Thank you for saying that."

"I wanted to pay it back, honestly I did. But nothing worked. I was getting in deeper and deeper, and soon it seemed like the best option would be for me to close the business entirely. So, that's what I did."

"And then you ran away from the mess you made," Cindy added.

He shrugged. "I didn't know what else to do."

"You could've faced it. We could've faced it together, the two of us."

"You'd have hated me," he repeated. "I couldn't take that on top of everything else."

She sighed, shook her head. "Well, you've made a right mess of everything now. Haven't you?"

His lips pursed. "Keisha hates it in Tweed Heads. She wants to move back to the Cove. Says her family's here and she's lonely."

Cindy's eyes narrowed. "What are you saying, Andrew?"

He sighed. "I'm telling you that Keisha and I are coming home. We're moving to Emerald Cove."

CHAPTER 41

SARAH

*S*unlight glinted off the pen poised between her fingers. Sarah glanced up as a cloud skidded into place, throwing shade across the porch. A wind kicked up in a burst, sending the top sheet of paper in her lap flying. It dipped and spun, soared then fell onto the newly stained hardwoods that made up the finished porch.

With a sigh, she stood from her comfortable white Adirondack chair and reached for the paper, then slid back into the seat. The scent of salt and freshly cut grass on the air tickled her nostrils, and she smiled as Oscar padded across the lawn in front of her with a stick wedged in his mouth. He lay on the grass, positioning himself so he could see Sarah, then set about gnawing at the stick, pulling the bark off it in strips.

"It doesn't get much better than this. Right, Oscar?" she called.

The dog's tail thumped on the ground, but he didn't look up.

She grinned, scanning the outlook with one hand shielding her eyes from the sun's glare where it reflected off the porch railing.

The cottage was finished. It was too pretty to live in. At least, that was what she'd told her mother. She almost hated to use the new porcelain sink in the bathroom or the gleaming stainless steel stove. She'd never owned a home before. The unit in Sydney had been rented, and before that, she'd been a student living in a dormitory. It was strangely exhilarating, knowing that the cottage belonged to her.

And now that Mick no longer worked for her, she was curious to see what their future might be. Not that his professional relationship was the cause of her reticence. It's what she'd said, what she'd tried to believe, but it wasn't true. Sure, it made sense to keep their connection professional, but her fears were more abstract than that. More grounded in the failures of her parents' marriage, a marriage she'd failed to truly understand for her entire life until the moment her father left her mother, left them all, really.

If she was being entirely honest with herself, she was angry at him for leaving her as well. She hadn't wanted to admit that, because it made no sense - she didn't live at home, wasn't a child any longer, but he'd abandoned them all when he left the way he did.

He hadn't talked to her about it. She didn't know how unhappy he was - of course she could look back now with the clarity of hindsight and glimpse the warning signs. But at the time, she'd thought of those things only as the quirks of a happy marriage between two very different people. They'd successfully shielded their children from the ugliness of open conflict, instead hiding their strife behind a veil of normalcy, polite exchanges and separate lives filled with the busyness of work, activities and friendships.

She'd seen her relationship with Jeremy through new eyes when her parents' carefully constructed ruse fell apart. Now she wasn't sure she could trust a man with her heart. What if she did it again - got deeply involved with someone who wasn't what he seemed? Mum had done it with Dad, Sarah had fallen for Jeremy - perhaps Mick wasn't the man she thought he was and she was simply unable to see it. Maybe it wasn't that she didn't trust Mick, but that she didn't trust herself.

Still, she'd miss having him around - climbing ladders, wielding hammers and play wrestling with the dog when he thought no one was looking.

The crackle of tyres on the freshly poured gravel driveway made Oscar's ears prick. He rushed around the side of the house barking, his tail held high.

She probably should rescue whoever that was. If it'd been Mick, her mother, Vicky or Meg, Oscar would've stopped barking by now. But the sound of his consternation rang out loud and clear across the lawn.

With a sigh, she set the manuscript on a small, round wicker table and pushed out of the chair. She strode to the front door and swung it open.

"Oscar! Come here, boy." She tented a hand over her eyes and peered into the blinding sunlight, her vision struggling to adjust after the relative shade of the porch.

She didn't recognise the vehicle. Some kind of sedan, a new one by the look of it - white, nondescript. A rental car company logo stuck on the back window.

Oscar backed towards her but didn't stop barking. She grabbed him by the collar and held on while he strained against her hold.

The driver's side door swung open, and a head poked out, sunglasses pushed up high. "You got a dog?"

"Jeremy?" Sarah's heart skipped a beat. "What're you doing here?"

He climbed from the car, all long limbs and fashion labels. "I came to see you, sweetheart." He scanned the cottage. "This is nice."

Her stomach clenched at the term of endearment. "Thanks, I did some renovating. It was a little more rustic when I bought it."

"Aren't you full of surprises? Dog owner and house renovator...very impressive." He stepped closer, still a little leery of the dog attempting to leap at him, teeth bared. "Does it bite?"

"Who, Oscar?" she began, studying the dog's lurching head. "Actually, I'm not really sure. So far, I've never seen him bite anyone, but I haven't known him all that long. He kind of adopted me." She pushed Oscar into the cottage and shut the front door. "Let's walk around to the back porch. He's fine inside for a few minutes on his own."

He grabbed her hand and leaned forward to kiss her, but she turned her face just in time for him to connect with her cheek instead. He lingered there, his breath hot on her skin. "It's really good to see you, sweetheart."

She pushed a smile onto her face. "Yeah, you too."

He wasn't going to release her hand, so she tugged it free. While he followed her around the cottage, her mind raced. What was he doing here? What should she tell him? There was so much he didn't know, and he was acting like he'd stepped right back into her life without a moment's pause, calling her sweetheart, kissing her...or, at least, attempting it. What was he up to?

She showed him onto the porch and offered him one of a pair of white timber chairs. He sat, his eyes widening. "Phew! Will you look at that view. Wow. Now I get why you moved here. This is stunning, Sarah. Really, it is. I could give up the city life for a view like this. It's inspirational."

She chuckled. "Yeah, it is. I've been working out here, actually." She waved a hand at the manuscript held down by an empty coffee mug on the side table.

His eyebrows arched high. "Well, I'd take this office over mine any day of the week. Although, I'm not sure how much work I'd get done."

She tucked her crossed legs up on the seat of the chair, held onto her knees with her hands and studied the view. It wasn't something she'd ever take for granted. Every time she took it in, it stole her breath for a single moment with its beauty.

Squat bushes and shrubs shuddered in the strong sea breeze. The cliff fell away, and beyond it, white-capped ocean peaks broke and sprayed, then hid themselves in the blue depths before peaking all over again. Grey clouds rolled across the sun, as if working themselves up to an afternoon thunderstorm.

"I came here to talk," Jeremy began.

She faced him, drawing a deep breath. What did he hope to gain? She'd told him everything she wanted to say in Sydney. Told him she didn't want to see him again. Yet here he was.

"Okay. I'm listening."

He sighed, reaching for her hand. "You and I are so

good together. I don't know why you keep fighting the pull we have. We're never going to be able to walk away, it's too strong - the love we share. I've tried... Trust me, I've tried to get you out of my head. But I can't. It's a lost cause. We have to be together, because being apart isn't an option."

She listened, her head cocked to one side. "Jeremy, I don't want to hurt you, but you're terrible at listening. This was one of the problems in our relationship. You decide what you want, and you go after it..."

He frowned. "Yeah, of course I do. I know what I want, and you're it."

"I know, I get it. And that works really well in your career - it's one of the reasons you're so successful. But in love...well, it takes two people. We both have to want it for it to work, and I don't want to be in this relationship any longer."

He hesitated, his eyes narrowed. "Why do you keep saying that? I know you feel what I feel..."

She shook her head. "Not anymore, Jer. I don't love you that way. I'll always care for you as a friend, as a writer, but not the way you want me to. I haven't for a long time. I thought I'd be able to work through those feelings, that we were just going through a rough patch and we'd sort it out. But it wasn't a rough patch... We're not right for each other."

His head fell into his hands, and he stared at the timber slats beneath his feet. "Is it because of Leander?"

Sarah's gut twisted into a knot.

"Because if it's her, I'm sorry. Okay? I'm sorry, and it's over anyway. So, you don't have to worry about that. It's behind us."

She shook her head. "No, it's not because you had an affair with your intern, Jer. Well, not entirely..."

He'd never openly admitted cheating on her before. She'd suspected a lot of the women who'd come into and out of his life over the years, but he'd always denied any allegations. Still, his words cut her even though she'd put it behind her - he'd cheated on her, he was admitting it. How could she have let their relationship continue for even a moment after something like that? She should've ended things between them a year before she had, back when her intuition first told her something was wrong.

He raised his head, eyes glistening. "Well then, what?"

"We're not right together. I don't love you. I don't want to marry you. And yes, I can't trust you to be faithful."

"You can't walk away from what we had, Sarah. I know you, you don't mean this... You're only trying to hurt me because I cheated on you. You'll regret this... I know you will. You'll come home, and you'll wish you hadn't wasted both our time..."

She knelt in front of him, cupped his cheeks with both hands and stared into his eyes. "I need you to hear this, Jer. It's over. I'm walking away from what we had, and you need to leave."

His eyes darkened. He shook her hands from his face, stepped around her and strode away through the yard. The sound of his tyres spinning on the gravel was his only goodbye.

CHAPTER 42

SARAH

*S*arah lifted her legs and bent her knees, then grasped both arms around them, pulling them close. She held herself that way on the porch for a few minutes, breathing slow and steady. Intentional breaths, to ward off the tears that threatened and to loosen the lump in her throat.

She'd done her best to be firm, to be clear with Jeremy. He was beginning to scare her, wouldn't seem to listen when she told him it was over between them. Of course, he was that way about everything - as his editor, she hated getting back to him with edits that required anything more than minor changes to his stories. He'd stand his ground and argue until she gave up and he got his way. He was stubborn, determined and difficult - but she'd seen him as charming, a champion of his own work and confident in his abilities when she'd first met him. Now, she wondered how she'd ever let herself fall for someone like Jeremy Goodall.

"Sarah?" Mick's voice startled her from her reverie. Then she heard Oscar keening at the door.

"I'm on the back porch!" she called. She jumped to her feet to let the dog out. He bounded around her, tail wagging as he licked her legs. She laughed, dashed the last of her tears away with the back of one hand and bent to rub Oscar's back.

"Hey, boy. You're a funny one, aren't you?"

Mick rounded the corner, one eyebrow arched. "Who was that burning rubber back there?"

Her nose wrinkled. "That was my ex-fiancé."

"Right. He seemed angry." A muscle in his jaw clenched. His eyes fixed on hers, calm, full of concern as he stepped closer. Her heart softened. "Are you okay?"

Mick wrapped her up in his arms, and her throat tightened all over again. She inhaled a quick breath. "Yeah, I'm fine. He wanted me to come back to Sydney with him, give us another chance, and I told him no."

Mick pulled back to look at her with a slow nod. "I'm glad to hear it."

She sighed. "I've told him over and over that I don't want to marry him, that we're done, but he isn't the type to take no for an answer. He's pig-headed that way."

She rubbed both hands over her face and sat on the edge of the chair. Oscar leaned into her, ears back and tail planted beside his rear end on the porch, thumping every few seconds.

Mick sat beside her. "I'm sorry you had to deal with that...again. But it sounds to me like you made the right choice. I'd hate to be married to someone who can't hear what you're saying or doesn't respect you enough to do what you're asking them to."

She dipped her head in agreement.

"Of course, I'm a little biased, since I really don't want you to leave..." He cupped her cheek with one hand.

She placed her hand on his, then stood, pulling away. "I'm not going anywhere." She opened the back door and stepped inside. "Want a cup of tea?"

He followed. "Sounds great, thanks."

She put the kettle on to boil and busied herself getting out cups and tea bags. He sat on one of the bamboo barstools with white cushions she'd found at another garage sale on the other side of the Cove.

Mick was wonderful. He was everything she was looking for in a man. But Jeremy's visit had shaken her. She felt like running and hiding herself away so that she'd be safe. And Mick showing up when he had only added fuel to her growing anxiety.

"Is everything okay?" he asked.

She nodded. "Of course." She offered him a half smile as she poured the hot water over the tea bags.

"I came over to talk to you about something...about us," he began.

She set down the kettle, her heart pounding in her chest. "Okay."

"I'm ready for more. I want to take the next step in our relationship. I want us to commit to each other - be on the same page about where this is going."

"And where is that?" she asked, her heart thudding.

"Love, commitment, family..." His words drifted to nothing. He watched her, eyes alert, seeming to wait for a reaction. They were deep, dark and mysterious as the ocean, boring into her, reading her thoughts.

She turned away with the excuse of looking for milk in the fridge. If he'd come over yesterday with those words on his lips, she'd have jumped, all-in, but now…now all she needed was some time alone.

With the milk still swirling in the cup, she handed the tea to Mick and settled onto the stool next to him with her own and took a sip.

"I hear what you're saying," she replied. "And I like you a lot… That doesn't really sum up my feelings. I care for you. We've known each other a long time, and yet we still don't know each other with any depth - the adult versions of ourselves, that is."

"We haven't changed…" he interrupted, his voice smooth as he reached for her hand, caressing it with his fingertips. "I know you, the essence of who you are - you're still the girl with no fear who'd take on the fiercest wave, while laughing. You're the woman who's so beautiful she turns heads but doesn't notice…who's smart, good and kind to everyone no matter who they are. You're the same person I remember from high school, and I'm the same as well."

She swallowed. "You knew all that about me? I thought… Well, I didn't think you knew me very well at all. It's a funny thing, the way childhood friendships exist, like deep water below the rolling waves, steady, constant, cool. When you're a kid, you surf with people, maybe play a sport, go to a dance, you think you don't know each other very well until you get out into the world and realise there were things you shared with your hometown friends that no one outside that town, that life, will ever understand in the same way. You share something profound, know the measure of people, without even realising it." She sighed. Mick smiled at her, eyes gleaming.

"But the thing is, I *feel* like a very different person than who I was. Breaking up with Jeremy was hard for me. He and I spent so much time together - we worked together, we dated, we were engaged and planned on spending the rest of our lives together. But I knew it wasn't right between us. Once the haze of infatuation passed, I began to see what he was like underneath the charm, the talent, the passion, and it wasn't good."

He nodded, his brow furrowed. "I understand."

"I don't think I'm ready for something new, to be honest." As the words left her mouth, they tore a hole in her heart.

He inhaled sharply. "I see."

"I've spent the past decade obsessed with building my career, networking with all the right people, making my life into something I thought I wanted - and part of that was dating a talented, successful author with a pretty face and smooth lines. But I'm older now, I've grown so much lately, especially after what happened between my parents. It shook me, made me see more clearly the things that matter in the end. And I had to walk away from everything I'd worked so hard to create for myself. Now...now I don't know what I want. I don't even really know who I am."

She ran a hand over her face, shook her head slowly. "I'm sorry, Mick. I don't think I can give you what you want. Not now. I don't want to hurt you, but I can't be who you need me to be. I'm still trying to find my way forward after tearing my own life apart. Seeing Jeremy... It reminded me that I loved him, thought him the best man in the world for me. I was so wrong about him, I don't think I can trust myself to make the right decisions when it comes to my heart.

I'm afraid... I don't want to wake up in thirty years to find my husband gone and realise I never knew him... It terrifies me to imagine making that kind of mistake."

He stood, shoved his hands into his jeans pockets. When he turned away, the hunch of his shoulders deepened the ache in her chest.

With a sigh, he faced her. "I get it, I guess. Although I'm not sure I like being called a mistake...or a potential mistake." A muscle in his jaw clenched; his eyes flashed. "I'm not your dad, and I don't know your ex, but I don't think we'd share much in common from what I do know of him. I care about you and want you to give us a chance. But I can see you're not ready for that. Thanks for being honest with me, even if I do think you're wrong." He ran a hand over his lips, shook his head. "I hope you don't mind, but I'm going to let myself out."

"Okay." She didn't want him to leave, not like that, but she couldn't think of anything else to say. Her throat ached.

"See you around, Sassy." He wandered out the front door, shutting Oscar into the cottage before he could dash outside. Then he was gone.

* * *

IT WAS dark in the cottage. Sarah leaned back on the couch, her legs crossed on the futon in front of her. She had a blanket draped over her legs, and an open carton of Chinese food sat on the side table, a pair of chopsticks jutting out at odd angles.

The television set blared, a romantic comedy. She couldn't concentrate on the storyline, couldn't think about anything other than the way Mick had looked when he walked out the door. She shouldn't have said what she did - should've asked him for more time instead. Now, he was gone. She doubted he'd ever want to speak to her again. And she wouldn't blame him.

With a sigh, she reached for the food, ate another bite, then set it back in its place on the table.

Her mobile phone rang, and she answered with a brusque "hello".

When all she heard on the other end of the line was sobbing, she straightened in a moment, her eyes wide. "Hello?"

"It's Meg," came the response, followed by sniffling.

"Meg, what's wrong? Are you hurt?"

Meg coughed. "No, I'm fine. I only wanted to talk. I visited Brad in Brisbane."

"When? What happened? Is something wrong?" Sarah asked, the questions pouring from her mouth.

"He's okay, he's with his parents. It's not that. No one's hurt. Only...I kissed him."

Sarah relaxed, a smile dancing across her lips. "Well, that's great. Isn't it?"

"Yeah, I thought so. But he didn't kiss me back, and he told me he doesn't love me anymore, doesn't want to be married to me." Her words ended in a wail, then were muffled by something.

"Where are you right now?" Sarah asked as a stone formed in the bottom of her gut.

"I'm at home. I had to work, but my boss sent me home because I couldn't stop crying. It's not like me. I'm not a crier. I never have been. I can go to a funeral and stand there with a dry face. I'm not one of those people who's so emotional, and yet today, I can't seem to stop." She sniffled again, then blew her nose.

Sarah grimaced, pulling the earpiece away from her head for a moment, almost deafened by the blast. "Okay, I'm coming over, I'll be there in a few minutes. Do you want me to call Vicky?"

"I already did, but she's not answering."

"I'll try her again. Okay? See you soon." She hung up the phone then rushed to grab her coat and car keys.

CHAPTER 43

REBECCA

"Got a tip on Thad Borseth," Franklin said as he strode past Rebecca's desk.

She reached for her hat, shoved it on her head and followed him. "Coming!"

Seated in the squad car, Rebecca stared out the front windshield.

"No sirens," Franklin said. "I don't want to give this lowlife a heads-up."

"Yes, sir."

They'd been looking for Thad for weeks, after two of the locals had sent them video footage of the waiter defrauding a cafe owner. Cindy Flannigan said he'd been doing it for months, but she hadn't realised what he was up to. Still, the moment he caught wind of their investigation, he'd disappeared. Franklin thought he must've left the state.

"Someone called in an anonymous tip. Turns out he's been bunking with a friend."

"Well, how about that," Rebecca replied with a shake of her head. "We only interviewed them all multiple times, and every single one said they didn't know anything about his whereabouts."

Franklin grunted. "I don't know what we're walking into. So, let's take it easy. We're just there to talk... That's what we'll tell him. Keep emotions steady until we know what we're dealing with."

She nodded, even as she checked her belt, gun and taser and patted the tight vest protecting her upper body. She was ready.

They followed the main road out of Emerald Cove south until they slowed at an intersection. Franklin turned east and headed along a narrow dirt track. They stopped at a gate. Rebecca climbed out to haul it open, then shut it behind them before they progressed up a steady incline and into a copse of coastal gums. The dappled light threw dancing shadows across Rebecca's arms and thighs. She watched it, then peered out the window, squinting against the afternoon sunlight as it glinted through the leaves in short bursts.

Finally, they reached the summit and descended down the other side. The road, such as it was, petered to a stop, then a grassy track with tyre marks veered off to the right.

Franklin pulled the car to a stop and turned it off.

"We'll walk from here."

She climbed out, hands tingling by her sides as her heart raced. The only thing she could hear was the distant crash of breakers against the sandy shore, hidden from view by wattle, bottlebrush and other dry, squat bushes. A seagull called, followed by another. Then, silence fell, and she could hear each puff of breath as it left her mouth and their quiet footfalls.

The grass-covered trail curved to the right, then into a clearing where a beach shack perched on a sandy hillock.

Franklin pointed at her, then indicated she should go around the back. With a nod, she followed his direction as he loped to the front door, hand poised above his gun.

Her mind flashed back to the last time she'd done this - the last time she confronted a criminal at the back door to his home. She wouldn't let herself be intimidated or pushed around this time. And she wouldn't let him escape.

She swallowed hard and drew a deep breath as Franklin pounded on the front door and called out, "Police! Open up!"

The back door in sight, she rounded on it silently, watching, her entire body tense, waiting. He'd run that way; she knew it. A quick glance revealed a dirt bike parked against a rotten timber shed. That was what he'd want - the best way to run from the police in this part of the country was on a dirt bike on unmapped sandy tracks. No doubt Thad had his route already planned out. He had to know this day was coming.

She focused her attention on the door, heard a commotion as Franklin pushed through the front. A shout. A bang, the thunder of footsteps on hardwood. He was headed her way.

With muscles flexed, she braced herself. He launched through the back door, long blond hair obscuring his vision.

"Stop! Police!" she shouted.

He hesitated for a moment, then surged forward, his weight knocking her down as he leapt. They landed on the ground as one, him on top of her. She grunted with the impact but held onto her breath. When he lurched to his feet, she jumped up behind him and ran.

He was quick, but so was she. He glanced over his shoulder at her, his feet slapping on the sand as he aimed for the bike. Surprise clouded his face when he saw how close she was.

Thad slowed as they neared the bike, fumbling in his pocket for something - no doubt he was looking for the keys. It gave her the chance she needed. She was a foot shorter than he was, so when she jumped, she made sure to aim high. Her arms went around him as her shoulder collided with his back, sending him flying. He fell forward, landing face-first in the grass with her on his back.

In a moment, he'd rolled over and punched her so hard on one cheek that stars danced before her eyes. When she punched him back, he shouted out a curse.

He landed a few more hits to her torso before she caught a hold of one hand and twisted it back. She forced him to roll over and cuffed him in one movement.

That was when she saw the knife. A short blade fell from his hand onto the sand by her foot. She studied it, her heart skipping a beat at the sight of blood on the blade. Whose blood? Had he been injured?

"Rebecca!" Franklin called, limping up behind her. He rested a hand on her shoulder. "Good work, Constable."

"Thank you, sir."

"What's that? A knife?" he asked.

She issued a quick nod. "Looks like it."

"Whose blood?" he asked.

She shrugged, even as a hint of pain began in her gut. She pressed a hand to it, then drew it back to see red. It was her blood.

Franklin took a hold of Thad by the cuffs and forced him to his feet, then walked to the shack while he relayed the arrest details to the office on his radio. He sat Thad on the back steps, finished up the call and fixed Thad's cuffs around the porch railing.

Rebecca lurched to her feet, her head a little light. She wandered in Franklin's direction, then sank to her knees. He saw her and ran.

"What's wrong? Are you hurt?"

She nodded, held up a hand covered in blood. "The knife..."

His nostrils flared. "Base, we need an ambulance at the previously relayed address. Officer hurt. I repeat, officer hurt."

He fell to his knees beside her. "Where is it?"

She lifted her shirt to show him a short, red line just below her body armour on the right side.

He shook his head, tugged off his own vest, then removed his white t-shirt and pressed it to the wound. "Hold this here."

She pressed her hand to the shirt as he donned his vest again. Then, she shifted until she lay in the dirt on her back. Her head spun. She hadn't lost much blood, so it must be shock. She was a little dazed, nothing too serious. If it was serious, she'd have bled more. Not that she knew it for a fact, not really. It made sense though. She was well rehearsed in how to get herself through the shock of an injury. She stared at the sky as gradually it turned a light shade of pink and clouds sailed overhead.

When Franklin took her hand, it caught her by surprise. She almost pulled it away but decided she liked the feel of it.

"What were you thinking?" he asked, his voice laced with exasperation.

"I wanted to stop him."

"Why did you go after him like that? Risk your life that way? It's not worth it. We would've caught up with him eventually."

She shook her head, winced. "I couldn't let you down again. I've got your back, Sarge."

He huffed and shook his head, his eyes gleaming. "You didn't let me down. Hold on, the ambulance will be here soon."

His other hand pressed on top of hers, so her hand was sandwiched in between his. Rebecca's eyes drifted shut as a smile tickled the corners of her mouth. She hadn't let another thug knock her around, not this time. This time, she'd won the battle, and she'd never let anyone get the upper hand on her again.

CHAPTER 44

MEG

$\mathcal{T}$he popcorn stuck to her lap - one piece here, another there. It was the caramel, she guessed. Caramel popcorn was stickier than the regular kind. Meg raised a hand and ran it over her hair - something sticky in there too. It might be more popcorn, or it could be the ice cream. She'd dished it out pretty liberally and hadn't washed it off her hands before pulling her hair back into a messy ponytail. That was probably it - ice cream.

Popcorn and ice cream weren't her usual choice for dinner, but what did it matter now? She only had herself to feed, and she hadn't felt like cooking after working overtime at the salon. Being on her feet all day, talking to every customer who sat in her chair, it all exhausted her in a way it hadn't ever done before.

She missed Brad. Somehow, she'd messed everything up. He hadn't written to her since her visit to

Brisbane and the kiss that'd ruined their visit. If only she hadn't tried to kiss him, maybe they'd still be talking or at least writing. Instead, he'd made it clear he wanted nothing more to do with her. Even Vicky had suggested, in her loving and gentle way, that it might be time to move on with her life.

With a sigh, she lifted the remote to flick through the channels. Beneath her, something sharp protruded into her back. She tugged it free – ah, that's where the cheese grater was. She'd been looking for it. Perhaps she'd left it on the couch when she was sprinkling extra mozzarella onto the pizza she'd ordered the night before, and it'd fallen into the cracks between the cushions.

She glanced around the small unit - she'd never been a slob in her life before, but now her apartment looked as though a dozen lazy teenagers all called it home.

There was a knock at the door, and the handful of popcorn she was holding scattered across the couch cushion. She watched the pieces roll into cracks and crevices and onto the floor with a grimace. Oh well, who was she trying to impress anyway?

She ran a hand over her hair and strolled to the door. The knock resounded again, echoing through the small unit. "Keep your pants on, I'm coming!" she shouted.

Who would be visiting her at that time of night anyway? She'd planned on falling into bed in a few minutes, completely and utterly exhausted from the day and from the sadness that had gripped her soul ever since she returned from Brisbane.

She flung the door open, a frown on her face. "Brad?"

He'd begun to wheel his chair back down the hall when she stopped him. He turned to face her. "Hi, Meg. Can I come in?"

* * *

MEG BRUSHED the popcorn from the couch with one hand into the palm of the other and hurried into the kitchen to throw it in the rubbish bin. The kitchen was awash with dirty dishes, plates and silverware. Half-eaten food sat out on the bench, open packets, rubbish and crumbs. Her face flushed with warmth.

"I wasn't expecting you. Did you call? I haven't been checking my phone much...worked all day."

He sat in the living room watching her, his eyes trained on her - there was warmth there behind the green. A warmth she hadn't seen in a long time.

"Come and sit down," he said softly.

"In a minute, the entire place is a pigsty. I'm sorry... Like I said, I wasn't expecting visitors, and I've been feeling a bit...well, sorry for myself, actually." Her cheeks burned hotter still. It was humiliating enough for him to find her in this state, to let him know it was because his rejection felt like a stab to the gut.

"I don't care about the mess, Meggy. Please, come and sit - I want to talk to you."

She threw a packet of half-eaten crackers that'd gone stale into the bin, then wiped her hands down the front of her shorts with a sigh. "Okay."

She sat, straight-backed, across from him. Whatever else he had to say, she hoped he'd get it over with as quickly as possible. There was only so much rejection a person could take - even Meg, after a lifetime of it, could only stomach so much when it came from the man she loved.

"Relax," he said with a chuckle.

She shifted in her seat. "I'm relaxed. What's up?"

"Why haven't you filed the annulment yet?"

Her lips pursed. That was what this was about? He'd come all this way to push her, to hurry the end of their marriage. Her throat tightened. She coughed to clear it, stuck out her chin. "I'll get around to it. Are you back at university yet?"

He nodded. "I'm enrolled, I'll be starting classes next semester. It's not the only thing that's changed, there are other things too…"

"I'm glad. I want to hear about all of it. I think it's really great you're doing that. You're going to do so well at whatever you put your hand to in life, I just know it."

His eyes crinkled at the corners. "We'll talk about everything, but first - you didn't answer my question. Why haven't you filed the annulment yet?"

She frowned. "I don't want to."

"Really? I thought we decided it was for the best."

"You decided," she interrupted. "I didn't, and I haven't made up my mind. I'll get to it when I'm ready, and right now, I'm not ready. What's the rush, anyway?"

He shrugged. "No rush, I only wanted to know what was holding you back."

She shook her head with a huff. "What's holding me back? Are you serious? I fell in love with a man, vowed to spend the rest of my life with him - which was no small thing, let me tell you. I'd decided I never wanted to get married after I saw the way my father treated my mother and the way they both neglected me - so for me to tell you that I loved you and wanted to commit my life to you was a big deal!" Her voice grew louder as she spoke, her cheeks flamed, and a lump filled her throat.

"And then you want me to annul that commitment, because you've been injured?" Tears oozed from her eyes. "I can't do it, Brad. Don't you see that? I love you, that hasn't changed. I don't have a family - you're it for me. You're my family, my love, my best friend. My whole world is wrapped up in you." She choked on a sob. "So, no - I haven't gotten around to filing an annulment just yet."

His eyes glistened with tears. "I was hoping you'd say that. I'm so sorry for what I put you through."

Her eyes widened. "Oh, Brad... It wasn't your fault."

He held up a hand. "No, don't say that. I lashed out. I didn't want you to be tied to me forever like this - I thought it would be best for you to let you go. So you could find someone else, make the kind of life with them that we'd talked about having. It wasn't fair to you...having to take care of me for the rest of your life." He choked on the words; his nostrils flared as he gathered himself. "But then you didn't sign the papers, didn't file. I gave you an opening, a chance to cut and run...and you didn't. So, I started to hope that maybe there was a chance you loved me more than I gave you credit for. Not just the man who was strong, virile, who won surfing championships on the telly, but the real me, disabilities and all."

She shook her head, unable to speak as tears slid down her cheeks.

"I was so angry, sweetheart. Angry at the world, angry at God, angry at myself... I took it out on you because I wanted you to walk away, to be free. But if you're not going anywhere..."

"I'm not," she simply said, her voice thick with emotion.

"I don't deserve you, and I don't know what comes next...but I'd like us to give our marriage a chance. That is, if you still want to."

She nodded, blinked against the flow of tears.

Brad wheeled his chair forward, reached for her face and cradled it between his hands. His eyes were full of love as they fixed on hers. He studied her with a smile that tugged gently at the corners of his mouth.

"What about...?" she began.

"Shhh," he said. "I love you too."

Then he kissed her. His lips connected with hers, their warmth sending a spark through her body. Her hands found him then, weaving around his neck, fingers entwined in his hair as she pulled him closer. He lifted her from the couch and sat her on his lap. She nestled against his chest, heaving as sobs burst from her mouth.

"Please don't ever leave me," she whispered.

His arms encircled her, pulled tight. "I won't."

CHAPTER 45

SARAH

*E*verything was in its place. Sarah lay on her back, hands laced together behind her head, staring at the ceiling and the small chandelier she'd hung moments earlier. The final touch to a room that felt warm, welcoming and like the home she'd longed for ever since she'd left her childhood one. Well, different than what she'd thought she wanted, but better. It suited her in a way she hadn't expected, and it felt like a victory, like she'd created a life for herself. She'd worked to build something unexpected yet beautiful, and it was hers and hers alone. A place to live her life, the kind of life that fit her more than any of the idea she'd believed was hers. A picture that stemmed from a desire to recreate a world that she could now see was nothing but a straw house destined to burn to the ground.

She hadn't realised there'd been a piece of her heart

missing until she'd recently begun having dreams. Every few months, she'd dream of the house she grew up in, of running into her mother's arms, play wrestling with her father, dolls with her sister, swimming in the pool with her brother. Then she'd wake up sobbing, pain throbbing in her chest, as intense feelings of homesickness washed over her.

Home.

It was something she hadn't had, ever since she'd left home at eighteen to attend university miles away from the Cove. The intensity of her desire to find a home left her feeling spent when she woke in the morning after one of those dreams. And now she had the cottage, and it finally felt like a home to her. She felt whole, complete; was content in herself and her life for the first time in a long time.

She grinned at the ceiling.

A glance at her phone revealed no missed calls, no waiting voicemails. It seemed Jeremy had finally gotten the message. He'd stopped calling, trying to get in contact, had even requested she be removed from his editorial team - which she'd agreed to immediately. He was finally out of her life, and it felt like a weight had been lifted. She wished him nothing but happiness, but whatever life he chose, she didn't want to be part of it.

Even though it was what she'd wanted, there was a hollow longing in her heart for what they'd shared. The early days of their relationship had her hoping about what was to come, how they'd spend their lives together, raise children, build a home. It'd been hard to walk away from all of that - things that she still truly desired, just not with Jeremy.

Her phone buzzed, jolting her from her reverie.

She'd been waiting to hear from Meg, had been checking on her daily to make sure she was okay. She and Vicky had teamed up to send Meg encouraging messages, call her before bedtime, then again in the morning. Between the two of them, they intended to help pull her from the miserable slump she'd fallen into since visiting Brad.

She held the phone to her ear. "Hello?"

"It's Mick, how are you?"

Her heart skipped a beat. "Mick, it's good to hear from you. I hung the chandelier in the living room."

"Oh yeah? How does it look?"

"It's looks perfect." She sat up, crossed her legs and spun in place to look around the cottage. "The whole place looks and feels amazing. I couldn't have dreamed of anything better - you and the guys did such a great job. It really feels like a home now. Thank you."

"I'm glad we could help out. Hey, listen - I heard what you said when I was there a few weeks ago, but I'd like to talk. Can I come over?"

"Sure, that'd be nice. I'll make us something to eat."

When she hung up, Sarah hurried to the refrigerator to look for something they could eat. She found some vegetables and cooked prawns, along with rice paper, and quickly got to work making rice paper rolls. By the time she'd made her favourite dipping sauce of soy, rice wine vinegar and sesame oil, the beam of headlights sliced across the kitchen wall through the shuttered window.

Her heart thudded against her rib cage, and sweat beaded on her forehead, even though it was cool in the cottage. She walked over to the oil heater she'd found in her mother's basement and turned down the dial just as there was a knock on the front door.

"Coming!" she called.

When she opened the door, she found Mick leaning against the frame - all lanky muscles and mussed blond hair.

She stepped aside. "Come on in."

They sat at the small, round dining table and ate, exchanging small talk. Then, they took glasses of wine out onto the porch. Sarah wrapped a thick, woollen shawl around her shoulders and shivered. "It's cold out here."

He laughed, shoving hands into his jeans pockets. "It's snowing in Victoria."

"Wish I was skiing at Fall's Creek," she said.

"You and me, both."

It was comfortable chatting together - talking but not saying much of anything at all. Although, Sarah was acutely aware that he'd come to see her for a reason, and whatever it was, he'd decided to wait before addressing it.

She sat in silence, her shawl pulled tight as she tucked her legs up to her chest and looked out at the clear night sky, stars winking close. If she tried she could reach out and pluck them from the inky blanket. She knew all of a sudden she was ready. For more, for him.

"I had to see you." His voice was deep; it drew her in.

She faced him, only seeing an outline in the darkness. He was backlit by the soft glow of the chandelier in the sitting room through the bifold glass doors.

"I'm glad you called. I've missed you," she simply said.

He leaned forward, took her hand and held it between his. "I know you said you weren't ready for anything more than friendship between us, but I can't stop thinking about you - about us and what we could be giving up. I've been down the road to commitment before, with the wrong person. I know what that feels like, and it isn't like this. This feels right in a way I've never experienced. I know you feel it too..." His voice trembled.

She held a breath deep in her lungs, the things she wanted to say, and her fear, fighting over the words that rose to her tongue. "I wasn't ready then...but the past few weeks have given me time to think, to heal. You caught me right after Jeremy left, I was upset, shaken... I wasn't ready then, but I am now."

He sat in silence, stroking her hand with his finger-tips. Then, he leaned forward and pressed a soft kiss to her lips. A deep passion welled within her at his touch. She pulled away to catch her breath.

"I want us to try..." he began. "I'm ready to commit fully to this thing between us, wherever it goes."

She kissed him then, and they rose from their seats at the same time until their bodies were pressed against one another. On tiptoe, she stared into his eyes. They were dark, but even in the dim light, she saw his heart. He was a good man - patient, strong, kind and part of the home she'd been searching for. "Even though I've known you my whole life, I think you're just the man I've been looking for."

THE END

* * *

Want to read more about your Emerald Cove favourites?

How about MEG & BRAD FALLING IN LOVE?
Find out how they fell hard and fast in an exclusive bonus scene...
TAP HERE: Give me this scene now please!

What's next?...
SEASIDE MANOR BED & BREAKFAST (BOOK 2)
Return to Emerald Cove for more of this heartwarming series & endearing characters...
TAP HERE: I want the next book in the series

ALSO BY LILLY MIRREN

THE WARATAH INN SERIES

The Waratah Inn

Wrested back to Cabarita Beach by her grandmother's sudden death, Kate Summer discovers a mystery buried in the past that changes everything.

One Summer in Italy

Reeda leaves the Waratah Inn and returns to Sydney, her husband, and her thriving interior design business, only to find her marriage in tatters. She's lost sight of what she wants in life and can't recognise the person she's become.

The Summer Sisters

Set against the golden sands and crystal clear waters of Cabarita Beach three sisters inherit an inn and discover a mystery about their grandmother's past that changes everything they thought they knew about their family...

Christmas at The Waratah Inn

Liz Cranwell is divorced and alone at Christmas. When her friends convince her to holiday at The Waratah Inn, she's dreading her first Christmas on her own. Instead she discovers that strangers can be the balm to heal the wounds of a lonely heart in this heartwarming Christmas story.

EMERALD COVE SERIES

Cottage on Oceanview Lane

When a renowned book editor returns to her roots, she rediscovers her strength & her passion in this heartwarming novel.

Seaside Manor Bed & Breakfast

The Seaside Manor Bed and Breakfast has been an institution in Emerald Cove for as long as anyone can remember. But things are changing and Diana is nervous about what the future might hold for her and her husband, not to mention the historic business.

Bungalow on Pelican Way

Moving to the Cove gave Rebecca De Vries a place to hide from her abusive ex. Now that he's in jail, she can get back to living her life as a police officer in her adopted hometown working alongside her intractable but very attractive boss, Franklin.

Chalet on Cliffside Drive

At forty-four years of age, Ben Silver thought he'd never find love. When he moves to Emerald Cove, he does it to support his birth mother, Diana, after her husband's sudden death. But then he meets Vicky.

Christmas in Emerald Cove

The Flannigan family has been through a lot together. They've grown and changed over the years and now have a blended and extended family that doesn't always see eye to eye. But this Christmas they'll learn that love can overcome all of the pain and differences of the past in this inspiring Christmas tale.

SMALL-TOWN FICTION

Home Sweet Home

Trina is starting over after a painful separation from her husband of almost twenty years. Grief and loss force her to return to her hometown where she has to deal with all of the things she left behind to rebuild her life, piece by piece; a hometown she hasn't visited since high school graduation.

GLOSSARY OF TERMS

Dear reader,

Since this book is set in Australia there may be some terms you're not familiar with. I've included them below to help you out! I hope they didn't trip you up too much.

Cheers, Lilly xo

* * *

Terms

Boot - car trunk

Pavlova - a meringue based dessert piled high with whipped cream and slices of fresh fruit.

"Love" - a term of endearment for friends and lovers alike

Tea - used to describe either a hot beverage made from leaves, or the evening meal

Unit - apartment or condo

Mobile - cell phone

Fringe - bangs

RSL Club - Returned Services League (war veterans) Club

Proby - Probationary Constable

Sarge - Sergeant

Senior Connies - Senior Constables

Biscuits - Crackers or cookies (could be either)

Sea Change - Moving to the beach from the city for a change of lifestyle

ABOUT THE AUTHOR

Lilly Mirren lives in Brisbane, Australia with her husband and three children.

Lilly always dreamed of being a writer and is now living that dream. She is a graduate of both the University of Queensland, where she studied International Relations and Griffith University, where she completed a degree in Information Technology.

When she's not writing, she's chasing her children, doing housework or spending time with friends.

Sign up for her newsletter and stay up on all the latest Lilly book news.

And follow her on:

Website: lillymirren.com
Facebook: https://www.
facebook.com/authorlillymirren/
Twitter: https://twitter.com/lilly_mirren
BookBub: https://www.bookbub.com/authors/lilly-
mirren